Gwendoline Butler

Gwendoline Butler is a Londoner, born in a part of South London for which she still has a tremendous affection. She was educated at Haberdashers and then read history at Oxford. After a short period doing research and teaching, she married the late Dr Lionel Butler, Principal of Royal Holloway College. She has one daughter.

Gwendoline Butler's crime novels are very popular in Britain and the States, and her many awards include the Crime Writers' Association's Silver Dagger.

When she isn't writing, she spends her time travelling and looking at pictures, furniture and buildings.

D1334758

A Dark Coffin
The Coffin Tree
A Coffin for Charley
Cracking Open a Coffin
Coffin on Murder Street
Coffin and the Paper Man
Coffin in the Black Museum
Coffin Underground
Coffin in Fashion
Coffin on the Water
A Coffin for the Canary
A Coffin for Pandora
A Coffin from the Past
Coffin's Dark Number
Coffin Following
Coffin in Malta
A Nameless Coffin
Coffin Waiting
A Coffin for Baby
Death Lives Next Door
The Interloper
The Murdering Kind
The Dull Dead
Coffin in Oxford
Receipt for Murder

GWENDOLINE BUTLER

A DOUBLE COFFIN

HarperCollins*Publishers*

HarperCollins*Publishers*
77–85 Fulham Palace Road,
Hammersmith, London W6 8JB

This paperback edition 1997

1 3 5 7 9 8 6 4 2

First published in Great Britain by
HarperCollins*Publishers* 1996

ISBN 0 00 649774 8

Printed and bound in Great Britain by
Caledonian International Book Manufacturing Ltd, Glasgow

AUTHOR'S NOTE

One evening in April 1988, I sat in Toynbee Hall in the East End of London, near to Dockland, listening to Dr David Owen (now Lord Owen) give that year's Barnett Memorial Lecture. In it, he suggested the creation of a Second City of London, to be spun off from the first, to aid the economic and social regeneration of the Docklands.

The idea fascinated me and I have made use of it to create a world for detective John Coffin, to whom I gave the tricky task of keeping there the Queen's peace.

A brief Calendar of the life and career of John Coffin, Chief Commander of the Second City of London Police

John Coffin is a Londoner by birth, his father is unknown and his mother was a difficult lady of many careers and different lives who abandoned him in infancy to be looked after by a woman who may have been a relative of his father and who seems to have acted as his mother's dresser when she was on the stage. He kept in touch with this lady, whom he called Mother, lodged with her in his early career and looked after her until she died.

After serving briefly in the army, he joined the Metropolitan Police, soon transferring to the plain-clothes branch as a detective.

He became a sergeant and was very quickly promoted to inspector a year later. Ten years later, he was a superintendent and then chief superintendent.

There was a bad patch in his career about which he is reluctant to talk. His difficult family background has complicated his life and possibly accounts for an unhappy period when, as he admits, his career went down a black hole. His first marriage split apart at this time and his only child died.

From this dark period he was resurrected by a spell in a secret, dangerous undercover operation about which even now not much is known. But the esteem he won then was recognized when the Second City of London was being formed and he became Chief Commander of its Police Force. He has married again, an old love, Stella Pinero, who is herself a very successful actress. He has also discovered two siblings, a much younger sister and brother.

1

John Coffin, Chief Commander of the Second City of London, sat in the sunlight at the desk in his office and allowed himself to feel surprise as the message came through. 'A Mr Bradshaw wants to see me? And urgently?'

He had been listening to Mozart, *The Marriage of Figaro*, and reading a travel brochure, while at his feet lay the new family dog, a white peke called Augustus. His old dog had succumbed to great years and an eventful life, both of which had done his heart in. The record player in the office and the presence there of Augustus were the work of his wife who had decreed that there must be a show of more civilization in the workplace. And what could be more civilized than Mozart (a dose to be taken once a day at least) and a Pekingese of impeccable breeding if of uncertain temper.

He had been content on this sunny October day. Content was now shattered.

'Richard Lavender wants to see me? Dick Lavender?'

His visitor nodded; he was a tall, thin man with crest of crisp hair just going grey. His eyes were an odd mixture between green and blue, attractive, Coffin thought.

'He does. Soon, if you please. Perhaps a first visit this morning?'

John Albert Bradshaw had come with an introduction from the Home Secretary and had laid his card on the table as soon as he arrived. Dr J. A. Bradshaw. Not a medical doctor, he had said at once – political science, Edinburgh. Coffin had the notion that this information was proffered to establish status. I am an important person in my own right, Dr Bradshaw was saying.

7

Coffin was interested, intrigued even, at what amounted to a royal command, from a great old man, but he played for time.

'I have a lot on hand at the moment, and I was thinking of going away on holiday.' Coffin did not take many holidays, too few, his wife Stella said, and they were going to have these few days on the Italian lakes. Or were they? Would he get away?

'You'll get away, he's thoughtful about that sort of thing. He goes away himself sometimes, he has a cottage in Fife.'

The Thane of Fife had a wife, but where is she now? recited Coffin to himself. Why did I think of that? And why this sudden quick wince of foreboding? And why do I think of his wife? Damn Macbeth. Shakespeare and Macbeth get everywhere. Aloud he said: 'I didn't know he was still alive.'

That got a reprimand. 'Indeed you did.'

'Yes, yes . . .' He did, of course, it was his business to know if the distinguished and important inhabitants living in his Second City of London were alive or dead. He was responsible for their safety.

Part of the job. He had taken on the task of policing the Second City of London some years ago now and had made a success of it. He had melded together the lively and criminous districts of Swinehouse, East Hythe and Spinnergate, with violent histories that went back before William the Norman, and helped them to live, not only with each other but with the new, up-and-coming areas like Evelyn Fields and Tower Hills. He had been a success, been acknowledged as a success, had a happy marriage with a well-known actress and had come through the threat of a serious illness. But nature had nudged him on the shoulder and said, in that sly, familiar way it had: OK, so you survived, but you may not come through next time.

It was a rough old world out there, the denizens of which had in their times troubled the Romans, the Normans and all rulers from the Plantagenets to the House of Hanover.

'You are quite right, I did know . . . but I never expected to meet him. And he wants to see me?' This was a surprise. He had made some good friends in his years as Chief Commander, and collected a few enemies. Which was the old man? They had never met, but Coffin knew you can make enemies without meeting them.

'Most anxious.'

He heard himself ask: 'Has he got a wife?'

'Widowed. Married twice, widowed twice.'

Coffin stood up and went to the window. 'I did see him once, I was only a kid, and he came through Greenwich . . . Election night, it was. The last big one he fought. Was he PM? I was too young to know. He looked like a film star.'

His visitor nodded. 'Remember it myself.'

'So what is it about?'

His visitor rose. 'He will tell you himself. Shall we go?'

Coffin stood up, his dog stood up too. 'Can he come?' He looked doubtfully at Augustus. 'He's no trouble, well behaved.' This was not true, but he had agreed with his wife Stella to offer this lie.

His visitor had a car waiting, he held the door open for Coffin and Augustus to get in. The car was an antique, a Rolls built in a style not used for many decades. Upright and sturdy with huge wheels and great windows, Coffin felt as if he was entering a hearse. Inside, the seats were covered in dark-grey brocade with a small silver flower holder by each seat. There were no flowers. On the air was a very faint smell of lavender and dust.

Coffin sat down, removed Augustus from the seat to which he had leapt, and stared at the glass barrier that separated him from his companion who was doing the driving. The car, old though it was, started without fuss and glided forward with an ease which was a testimony to the engineering which had produced it.

As a passenger, Coffin found you had to be prepared for the rolling motion which came with the steady regal progress through the streets. It was a bit like being on board a great liner; you could be travel sick. He also had to bite back a strong impulse to wave at the passers-by as he was driven along. Against his will, he found himself bending forward from the waist. Damn it, he was bowing.

He felt archaic, he was living in the past. Was the old man

living in the past? Well, I wondered if he was dead, Coffin reminded himself, so perhaps he is.

But he had been practical and shrewd enough in his day, or so the political memoirs said. Feared too, a magnificent, mesmeric figure. And a great drinker. Other pleasures as well, if all that was told was true.

Now he was a memory, but alive. Alive, and still enough of a power in the land to call in the likes of John Coffin when he needed help.

The car carried him through one of the more pleasant districts of his Second City to the riverside, where a modest block of flats overlooked the Thames. He had been here only once before, so the view was fresh to him. He could see across the water to an area of trees through which a large building just showed its roof. He did not recognize this either, but he decided it was a public park with a municipal building inside it, perhaps a museum or a picture gallery or one of the new universities. It did not look industrial, although it was true that many commercial enterprises were moving out of central London and establishing themselves in something as near a great country estate as they could achieve.

The car stopped and he stepped out into the chill, sunlight air. He nodded across the river. 'Do you know what that building is?'

'The Central Bank of Arabia,' said his companion briefly. 'Lovely building. Empty though, of course, since the bank went broke.'

Sign of the times, Coffin thought, banks created wonderful buildings for themselves, then could not pay their bills and went out of business.

'It was built as a prison in 1850 by Victorian reformers. Out of use as a prison a hundred years later, that is when the bank bought it.' He added without a smile: 'Himself admires the view, but I am never sure if he remembers it is no longer a prison.'

Not great on memory, then, Coffin thought. 'Does he remember who he is himself?' Better to establish that fact at once.

'He remembers who he was,' said his companion tersely.

'An old Prime Minister.'

'A former Prime Minister,' corrected Dr Bradshaw tartly.

Significant difference, Coffin thought, as he approached the flats' entrance. I am being taught my lines.

'I'll have to leave the dog in the car . . . Stay, Augustus.' The dog looked at him thoughtfully, seemingly content to stay where he was in the great car.

A small white van was parked nearby. 'Belongs to the old man's niece,' said Jack Bradshaw shortly. 'Uses it for shopping. Ferries himself in his chair sometimes.'

As he walked into the entrance lobby Coffin was remembering what he knew of the origin of this block of flats: they had been built by a housing association to provide pleasant, medium-priced homes for retired professionals. The rents were not high, nor meant to be.

The entrance hall was in line with what you might expect from this policy, being plain, with stone-coloured walls and tiling floor. There was a lift in one corner.

Surely former Prime Ministers could afford better than this? There was a pension, wasn't there?

'Hard up, is he?' Coffin asked. When you were nearly ninety (or over it, more likely) money might have dried up. Money had that way with it, sometimes seeming of organic growth, and a plant capable of drying up mysteriously and almost malevolently. Coffin had had this happen himself in his younger days and knew it could happen again. You had to watch money and water it with your attentions.

'No, or as to that, it's not my business to know, I don't touch his financial affairs, but I should say not. No, he lives here because he likes it. He was born here. Before they were bombed to bits in the last war, there was a tenement block here and in one of them he was born. The eldest son of Edward and Ada Lavender . . .'

'Yes, I know that bit – Dick Lavender,' said Coffin. 'It's in all the books. But I did not know this was his birthplace.' He wondered if it was true really. Even old Prime Ministers, sorry, *former* Prime Ministers, could have fantasies. Even tell lies. 'Do we take the lift or walk up?'

'Lift, he's on the top floor . . . that was the only thing

he asked for. Otherwise no favours, he took what he was offered.'

Took what was offered but took the best; the view from the top floor across the river must be splendid.

The lift delivered them to a plain lobby, the mirror image of the one below. There were two front doors.

'One other person lives up here then?'

'Yes,' said John Bradshaw, in his usual Jovian style. 'A tiresome person.' He did not add to the statement.

He rang the bell on the door nearest, and they waited.

'Lives alone, does he?'

'No, a niece lives with him. Runs the domestic side.'

'Hang on a minute,' said Coffin. 'Tell me a bit about why I am wanted. You do know, don't you?'

'Yes, I know,' admitted Bradshaw stiffly. 'You are wanted because you have the resources; it's a police matter. Of course, the Special Branch keep a watchful eye, but this isn't one for them.'

'I guessed that. Any connection with the tiresome neighbour?'

'No.' Bradshaw sounded surprised. 'None.'

'But it's a serious business?'

'Serious enough,' said Bradshaw, as the door opened. 'Death always is.'

The door was opened by a short, plump woman with a froth of white hair cut short, she wore bright-pink lipstick and blue-rimmed spectacles, a lively and cheerful figure. 'Oh hello, Jack, you've made good time, you're back sooner than I expected. Uncle's still dressing . . . Good morning, sir.' She turned to Coffin. 'I'm Janet Neptune . . . silly name, isn't it, but my own. Tell you about it some day if you ask . . . He's dressing but he's been up and about for some time.'

She too, knew why he had been summoned, Coffin was convinced of that, knew it was about death but was not letting it get her down. 'Miss Neptune or Mrs?' he asked politely.

'Miss, miss, I am not married. Asked for once or twice but never took on. It doesn't suit everyone, you know. Not to

12

be expected, is it? I mean, nature is prodigal and various in its arrangements.'

'I can see you and I have much the same notion of nature,' said Coffin.

'It's common sense, isn't it? Now come into the dining room the two of you and have a cup of something while Uncle is getting ready, we don't hurry him, sir, not at his age . . . Jack, he's turned up another great pile of letters, you'll never get that life of him written at this rate.'

'Is that what you are doing?' Coffin was interested. 'Writing his life?'

'Ghostwriting,' said Bradshaw without much expression in his voice. 'It'll come out in his name. Who but himself could write his life?'

A rhetorical question, needing no answer.

'It's not my only job; I have others.'

The room into which Coffin had been led was a step into the past. He felt he had been moved back in time by a hundred years. It was a small room made smaller by massive furniture in a style favoured by the merchant classes of Victorian England. In the middle of the wall facing the door was a large square looking glass of gilded wood, the sides fretted with little shelves for china pots and photographs. Coffin thought it must have been the devil to dust. Another wall was covered by a monument in dark wood with another mirror set in a nest of shelves and drawers. From his memory he dredged up the word chiffonier. An oval table of mahogany ranged around with chairs, the seats covered in red plush, filled the centre of the room. Underfoot was a dark Turkish carpet.

Janet Neptune saw Coffin looking around him as she came in with cups of coffee. 'He bought the furniture for his mother when he started to earn well, it was her taste. Made her feel a lady, he said. I think he likes it himself because he's never got rid of it.'

'What about his wives? How did they take it?'

'Oh well, I don't suppose they liked it, but the furniture lasted and they didn't.'

She was handing round the coffee, which was strong and good.

Janet Neptune said: 'I can hear noises, he's ready to receive company, I know that cough he gives.'

Several generations of MPs had known that cough too in the House of Commons before an important speech.

'Right.' Coffin stood up.

She bent her head towards him and said in a confidential way: 'Just one thing, I expect you will be calling on him again, but don't let him give you anything to eat or drink.'

After a moment of stunned silence, Coffin said: 'He won't poison me, will he?'

She put her head on one side. 'Not poison, no, we don't let him get his hands on anything really dangerous. He's on a few medications but we keep those out of his way. No, but sometimes he thinks it's funny to load a drink with a laxative or some such. Once he gave Jack here a gin loaded with hydrogen peroxide, didn't he, Jack?'

'If you say so.'

'Didn't half fizz; 'course it tasted terrible.'

'No worse than some drinks I've had,' said Bradshaw.

'It's a very Edwardian-house-party sort of joke.' Janet put her face near Coffin's. 'You can imagine . . . not his world, of course, but some of the ladies he went with later . . .' She shrugged. 'Upper class . . . Lady this and the Honourable that . . . they found him attractive, he was an attractive man, and he picked up a few of their ways.'

'Yes, I've heard that.'

'We'd better go in.' Bradshaw stood up.

'Yes,' Janet nodded. 'Finish your cup, sir, and we'll go on in. He'll be getting impatient. If you haven't got many years left you want to get on with things.'

She led the way out of the dining room, shutting the door carefully behind her, Across the hall, the door to another room stood half open.

Even half a glance showed Coffin that this room was a museum piece, crowded as it was with heavy, dark, ornate furniture. One wall was covered with a great bookcase in which the leatherbound books looked unread and unloved. The past was strong in this place.

Inside the room, the old man sat in a large armchair. His head, with its cockade of white hair, was supported by cushions so that he was upright and commanding. He wore a soft cashmere jacket with a tartan shawl draped over his legs. He looked old, elegant and in control. No loss of substance there, you felt at once. He might tire quickly, he probably did, but while he was functioning he would be acute.

Coffin was surprised how well he remembered the face. Likewise the strong head of hair seemingly so untouched by time that Coffin wondered cynically if it was a wig. But surely not, the old man's watchword had always been honesty and integrity, although exactly what that meant in political circles might be doubted.

And after all, many people had wigs. His own wife had several, which she said were essential to her professional life.

He fixed Coffin with a commanding blue eye. 'Good of you to come, sir. With all your responsibilities it cannot have been easy. I appreciate your courtesy.' It was a rich deep voice, but age had introduced streaks of lighter tones.

'You know who I am?'

'I keep up to date, sir.'

So you do, Coffin thought, noticing a small television set on a table by the chair. Shelves underneath the table were stacked with more modern books, and magazines. The present did get a look in then.

Janet fussed forward, adjusting his shawl. 'Of course you do, Uncle.'

He ignored her. 'Helped by my good friend, Bradshaw.'

'You pay me, sir,' said Bradshaw, somewhat sourly.

'Not enough.'

'Probably not enough, but I am bearing it.'

The old man chuckled. 'Other things make it bearable, eh? You enjoy working with me, and we will both make money out of my autobiography.'

'So you hope.'

This sparring is in fun, they like each other, Coffin thought. But even this might be wrong, you had to remember that

15

one at least of them was a politician, used to wearing a false smile, dissembling. Lying, in short.

'Nice collection of books you have there, sir. Dickens and a complete Thackeray.' Not many other houses in Spinnergate had a library like it, he guessed.

'My mother ordered me to buy them. Said it was what I should have, but I never opened them. I was a Shaw and a Gissing man, myself. She didn't read them either, not what she liked; Ethel M. Dell and Ruby M. Ayres, they were her goddesses. I don't think anyone has ever opened those books there. But they look good, don't they? Nice covers.'

'Very nice.'

'You're just making conversation, lad,' said the old man with a sudden shift of character from nostalgic son to old headmaster talking to a former pupil.

What a politician he must have been, thought Coffin, able to change his stance as it suited him. 'I have been wondering what you wanted from me.'

'And when I was going to get down to it?' He looked at Janet, who drew chairs forward for Coffin and Bradshaw, then retired quietly from the room. 'And you can shut the door, Janet,' he called out. 'She listens at the door, you know,' he said to Coffin in no soft voice. 'I know you are still there, Janet, I can tell.'

Bradshaw clicked his teeth. 'You're hard on Janet; you wouldn't find it easy to get anyone else to do what she does.'

'She doesn't like me, you know.'

'Do you want me to leave as well?' asked John Bradshaw with a show of irritation.

'You can stay.' The old man looked down at his hand. 'I'm dead in a way, dead to a lot of people, you probably thought I was dead, been off the scene a long while, a bit of old history,' he said to Coffin.

'English history, sir.'

'And that's how I want to stay. I want to be remembered for the good things I did for English society, what I opened up, what I swept away.'

'That's how it will be,' said Coffin, wondering what was coming.

'I was born round here . . . Different world then.'

'Born not so far away myself, sir.'

'Much later, you are a younger man. A different world even so and even then.' He got up and walked slowly to the window. 'All changed out there. New buildings, and an empty river. Different sort of people live here. When I was a kid, there was a tenement block here, dozens of families all crammed in with a lavatory and pump in the yard outside. I remember the stink.'

'We all have memories like that, sir. I remember when there were big ships on the river here, and barges.'

'And men at the dock gates, fighting for work, with the guv'nors coming out and picking and choosing . . . I remember that too . . . I helped put that away. Made a start.'

Still looking out of the window, he went on: 'At night, it's bright with lights, they shine across the water. Keep me awake sometimes.' He turned round: 'It was gaslight on the cobbled walks then, and not much light at all anywhere. Pools of light under the lamps and then blackness. A dark world. I want you to remember that.'

'I can imagine.' Coffin began to feel like Alice through the Looking Glass. Not going into another world, but back in time. He looked at Jack Bradshaw who gave him a faint sympathetic smile. He lives like this all the time, Coffin thought, walking in and out of the past.

'The streets were different too, narrower as well as worse lit, not so much traffic and a lot of it still horse driven. Court-yards with little houses round them. Broken windows with old clothes stuffed in them to keep the draughts out, unlocked doors – with so many souls under one roof, families crammed into one room, you couldn't keep the front door locked much. A thieves' paradise, and worse . . .'

Bradshaw met Coffin's eye and gave a small nod. He'll be out with it soon, the nod said. He has to work up to what's coming.

'We had a very hot summer the year I was thirteen,' Lavender went on, 'followed by a bad, foggy winter. I remember how the fog hung over the street we lived in and seemed to creep slyly into every crack of the little house. My school

17

was just around the corner and I spent as much time there as I could. There was a little library, I could get into that and sit reading, it was warmer than home ... quieter too. My mother used to take in washing, it was a common way then to earn some money, the washing was collected and taken home to be washed. Rubbed up and down a dolly board. We had a boiler in the kitchen with a coal fire beneath. I used to help my mother by delivering the clean washing in an old pram ... I had a younger brother, but he died ...'

'I used to do errands, delivering messages, collecting shopping, to earn a bit of pocket money,' said Coffin, dredging up a memory, long forgotten. Did he say it aloud? If so, the old man took no notice, but went on:

'So I was out and about the streets at all hours, sometimes early in the morning, sometimes late at night. I saw all things ... there wasn't much I didn't know about the ways of men and women and of men with women. Stood me in good stead, I can tell you, when I went out into the world ... But even so ...' He paused. 'There was a lot of violence on the streets that winter ... the fogs, I suppose, being particularly bad made it easier for attackers to get away. Four women were killed in Spinnergate and East Hythe that winter and spring.'

'You remember exactly?'

'I remember; there was a lot of talk and boys listen to that sort of thing ... One woman was found dead in a gutter, another in a park, another up an alley. And I have cause to remember.'

'Four, you said?'

'Yes, all strangled, just one killer for the lot. What we now call a serial killer. Monsters, was the word then, that last winter before the First World War.'

Lavender stopped, his voice had been tiring.

'You could do with a drink,' said Bradshaw, standing up. 'You should have let me tell all this.' He went to the door. 'Janet, bring a glass of water.'

Janet must have been at the door, she was in so quick, holding out a glass. 'Here you are, I dropped some whisky in it.'

18

More than a drop, thought Coffin, observing the colour. Still, she knew the old man and what he could take.

Dick Lavender took a sip. 'I came home one day of a deep fog, I'd been delivering the washing to a local pub: the Rock of Gibraltar . . . the Gib, we called it.'

'Still there,' said Coffin.

'I know . . . When I got home, my mother called me into the kitchen . . . I'd been meaning to sneak upstairs to read, I had a good book on the go . . . My mother was shaking and there was blood on her apron . . . She was a little woman and she was not drunk, she did not drink. She took me into the kitchen and told me that my father was the multiple killer and that he had killed one more woman and her body was in our back yard.'

The words fell into the room like little weapons, sharp and heavy. Are you sure about this, Coffin wanted to say. Not a kid's fantasy, remembered now for real? But he did not say it.

There was only one question to ask and Coffin asked it: 'Where was your father?'

'Gone.'

Then Coffin did say, he had to ask it: 'Are you sure this is real?' Later, he might take Bradshaw aside, and say: Is the old man mad?

'Oh, I am sure. My mother asked me to come with her to bury the body . . . I helped her put the woman in the pram, and I pushed it through the streets, and then I helped Mother bury her.'

Janet came in with the bottle of whisky, and handed drinks all round, taking one herself. She then withdrew, no doubt to listen at the door again.

Coffin received his drink gratefully, downing it in one long gulp. He felt steadier then, and able to move on.

'So where do I come in?'

Dick Lavender said gravely: 'I have had this on my conscience this long while.'

Did it worry your mother? Coffin wanted to ask, but he felt the answer would be that it hadn't. She had died happy and content.

'I want you to find out the names of the murdered women. It will be in the police records. I can give you the years.'

'It's been a long while, sir,' said Coffin gently. 'Why not leave it?'

Lavender went on, as if Coffin had not spoken: 'All the deaths were in Spinnergate or East Hythe, that should help you. The police investigation got nowhere, I can remember my mother worrying, but time went on and nothing happened.'

'You mean your father was never named?' Coffin was blunt.

This too was ignored. 'If you could find out the names and if there are any living relatives of the dead women, then I would try to do something by way of reparation. Anonymously, of course.'

I was right, I am going to be a time wanderer, Coffin thought, feeling dazed. Wandering around in the past. If I am not careful I shall never get out.

'And I would like the woman my mother and I buried to be dug up and given a proper funeral.'

Coffin was silent. 'Let me think this over, sir. I can see difficulties.' Finding the grave, digging up the corpse, the holding of an inquest ... the press would be there like vultures.

'I can tell you where we buried her. I remember very clearly.' Dick Lavender nodded at Bradshaw. 'Get us the map, Jack.'

'He knows all about it?' Coffin looked at Bradshaw's retreating back.

'Of course, I trust him. He is writing my life, but he will only put in what I tell him to.'

I wonder, Coffin thought.

'And Janet?' Who listens at doors.

'She won't get a penny from my will unless she has been discreet.'

'And you trust me?'

Dick Lavender gave him the famous smile, the one that had ravished the hearts of those beauties long ago. 'I do.' He bent his head in a kind of noble obeisance.

20

Oh, you charmer, you, thought Coffin. But what is it really all about? He had the distinct feeling of being led into a maze.

'I can't guarantee either success or complete secrecy. Just not on, sir.'

Bradshaw appeared with a map of the district, which he handed to his employer.

'You may remember where you and your mother buried the body all those years ago, but there has been a war and a lot of rebuilding . . . the spot may have a tower block sitting on it, or a factory.'

'We think not,' said Bradshaw. 'It was open ground then, and it still is so.'

'It was the old churchyard, even then unused, hard by St Luke's Church.' Dick Lavender smiled again. 'You will know it.'

'Oh, I do, I do.' One by one, facts were slotting into place. Not only was he Chief Commander of the police of the Second City, and thus in the first position to investigate a series of murders long ago, even if the investigation came to no resolution, but he also lived in the tower of the old St Luke's Church. Former St Luke's Church, he corrected himself. 'It is a small public park now, over the road.' The road, he supposed, was relatively new but before his time.

'I have seen your wife act,' said Dick Lavender. 'Not recently, of course. I no longer go out. A beautiful lady.'

'I think so . . .' Coffin gathered himself together. 'Sir, as I said before, all this was a long time ago . . . Why not let it rest?'

Dick Lavender looked at Bradshaw, and gave a small nod.

Jack sighed. 'A young woman, a freelance journalist has been around, asking questions . . . she may have flushed something up . . . If so, she will certainly publish.'

'I must be there first,' said Dick Lavender. 'I value what reputation I have.' He read the expression on Coffin's face accurately. 'But it is mostly conscience. I have enough in my life to regret. Of this particular crime, I want to be relieved.'

'Your father and your mother are dead . . . they were the guilty ones, you were young, not to be blamed.'

'I do blame myself,' said the old man simply. 'Guilt grows

on you with age like a mould. You will find that out for yourself one day. I do not want to die covered in mould.'

Coffin stood up. 'I will think about it, sir, and come back to you when I have made up my mind.'

Dick Lavender bowed his head again, in dignified acceptance. 'Please let me know.' He leaned back in his big chair, closing his eyes. 'Jack, show the Chief Commander out . . . I thank you for coming.'

Bradshaw took Coffin to the door, avoiding Janet who was hovering, then took the lift down with him.

As soon as they were in the lift, Coffin said: 'Is this all serious?'

'You know it is.'

Coffin was silent till they came to the ground floor and the lift door opened. He walked out into the air, taking in deep breaths. 'I don't know, I don't know.'

He turned to Bradshaw. 'Is he mad, or senile?'

'No, not mad . . .' He gave a slight smile. 'He always remembers he was PM, but sometimes I have thought he believed he was Mr Gladstone, going out to save fallen women . . . the story he told you has some relevance there. And once he seemed to act as if he was Pitt the Younger, taking on Napoleon Bonaparte.'

Coffin digested the comment, half satirically meant and the more interesting for that. 'This young journalist . . . she really exists?'

'She does. No one invented her.'

'Then let me have her name and any address you have.'

Bradshaw nodded. 'I will send round all I have. There isn't much. Marjorie Wardy was the name she used when she came round, may be a pseudonym.'

'Let me have what you've got. I will let you know what I decide.'

Jack Bradshaw hesitated. 'There's one other thing . . . it has certainly been on the old man's mind, may have motivated him to call you in. He has had two letters threatening him . . .'

Coffin gave him a quick look.

'He knew I would tell you,' said Jack Bradshaw. 'Meant

me to. It has made him nervous. He thinks it may be something from his past.'

Once again, Coffin had this feeling of being caught up in a maze. Every time he felt he was on solid ground, the ground was moved.

'Send me all the information you have, including the letters, and I will say where we go from there.'

2

Coffin went home to his wife, Stella, whom he found lying across the bed, wearing a red satin trouser suit, and painting her nails in a very delicate shade of pink. He liked her in red, but it made him nervous. It betokened what he thought of as her flighty mood. This was a mood which he loved but feared because you never knew how it would take her.

'My darling,' he said. 'How glad I am that I am married to you.'

Stella sat up. 'So am I, my dearest. It is very nice for me.' She sounded slightly surprised. But she was a generous woman who liked to return praise for praise. Even if it was not strictly true, since they had their ups and downs and she could not deny that she sometimes found her husband tiresome. It was part of the function of being a husband, perhaps a necessary one.

'I love you, darling.' She held out her arms for a kiss.

They had hitherto conducted their marital conversations rather in what she called the 'Noel Coward style'. In other words, relaxed, amused and detached. Except when they were quarrelling, when there were no holds barred. Stella enjoyed the quarrels, she said they gave her scope. As a dramatic actress, she needed scope.

It occurred to her to say: Mind my nail varnish, but this would have been both unkind and bad manners, so she enjoyed the embrace, only turning her eyes for a quick glance as she emerged. All well, no smudging.

'What's up?'

'Why should anything be up?'

How to put this tactfully? 'That was kind of a desperate kiss.'

'You certainly know how to cut a fellow down to size,' said Coffin, rolling over on his elbows on the bed, but he was more amused than angry. 'Not desperate, just bewildered.'

'That isn't like you.' Stella rescued the bottle of nail varnish, and put it away tidily in a case. It was true, her husband was usually in control of himself and the scene: sometimes angry, sometimes depressed, but always sure he knew where he stood. Or that was how she saw him.

'I have just listened to the most extraordinary tale and I don't know whether I believe it or not.' He stood up, and walked to the window. There just in view was the old churchyard. A woman was pushing a pram round it, and there were two dogs behaving the way dogs do. An old man was sitting on a bench, apparently asleep. It was not going to be an easy area to excavate. If he decided to do it.

'I suppose it is one of those cases you can't talk about,' said the experienced Stella.

'I am going to talk about it to you.'

'Oh, thank you.' Stella appreciated the compliment.

'You're sensible.'

Ah, the compliment shrank a little.

'So I am,' she said, getting up, wrapping the silk jacket – which the warm embrace had disarranged a little – more closely round. 'What are you looking at out there?'

'The old churchyard.'

Death again, she thought, there's always death in our life. My husband's career has been largely built on the deaths of men, women, and children.

'It figures in what I am asked to do: I am asked to investigate a serial killer who did the deeds over eighty years ago (only they were not called that then but monsters), and find the grave of one of his victims.'

'It's a joke?'

Coffin shook his head. 'No, it wouldn't be funny if it was, but it isn't.'

'You can ignore it, say you are too busy to investigate deaths so long ago.'

'I'm too busy all right,' said Coffin gloomily.

'Who is it who is asking you to do such a thing?'

Coffin took a deep breath. 'Richard Lavender, former Prime Minister.'

'I thought he was dead. No, that is not true, I didn't think about him at all. Past history.'

'Go on,' said Coffin, still gloomily. 'You aren't cheering me up, but it's what I thought myself. More or less. He is not dead, very old, but alive and articulate. Also, it seems, the possessor of a conscience that must be assuaged.'

'He didn't do the killings? Don't tell me he was the mass murderer! What a play it would make.'

'It would take a Shakespeare to do it justice ... but no, he said it was his father who did the killing. He and his mother did the burying. At least, if we can believe him.'

She caught the note of doubt in his voice. 'You don't believe him?'

'I don't know. I just don't know. Come on, what do you think, you're outside it, what do you think?'

'Be sensible, you mean.' Stella sat down at her dressing table, and studied her face. She drew her mouth down in an ageing but sensible expression. 'Well, why should he lie?'

'That's it. What is the motivation? I can't make it out. He says he wants to die with a clear conscience.'

'We all want that, I suppose, but it hasn't worried him all these years.' A thought struck her. 'He must have been very young, you can't blame a child.'

'Not quite a child. A very clever one, too. And then all those years in power, controlling London. Why didn't he do something then?'

'He does believe it?'

'Mm, mm. I think so ... but I feel he might be under the influence of the people he lives with ... A man called Jack Bradshaw.'

'Oh, him,' said Stella.

'You know him?'

'Comes to the theatre, belongs to the Theatre Club, even does the odd review for the local paper. Yes, I know him.'

'What do you make of him?'

'I like him, I think he's got a sense of humour.'

'Perhaps this is his joke,' said Coffin, gloomily again.

'He may not be kind,' she added thoughtfully. 'I don't think I would count on him to do the kind thing. It might not be a kind joke.'

'It wouldn't be, but unkind to whom to rig this up? Apart from me, of course. He'd have to hate the old man to manipulate him in that way. He could do it, I suppose, he's writing his life. Perhaps old Lavender is senile.'

'Does he look it?'

'No, but it might need a trained observer.'

'Aren't you one?'

'In a way, yes . . . This conversation isn't getting anywhere. Give me a new start.'

'Does he live alone? Is there anyone else?'

'He may have more of a circle than I know. I could find out, and there is the niece. Great-niece, but she is just a domestic character.'

Stella shook her head. Women are never just domestic characters. Inside they are plotting another world like everyone else. Probably even animals did it in their own way. Cats certainly did, she thought, looking down at her own cat, former lost cat, ex-warrior of the streets, now an aged domestic retainer in a livery of tabby.

'Do you think he is mad?'

'He could be. With the sort of madness that can come sometimes with extreme old age . . . Not exactly madness, really, just too many memories, too many dreams remembered.'

'It seems to be the memories that are the trouble.'

Coffin went to the window to look down on what he could see of the former church below, now part of the St Luke's Theatre Complex, and then beyond to what had been the old churchyard, with the aged tombstones ranged around it like dead teeth.

The church was a solid Victorian building which had survived two world wars, much bombing, only to fall victim to the decline in churchgoing. The church had been deconsecrated, and converted into a dwelling in the tower, into which Coffin had moved, while the church itself had been turned into a theatre, and a theatre workshop and an experimental theatre.

'It was a different world outside there then, when he was a boy. The London of his childhood was rougher and nastier and poorer in so many ways. Dark streets, and cramped, crowded living places.'

'Oh come on. Dickens was dead, you know.'

But Coffin would not be stopped. 'As a boy, he must have heard all about the murdered women, read about them in news sheets. Talked about it. Perhaps he buried it in his memory through the years as he became rich and successful. Now he has let the memory out, and he has taken on the guilt.'

Stella said: 'I must think about that . . . perhaps there was something in those days that he had guilt about and he has transferred it . . . Make a good play.'

'Jack the Ripper was not so far off in the past. Still a terrible name to conjure with. Talked about at the time . . . People would have been reminded of him. It would have been in his mind.'

'Perhaps his father was Jack the Ripper,' said Stella lightly. 'Come back for a second go.'

'That would be something, to identify the Ripper after all this time,' said Coffin, 'and to have him father a Prime Minister.'

It was not quite a joke.

As he looked out of the window, he saw a tall figure going into the old churchyard; Coffin watched as the young man threw himself full length under a tree and buried his face in his hands.

An actor, of course. Only an actor walked with that air of ease and elegance, and then behaved with so much emotion. Unless he was a duke.

'Who is that beautiful young man who crossed the road with such consummate grace and then fell on his face?'

Stella got up to look. 'Oh, that's Martin. Martin Marlowe. He's just joined the company. He is lovely, isn't he?' There was frank appreciation in her voice: no one liked a beautiful

28

young man more than Stella. Usually it went no further than detached admiration, but possibly not always.

Coffin looked at her and shook his head. 'Not for you, darling.'

'I wouldn't think of it.'

'You may think. Look but don't touch.'

Stella laughed. 'You are a pig. Or you can be. But bless you, I promise you that boy has enough emotion in his life without me joining in.'

'I thought that from the way he fell upon the grass. Hamlet himself.'

'Oh, do you think so?' Stella was appraising. 'I see him more as Romeo. Romeo after he's lost Juliet.'

'Has he lost his Juliet?'

'Not yet, but he's well on the way. He's had a noisy row with his girlfriend, everyone heard, he was most articulate. So was she, come to that.' She didn't sound too miserable at the thought. 'It will give depth to his acting, of course.'

Coffin was still looking out of the window. 'That must be why he is beating the grass with his fist. Is that sorrow? I am bound to say it looks more like anger.'

Stella came to look. 'I expect he is just rehearsing his part.'

'What did you say his name was?'

'Martin Marlowe.'

Coffin was thoughtful. 'Real name or just for acting?'

Stella said slowly, 'His real name.'

'Ah.'

There was a pause, then she said: 'You know who he is?'

Coffin said slowly but without emphasis: 'I know.'

'I suppose you usually get to know things like that.'

'It's part of the job. As you say, I get told that sort of thing.'

'He doesn't talk about it a lot, but he understands that people know and do. He doesn't hide it, I call that brave.'

'I didn't know he was in a cast here.'

'He's only just joined. I went down to Bristol to see him act there, liked what I saw and offered him a part. He's very young still . . .'

'I could see that.' It had been a very young man who had flung himself on the grass, and then to hammer it with his fists. An emotional young man. He did not accept Stella's comment that he was rehearsing his part.

'He did well at RADA, didn't win any prizes, but we all know that prizewinners don't necessarily have the most brilliant careers.' Stella herself had never won a prize as a young actress, but her career afterwards had brought her several; she was up for a BAFTA award now. 'But he has a way of getting straight at the audience that will stand him in good stead.' She added: 'Of course, he knows some people remember what took place and will talk about it. He accepts it. He told me that he doesn't remember much . . .'

'Do you believe him?'

'He was only eight.'

'You can remember a lot of what happened to you at eight,' said Coffin. 'And death . . . murder . . . your own father.'

'But that is just what would block it.'

'What about the sister?' The sister had been much older, about sixteen.

'She is a surgeon in a hospital in East Hythe.'

'Isn't it unwise to let a young woman so well acquainted with a knife become a surgeon?'

Stella was angry. 'That is very unkind. And not like you.'

'Yes, perhaps it is in bad taste.'

'She is a different person from the girl who stabbed her father.'

But Coffin had read the official reports on the murder, had read the pathologist's notes and seen the photographs of the victim. None of these had been seen by Stella.

Fourteen years earlier a family tragedy had been played out across the river in Chelsea. Henry Arthur Marlowe, a reasonably successful barrister, but a heavy drinker who became violent when drunk, was stabbed to death by his two children: a son, Martin, aged eight and a daughter, Clara, then sixteen. They stabbed him to protect their mother whom her husband treated savagely when drunk. Within a few weeks, the mother killed herself. In spite of everything, she had loved her husband. The girl Clara was in deep shock, inarticulate, not able to talk freely; not willing to, either.

The sitting room in the house in Vernon Gardens was full

of blood, there was blood on the stairs, blood in the bathroom and blood in the bedroom where Averil Marlowe lay deeply asleep; she had taken a sedative.

The victim was lying, his body half across the doorway into the hall. He had been stabbed several times. Each wound penetrating deeply. This had been no quick killing.

The girl had let her mother have her sleep out before waking her with a cup of tea to tell what they had done. She herself telephoned the police, confessing to the killing.

When the police got there, the boy was found, asleep with the knife clasped to his chest. Both he and the girl were covered in blood which they had not washed off.

From prints on the knife the boy had certainly held the knife, and there was a bloody thumbprint on his father's shirt.

But the girl did the main job, Detective Inspector Headerley had said. And he had added a scribbled note to the report that Coffin had seen: 'And she wasn't joking, every blow was meant.'

The boy, being so young, was not charged with any crime and could not be charged – he was sent to live with foster parents. The girl was put into a special establishment for disturbed and violent children, where she had a breakdown but responded to treatment, and after she was calm and cooperative, no trouble to anyone. Being highly intelligent, she had no trouble getting the exam levels demanded by the medical school of her choice. Her background was known, but after several interviews she was accepted. She was the best student of her year, but she had one little idiosyncrasy: she never spoke unless spoken to.

Still looking out of the window, Coffin said: 'Do they still see each other, the brother and sister?'

'I believe so,' said Stella. 'But I am only just beginning to know him, and I have only seen her once.'

'Did she speak to you?'

'No, that's how it goes, I believe.'

'Hard on her patients.'

'Martin says she has a professional technique for work. I

31

think they fill in a questionnaire and read it to her, that gets her going.'

Coffin still had his eyes on Martin, then he turned to Stella. 'I have always had a feeling that we got something wrong about that case.' He shook his head. 'And yet I don't know what.' He looked out of the window again. 'He's getting up.'

'Rehearsal over,' said Stella cheerfully.

Coffin watched Martin's progress; he certainly was handsome, and strode forward with a gentle, elegant air that was attractive. 'He's coming this way. I believe he is going to call on you.'

'I wouldn't be surprised,' said Stella. 'I asked him over for a drink.'

'Stella,' said Coffin warningly.

'No, of course not.' She sat up very straight and managed to look indignant. 'Nothing like that. Why, he's a baby.' Then she said sweetly: 'You'll get a stiff neck if you look out of the window at that angle, and you know policemen are very prone to stiff necks . . . it's an occupational disease.'

It was very hard to get the better of Stella, reflected Coffin as he went down the long staircase to let Martin in and take him to the sitting room, which, like the bedroom, overlooked the churchyard. It would be flooded with sunlight, and Stella had recently redecorated it in soft yellow. He was still laughing when he got to the door.

Martin stood outside on the low step, running a hand up and down the soft silk sleeve of his jacket. He looked expectant but smiled tentatively. 'Stella asked me in for a drink before dinner.'

'I expect she will ask you to dinner too. Come on in.' Coffin held the door.

'Oh, I never think of her as cooking.'

'Oh, she won't cook it.'

Martin looked at Coffin with surprise and query.

'Not me either,' said Coffin. 'I expect we will go to Max's or get him to send something over.'

The young man tripped on the stairs and apologized. 'S-sorry.' He had a little stammer.

'This is a difficult staircase. Copied from a Norman trip

stair in castles, I always say,' joked Coffin. He put out a hand to steady the lad.

'S-sorry . . . I'm not usually so clumsy.' Martin had this slight but not unpleasing stammer. 'I'm always nervous with a policeman.' He looked at Coffin. 'I've got a bit of a past, as you know.'

Coffin nodded silently.

'I always tell people if they don't know, just to get it out of the way.'

'You had no need to tell me.'

'I expect you knew anyway. You probably know more than I do. The thing is, I've forgotten. Silly, isn't it?'

'No, not silly at all. It's probably a sensible way of dealing with it.'

Martin looked at Coffin as if he didn't know exactly how to take this. Then the sitting room door was opened smartly and Augustus burst forth with a little bark. Stella followed, red satin catching the light. 'He says he needs a run,' she said, holding out her hand to Martin. 'Come in, Martin.'

Martin bent down to pat the dog. 'Good boy, nice fellow.' He looked up. 'I'll take him, Stella. Just across the road to the park.'

'I don't know if dogs are allowed there,' said Stella doubtfully.

'Oh, this fine fellow won't be stopped. He's a real beauty. You were right to get him, Stella.'

Augustus and Martin seemed acquainted, which Coffin found mildly irritating. 'You know the dog?'

'Oh yes, isn't he nice? He's from the Deddington kennels . . . they have a lot of the old Alderbourne breed in them which makes them special. I knew it was the right place to go to.'

'I've always had mongrels before,' said Coffin, thinking of his last dog and the dog of his troubled boyhood, who had appeared out of a bomb shelter, the only survivor. Coffin had always felt that he and that first dog had a lot in common. But then he had felt the same about the second, only a mongrel, a rangy beast and a good fighter.

'Oh, they're the best of all,' said Martin, 'if you can get a good one, but if not you can't go wrong with a peke.'

'And so you told Stella?'

'Yes, she took my advice.' Martin bent down to pat the dog. 'Come on, Gus, off we go.'

They bounded down the stairs, sure-footed this time.

'So he chose the dog for you,' said Coffin, coming back into the room and throwing himself on the sofa. 'Let's get out the champagne.'

'Oh, come on.' A flutter of red silk settled beside him. 'Don't be childish, besides, he's your dog, I bought him for you. He's Augustus, his mother was called Empress and his father was Pompey, Policeman of Rome.' And she laughed.

Coffin laughed in spite of himself. 'You are making that up.'

'You can look at his pedigree.'

He stood up. 'I don't believe a word of it, but I will get the drinks out. And do you want champagne?'

'No, of course not, he's far too young to give good champagne to, let him have gin and like it. Or a nice sweet white wine, much more his style.'

'I'd be surprised,' said Coffin, as he moved away. 'He has obviously got good taste.'

He got the reward for his good humour because Stella came up to him and kissed his cheek. 'That is a lovely compliment, thank you.'

'He's back, there's the bell.'

Dog, Martin and Coffin, with a tray of drinks, came back into the living room together. By this time, Stella was standing by the window staring down across the road to the old churchyard. Last year it had been turned into a small park, and all the dead, long dead they were by then, were disinterred and buried in one big grave in the new cemetery in East Hythe Road, where one great stone was their memorial. The old headstones were placed like a stone fringe in the former churchyard. The years had worn away most of the inscriptions but some could still be read: she remembered a Duckett, several Cruins, and many Earders, all of which names the district still knew. Families seemed to stay in Spinnergate over the generations.

Surely. she asked herself, when the churchyard was turned into a park, and graves were dug up, they would have found a body if one had been buried there?

As Coffin came up to her, offering her a glass of wine, she looked towards where Martin was playing with the dog, and murmured: 'But wouldn't a body have been found last year when the graves were dug up?'

'I have been wondering about that myself,' he said quietly. 'None was found as far as I know, and I think I would know, but as I remember only the central area of the churchyard was excavated, and a wild area with shrubs and grass around left.'

He moved away to give Martin his drink. Martin stood up and smiled. 'Thanks, I feel better already. I felt suicidal before I came . . . this is my big chance' – he looked at Stella – 'and I don't want to fluff it . . .' He walked over to her, drink in hand, and followed by Augustus. 'I really have a problem with Shakespeare . . . I know you are not supposed to say so, but the verse is so difficult . . . it's dialogue, right? I want it to sound like dialogue and not verse.'

'Well, Olivier managed it,' observed Stella, 'and Gielgud managed to combine both.'

Martin groaned. 'Have a heart, please. I am not in their class. Not yet.'

'What's the part that worries you?' asked Coffin, trying to take his own mind off a dead woman who might not be there.

'Malvolio, a tricky part at the best and I have to get it across to an audience of schoolchildren.'

Stella explained: 'It's an examination text this year – we always try to do a performance of the play if we can. We get a grant from the Schools Theatre Society on condition we do it. Short run and full houses . . . the kids are conscripted.' She turned to Martin. 'Best part in the play, and you know it.'

'And the most difficult . . . I've always fancied Sir Toby Belch.'

'You will have to wait a decade or two to do that.'

'Or Maria . . . good part, that.'

'Don't go bisexual on me.'

Coffin watched them gloomily: they were flirting, it was only a theatrical flirtation, which did not usually mean much, but he found it hard to handle. And you never knew where it could go: to bed quite often, and then best friends for ever, only they might never meet again – that was the theatre world.

I'm afraid, he said to himself, that's it. I am afraid. I fenced myself in, I built a wall and felt safe inside it. Stella broke down that wall. I can't risk anything with Stella and nature has not made me a trusting customer.

Nature and his profession. There he was again, thinking about Dick Lavender and his astonishing story. He wondered if he could get away with doing nothing, and telling the old man that there had been nothing to find.

But bodies and bones have a way of outing themselves when least you want them to.

He raised his eyes to Martin, who was saying that in many ways Shakespeare's tragedies were easier to act than his comedies. 'We laugh at different things now compared with Tudor England, but we cry at the same. I could manage tragedy.'

No doubt, thought Coffin. Perhaps we all can.

'Depends on the part,' said Stella, always willing to enter into a good theatrical discussion. 'I defy anyone to call Hamlet easy, or Lear.'

'They support you,' said Martin with animation. 'Iago must be a wonderful part to play.'

'We don't do *Othello* much for the school and college audiences,' said Stella drily.

Augustus sidled up to Stella, opening his mouth and looking at her intently. He gave a little bark.

'He wants a drink.' Martin reached out a hand to pat the white head.

'He's not having gin or wine.'

The loose sleeve of Martin's jacket had fallen back; Coffin saw a line of just-healed scratches on his arm. Three ragged, not parallel but haphazard, lines. Gouged out. They didn't look like loving but overpassionate scratches, more as if delivered with a sharp instrument. Say a knife. To his experienced eye they looked both deep and sore. Fairly new, also.

'I'll get a bowl of water,' Coffin said. A self-mutilator? Or how much did the lad see of his sister of the knife?

The conversation was going on when he got back. Stella was showing Martin a book of her press cuttings; she was unusual among actresses since she kept bad notices as well as good ones. 'Look at that one' – she pointed – 'the stoat ... never got a good notice out of that man, I always got the parts his girlfriend wanted. Even when he decided that he wanted a boyfriend and not a girlfriend, he didn't change to me ... Now this one, bit sharp, but not bad. I was a bit facile in those days.' She frowned. 'I think I have got over that, life knocks it out of you in the long run.'

Martin picked out a review. 'You know, I couldn't do that ... keep the bad notices. I'd have to tear them up, pretend they hadn't happened.'

'It's one way,' said Stella, closing the book.

'That's what makes Jaimie so mad with us ... my girlfriend,' he explained. 'She says I bottle things up. So I do, I suppose.' He sighed and suddenly looked very young.

'Jaimie is not usually a girl's name, is it?'

'Can be. She's very strong, is my Jaimie, but we do get across each other,' he said sadly. 'I expect we will split up. She says I'm a dreamer, not focused and too repressed.'

'She does love you.'

'I daresay it is true ... she's very focused herself.'

'What does she do?'

'A writer ... freelance journalist ... she says I am a table for one permanently reserved.'

'She has a good turn of phrase.'

'She's very clever; she's on to a good story at the moment.'

'Oh?'

'No, she hasn't said much, probably afraid I'll talk too loudly. Something from the past is all I know.' He had seen Coffin notice his arm and he smoothed the sleeve down in a protective way. 'Never keep a cat,' he said lightly.

'We do, but it doesn't scratch.' Not quite true because Tiddles not only put out a sharp paw on occasion but had been known to bite as well. Lovingly, Stella always said, but Coffin wondered.

When the telephone rang, Stella, who was nearest, picked up the receiver. Her voice registered surprise. 'It's for you, Martin.' And she handed the telephone over.

'Jaimie, hello. Yes, I'll be there . . . d-down . . .' He was stuttering again. He turned to Stella: 'It's Jaimie, I asked her to pick me up here.'

Stella nodded. 'She's on the way then?'

'Down below, mobile phone.'

Stella decided to be gracious; she was also curious. 'Ask her to come up for a drink.'

Martin stood up, a wary look on his face. 'Thank you, I know she admires you. She would l-love to come.' Once again he stammered.

They heard him clattering down the stairs, the door open, then silence.

There was a long wait.

'She doesn't want to come,' Coffin said.

'No, in spite of admiring me so much . . . Wonder what she's like.'

'Tough, I guess.'

'Wonder if she gave him those cuts on his arm?'

'You saw them?'

'Of course, and no cat did them. She did. Love and hate.'

Coffin stood up. 'I think they are coming.' He held up a hand. 'Listen.' Someone fell up the stairs, then laughed an apology, getting only silence in reply.

Martin was first into the room; he was followed by a tall, young woman with a mane of fair hair, unbrushed, wearing dark jeans and a dark sweater. She had a small, lovely face, but she looked cross.

Proudly, Martin introduced her: 'This is Jaimie.'

She held out a hand. 'Jaimie Layard.' The hand was not directed at anyone in particular.

Stella took the hand, pressing it gently before returning it to its owner. 'Jaimie is a pretty name, but unusual.'

Jaimie's face did not change, but she was willing to provide some information. 'I took the name myself, I got it out of a

38

book at the time – I was aged eight. I was christened Jessamond and it wasn't right for me, I didn't want to go through life as Jessamond. Jaimie did me, I might have chosen anything though. I don't see why you shouldn't change your name as you grow.'

'Actresses do change their name,' said Stella. 'I use my own, but it might have suited me to change it. And if there had been another Stella Pinero on the boards, then I would have *had* to change. Couldn't have two of us.' She smiled at Jaimie. 'A professional matter. You are a writer?'

'Journalist.' Jaimie accepted the glass of wine that Coffin was offering to her.

'Which paper?' asked Coffin.

Jaimie drank some wine. 'Freelance,' she said after a pause.

'Martin says you are working on a story?'

She shrugged. 'Oh, it's something or nothing. I may drop it.'

How does a freelance journalist live, if she drops her story without getting it into print? Coffin asked himself. Jaimie, although plainly dressed, was not poorly dressed, her clothes were expensive, the bag thrown over one shoulder was beautifully shaped and of very good leather. Even her hair was designer-unbrushed. Then he remembered her name was Layard. Money, there. He remembered something else about the Layard family too: soldiers, fighting men all, Jaimie looked a fighter.

At the moment, she looked a cross, aggressive fighter who was not pleased with Martin, not pleased to be dragged up the tower, and even less pleased to meet a policeman and his actress wife. Maybe she suffered from jealousy and if so he had a fellow feeling.

The telephone rang on the table by his side. He picked it up.

'This is Dr Bradshaw . . . May I speak to John Coffin?'

'Speaking.'

'It really is John Coffin himself? This is such a very confidential matter.'

Coffin covered the telephone. 'Stella, I will take this call downstairs. Please excuse me, everyone.'

In the kitchen, he asked what the call was all about.

'First, here is the telephone number of the journalist.' Jack Bradshaw read it out. It was a local number. 'But I have not succeeded ever in talking to her directly, you get the answerphone and later she rings back.'

A phone in a rented room, Coffin thought. But we could trace it easily enough.

'Her name,' Jack went on, 'did I say, is Marjorie Wardy?' His voice dropped.

Coffin held the receiver to his ear: And I might already know who she is.

'Can you describe her?'

'Tall, wearing dark spectacles, with curly black hair.'

Ah. Well, there were wigs.

'I expect I can find her. And she is digging around in the story?'

'I think so, from the questions she asked. But I cannot imagine how she got on to it.'

'Dick Lavender hasn't spoken of it to anyone?'

'Not that I know of, he's only recently told me. I could sense he was working up to something but he took his time. To tell you the truth, I believe it was her questions that made him feel he must unburden himself before it was done for him.'

'Would it be so terrible if it came out? It will in the end if I go investigating.'

'He thinks so. If it comes out that his father was a killer of women, then he wants to be the one who tells the story.'

'Yes, I see the force of that.'

'But there is something else: I told you he had had anonymous letters . . . Today there was an attack on him.'

'What? Is he harmed?'

'A big bunch of mixed flowers was delivered . . . it was covered in transparent paper; when it was opened it appeared that the flowers had been covered with some sort of irritant powder affecting the eyes, nose and throat.'

'So what happened?'

'It was opened by Janet, she deals with all parcels, he never came near it, but it was meant to hurt. For an old man the result might have been serious. No, it was sent by an ill wisher.'

'Not one who knew the ways of the household, though.'

'True. So no one close. There is hardly anyone, to be honest, only Janet and the woman who comes in once a week to help with the laundry – the old man likes all his personal linen washed and ironed by hand, no laundry. But Lavender thinks, and I think too, that it is someone who knows the story. And wants . . .' He hesitated.

'Vengeance? It's been a long time coming. Hardly likely to be a contemporary of Lavender as a boy.'

'No, but possibly the descendant of one, someone, man or woman, who knew about it from parents or grandparents. Seriously, I believe there is someone out there who is after the old man. And I cannot believe it goes back to his days in government, although God knows he made enough enemies then. But most of them are dead. No, this is someone else.'

Oh good, Coffin thought, not only do I have to find the remains of a long-dead woman, but I also have to find a hunter in the shadows.

He went to the kitchen to look out; he was nearer to the old churchyard on this lower floor. A child was playing on the grass while his mother stood watching. An older woman was walking towards one of the flower beds. An old man sat on one of the seats, smoking and reading a paper.

Peaceful scene, Coffin thought. I may be about to turn it into a less tranquil place. He could imagine the digging, the police screens set up to shield what they might have found.

He turned away. I have been told an extraordinary story. The threatening letters to Richard Lavender, and now this bunch of flowers, they are not dangerous episodes in themselves, but there is a threat.

He heard Martin and Jaimie tumbling down the stairs, he could hear voices which sounded angry. He thought he heard her say she didn't want to come to this house again.

Upstairs, Stella was finishing her drink with a thoughtful look. 'I didn't ask them to stay for a meal, I think they are about to have a quarrel. One of many, I fear. So I encouraged them to go.'

Coffin sat down beside her, he picked up the end of the silk girdle that went round Stella's waist and was tied up on the side. 'Do you think you could hide all that fair hair of hers under a wig?'

Stella shrugged. 'I expect you could. Yes, I daresay. Why?'

'Tell you later, but I feel as though I am being led into an unpleasant business.'

And as if the past had reached out a bony hand to tweak him. He did not enjoy being reminded of his own boyhood and youth, when he had felt that he might get stuck in a world he did not like and when he knew it was up to him to fight his way out.

He was going to need assistance with the problem the former Prime Minister had set. It was like being given an errand by Mr Gladstone, the moral imperative was strong.

Phoebe Astley, he thought, he would set her to work.

He looked at Stella; if she was jealous of any other woman in his life, then it was Phoebe.

3

Phoebe Astley was a senior police officer who had been brought into the Second City by John Coffin to head a special unit. Since one of the purposes of this small and secretive unit was to check on the performance and behaviour of the local force, he had taken Phoebe from another county. Phoebe was a forceful, dark-haired woman with great energy. Charm too when she chose to use it, but because of the delicacy of the tasks she was given, she preferred a smooth neutral manner. Archie Young was her nominal chief but she reported directly to the Chief Commander.

Underneath, however, she was never neutral, as Coffin knew well. Their paths had crossed in the past, tangled together, you might say, and the memory of their past relationship was something they chose to bury. What remained was trust and friendship, and that was good. In his career Coffin had found that you needed a colleague you could trust, and there were not too many of them. In Chief Superintendent Archie Young he had such a one, and he was coming to feel that his young assistant Paul Masters was another.

He considered Phoebe for the task; in the past, the joke had been that work was her love and sex was her hobby. These days she seemed to be keeping that side of things discreetly in the background. He doubted if she had turned into a nun, but there were no tales and no gossip. Yes, he could use Phoebe Astley without the fear that she would meet the scholarly Jack Bradshaw and eat him up. The old Phoebe might have tried a nibble or two, because there was no denying that Dr Bradshaw was attractive, if dry and occasionally pompous. A scholar, he said to himself, probably cannot resist having that manner.

Phoebe's office was tucked away, hidden almost, on the top floor of the new police building. She had three anonymous-looking rooms, which suited her, finding she did not mind in the least that the furniture was standard equipment with little charm but very practical. The great pleasure was the splendid view from windows over the Thames and the Second City. Phoebe drew strength from the panorama stretched out below her which she stood looking at when she had a problem to solve. The shifting light on the Thames seemed to illuminate her mind.

Her home, if you could call it that, because she never seemed to settle, was at present in a one-room flatlet on the Isle of Dogs from which she commuted by means of the Dockland Light Railway. Her flat was minimum care and since she never did anything but sleep in it, eating always on the job and drinking black coffee as soon as she got to work, it suited her. She said her only virtue as a housekeeper was that she did not smoke. Even this had not been true a few years ago when a bad health scare had put her in hospital and given her pause for thought. Now she ran and swam as often as she could.

She had a staff of two, a man and a woman, who managed the computer and the equipment added to it, and unobtrusively worked with her. To be unnoticed was part of the job. Coffin knew her well enough to be sure that Phoebe maintained an active social life in districts well beyond the Second City.

She was always at work early, so that she was there when Coffin telephoned her the morning after his meeting with Richard Lavender and Jack Bradshaw.

'I want to talk to you.'

'Is it a job?'

'Yes, one for you alone.'

'Aren't they always?'

'It's an odd business. One you may not care for. Or you may be greatly interested. Either way it needs careful handling. It might be as well if you did not involve Gabrielle or Leander.'

'That might be hard to do.'

'As little as possible then.'

'I'll be over, if it's that confidential you'd better send Sylvia and Gillian out.' Coffin was silent, his two secretaries did not listen at doors, but Phoebe must be allowed her jokes, she was often a bit sharp about other women. (It worked the other way too; Stella for instance treated Phoebe with friendly caution.) 'Will Archie Young be there?'

'No.'

'It is secret then.' Phoebe gave herself an invisible pat on the back. Although she liked Archie Young, who never got in her way, she was a natural competitor who liked to outscore others. Every case to which she was privy alone, she regarded as a top mark. But she was fair and did not regard this as one of her better traits, only a natural one.

She walked into Coffin's office, passing Paul Masters, who was talking to Gillian, with a wave. He moved quickly to get to Coffin's door but Phoebe was quicker. 'Expected,' she said blithely.

Paul turned to Gillian. 'I'm supposed to check everyone who goes in.' But he said it without rancour: he liked Phoebe.

'Take a tank to stop that one,' said Gillian.

Coffin stood up politely as she came in. 'Thank you for coming round straight away.'

'You're the boss. I have plenty of work on hand, the Pickles case to begin with, but I walked right across.'

'It's something I have promised to do myself.' He paused. 'But I need help.'

He told her the story, complete with names and personal impressions. She knew the name Lavender, she said, it was in her schoolbooks, and she knew he wasn't dead, but she had never thought of him as a live person moving around the London scene, somewhere between a ghost and a memory.

Now it turned out he had a secret. Either that or he was nursing a little madness.

'I believe I have met Dr Bradshaw . . . He gave a lecture at the John Evelyn Public Library on the writing of history.'

'Sounds incredible, doesn't it? Can you believe it?'

'Yes, I think I can. People do have family secrets. Traumas buried deep. I am not saying I believe it was all as Richard Lavender said – he may not remember accurately, he may be indulging in a fantasy, hanging on to a false memory. It happens.' She thought about the story, then said:

'But something is there.'

Coffin trusted Phoebe's judgement. 'I believe you, I feel the same. But whatever is there is bloody, murky and deep-buried.'

Phoebe said: 'But I can't think why he wants to dig it up. He knows all sorts of things come out in a murder case.'

'He wants to repent, to make amends,' Coffin explained. 'Also, there is a young journalist going round asking questions as if she knew something.'

'Now that *is* interesting.'

'And the Grand Old Man wants to get his story in first. He still has a lot of political sharpness.'

'I wonder what part Jack Bradshaw has in all this? Could he have fed this story to the old man?'

'I don't know what his purpose could be.'

'He's writing Lavender's life: a tale of murder would certainly take it to the top of the bestseller list. But who's to know about motives?' She added thoughtfully: 'He looks to me like a man who could keep a secret.'

'The old man trusts him.'

Phoebe said: 'Well, we will do what we can. An interesting problem, quite different from anything I have ever done before. I think I might enjoy it. No idea where to start.'

'I'm damned if I know either.' He got up and started to walk round the room. 'I don't know why I said yes, but he still has power to command, that old man.' And then he said guiltily, 'And I have to admit the idea of tracking down a multiple killer from the past had its attraction for me. Can you understand that?'

'Yes, sure. I've always understood you more than you knew.'

There was a silence between them.

'We could have ruined each other once, Phoebe, you know that? We nearly did.'

'But we didn't.' She smiled.

'No. We drew back. I wonder why?'

'Natural sense of preservation, I suppose,' she said lightly.

'No, I think it was something other . . . we didn't want to lose what we valued in each other.'

Phoebe smiled again. 'I would remind you that we didn't meet for about ten years after that. Small value.'

And when he just gave a smile back: 'How's Eden?' she asked.

Coffin shifted his mind away from this dialogue with Phoebe to consider Eden. Phoebe had shared a flat with Eden in her first weeks in the Second City. Eden had then managed a shop selling expensive fashion clothes; when it folded she had taken a job in the theatre in the costume department. 'Oh, doing well, as far as I know.'

Eden was small and very pretty. The theatre gossip was that she was in love with Martin. Not difficult to believe.

'She's happy working in the theatre. Did you know her name was really Edith?'

'I'm not surprised,' said Phoebe. 'I met her mother once and she did not look the sort of woman to call her daughter Eden. Come to think of it, I heard her call her daughter Edie. Of course, I thought it was short for Eden.

'Has it occurred to you that you yourself might be at risk? That you have been drawn into this investigation to drag you into trouble?'

'Yes, it has occurred to me,' Coffin said soberly. 'I always look for things like that. A suspicious nature after years on the job.'

'So?'

'I am going ahead.'

'I thought you would say that.' Phoebe hitched her shoulder bag over her right arm and gathered up her document case with her left. It was raining outside so there was a raincoat as well. 'And you want me to make a start? Not sure where I do that, never done this sort of case before. You could call it historical research.'

'I hope we can continue to think of it that way . . .'

'I might enjoy it. I have always liked thinking about the past.'

'Think of it as writing one chapter on "Death in the Old East End of London before the first Great War" . . . Begin with the written records.'

'Death certificates?'

'And the old local newspapers . . . Most of them have folded, so see what the Second City Public Library can do for you.'

'You need a scholar not a police detective,' said Phoebe, giving her bag another hitch, she seemed to be treating it like a weapon.

'Pretend to be one.'

'I can't give all my time to it. I have plenty of other work on hand.'

'Wouldn't expect you to. I'd call it important but hopeless . . . You may never get anywhere.'

'As long as you know.' They eyed each other. 'I will make a start.'

He handed over his folder with all the notes he had made. He did not say to her that he had identified the woman journalist who was on the prowl as Jaimie, a girlfriend of a promising young actor, partly because he wanted to think about that and partly because he wanted her to make the identification for herself.

'Come and have dinner with us tomorrow night, tell me what you've got.'

'Will Stella like that?' Phoebe had no illusions of how and why Stella was not too fond of her; she liked Stella, admired her, but had no desire to get closer.

'She will.'

Stella would not be there, though, he knew very well she would be in the north, seeing a possible new production and that he would take Phoebe to Max's restaurant and talk to her there. To make sure, he rang up and booked a corner table for tomorrow night. Less easy to be overheard in a corner. Also, Max understood about corners and he had some nice private ones where you could hardly be seen at all.

It was nothing to do with him and Phoebe in the past, or any possible relationship now, there was none, but he did not want any questions about this piece of investigation floating around the Second City.

Once again, he found himself thinking about the girl Jaimie, she struck him as a clever, pushy young woman.

After leaving Coffin and Stella the evening before, Jaimie and Martin had quarrelled, or rather, let the anger surge up again. It was one of their better quarrels in as much as after a certain amount of pummelling and throwing of china, accompanied by the shouts that sooner or later one of them would kill the other, they ended up in bed. But the resentments between them were still there.

'You knocked me over,' said Jaimie, examining her bruises.

'You fell,' said Martin in a tired voice. He was not unscarred himself. He put his arm round her and nuzzled her head. He was all for peace now, spent, worn out.

Jaimie rolled over on her back and looked at the ceiling.

'Every time you touch me, I feel as though you are touching your mother.'

Martin shot away, his skin tingling. 'Damn you, damn you, damn.'

Although it was in the small hours, he got up and banged out of the flat.

'Goodbye, Jaimie, or whatever you call yourself.' He shouted it out over his shoulder.

'It's true,' she shouted after him. 'True, true, you think about your mother when you make love to me. Run away if you like, you always run away.'

'I'll come back and kill you,' he shouted back at her. Then he slammed the door and walked through the rain to his sister.

His sister lived in part of a house near the hospital where she worked which she shared with another doctor. She had the ground floor and a dark basement which led on to a tiny garden where she grew plants in pots. Her rooms were painted white and sparsely furnished, there was no untidiness; you got the impression that every object had been chosen with great care. She said herself it was the only way to live after her years in a controlled world. Another sort of person might have burst out into wildness, but she had come to like the idea of smallness of choice. It was not without significance that she specialized in microscopic surgery. Knives hardly came into it.

Clara was as tall as her brother, as blonde as he was and almost as tall. She was always beautifully if casually dressed, with her hair cropped short. She remembered her parents and knew that she looked like both of them.

She came to the door to let her brother in. 'I knew it was you. Only you, Martin, could ring the bell at three in the morning ... I am on call, so if I have to leave, you are on your own. What's the trouble now? But need I ask?'

He came in, shaking the rain off his hair like a dog.

Clara tossed him a towel. 'Here, dry yourself.'

'One of our worst rows ... Jaimie really is the end. It's terrible to love someone you cannot stand.'

Clara kept silent. She remembered her mother and wondered what else you could inherit besides hair colouring and blue eyes. Was there a gene for loving the wrong person?

'She thinks I want to kill her,' said Martin, rubbing his hair.

'And do you?'

'No, consciously, no. What do you think I am?'

'I don't know, my dear,' said Clara, sitting down and looking at him. 'I don't know what either of us are.'

'Oh Clar, darling, don't go all philosophical on me. I just need a bit of home comfort.' He had finished drying himself. 'She brings out the worst in me, that's all. I'll get over it. Can I stay the night?'

'Just for one night ... I don't want you staying here. I have enough watchful looks to contend with without them adding incest to the list.'

She did not hide her identity from those who wished to know, but she had changed her name, thinking, and rightly, that here patients might not care for a surgeon so handy with a knife. She was Miss Clara Henley, FRCS. Henley had been her maternal grandmother's name. She was training herself to speak freely.

'Don't,' said Martin, flushing, remembering what Jaimie had said about his mother. 'Clar, there's something I ought to tell you about Jaimie ... You know she's a journalist? Well, she's been researching some story, but she wouldn't say much about it. I thought it was about some long dead-and-gone figure ... well, maybe it is, but maybe not. I think she's been researching us, and that's what she is going to write about.'

'There can't be much left to say.' Clara took a deep breath.

'She'll find something,' said Martin with conviction. 'I think that's why she moved in with me. She's going to make a story out of it.' He looked at his sister's face. It wouldn't do him much harm, and the publicity might even help him, but Clara, that was another matter. He knew how hard she had struggled to get where she was, and how even now she was working in a lower position than her age and qualifications merited, but she had started from a low base. 'I'll kill her, I really will kill her.'

'Oh, go to bed,' said Clara wearily. 'You can kip down on the sofa. Good night.' At the door, she turned back. 'Don't worry if you hear me go out, it's just that I am on call. I will take the phone through so it won't disturb you.'

He thought he did hear her later, the door seemed to open then close quietly, and in the morning she was dressed as if she had been out. 'Yes, I had a call. One of those emergencies which call me out but not my consultant. I hope I didn't disturb you.'

Martin had not been disturbed by any noise, but he had had bad nightmares on and off through the night.

Coffin knew nothing of Martin's disturbed dreams, although later he was to hear of them.

He worked on routine matters all the rest of the day. There was an arson case in an electrical factory that was getting a lot of attention, and a police officer had been shot at, not hit, thank God, but lucky to be alive; the newspapers were giving both cases the big treatment and were not full of praise for the Chief Commander.

Perhaps Phoebe was right, he reflected as he drove home, and he was being conspired against. He knew he had enemies. It seemed a roundabout way of doing it though, and it wouldn't put a gloss on the name of GOM Lavender. There must be easier methods of bringing down John Coffin.

He could think of at least three. He allowed himself a smile as he parked the car. Someone who had lived his sort of life had left plenty of strings for enemies to pull upon. He had lied at various times, knocked one man unconscious and killed another, all in the cause of duty, of course, but you weren't supposed to do it. No malice. That is one thing you can say about me, he said to himself, as he opened the door, there is no malice in me. Anger, yes; resentment occasionally; jealousy at odd times; and the other lusts of the flesh as the occasion called out for.

Tiddles met him at the door.

'She's out, is she?' Coffin knew the signs.

The dog came down the staircase more slowly, since his short legs found the risers taxing.

At their silent but earnest request, he went into the kitchen to open tins for both. Both were eating dog food tonight; sometimes they both ate food marketed for cats, but they never seemed to notice the difference.

A savoury smell coming from the oven hinted that someone, probably not Stella, had been preparing an evening meal. He opened the oven door to make an inspection. A large casserole was simmering away.

'I didn't know we had one of those,' he said aloud.

From the door, Stella said: 'We don't. One of Max's assistants from the restaurant comes round to do it, this is chicken and ham.'

'Smells like it.'

'It's a very good new service that Max is thinking of starting up. Kind of luxury meals on wheels. You can choose from three menus and Max says they will change from week to week, according to what is in season.'

'How long has it been going?' asked Coffin suspiciously.

'Just started, we are the first to use it. Max suggested it to me. If it's a success, he will build it up.'

'We are an experiment then. He's trying it out on us.' Coffin liked Max and appreciated his food, but he also saw that Max aimed his arrows at Stella. Celebrated, fashionable, much-photographed Stella who brought in the smart customers.

'Well, you know Max, he's very adventurous.'

Some years ago now, when Coffin had first come to live in St Luke's and Stella had only just started the theatre in the old church, before they were married, in fact, Max had opened his first eating place. He and his daughters, the Beauty one and the Clever one and the Married one, had run it between them. Since then he had prospered and taken on the catering in the theatre. Max's restaurant was now a smart place to eat in the Second City, which was not famous for good food.

'He ought to pay us,' he protested.

'This meal is a present,' said Stella, showing that she too had a business head. She had learnt a lot from Coffin's half-sister, Letty, who always knew where a bargain was to be negotiated. She was at present in Hong Kong, where she was doing business. Letty was a backer of the theatre, for which Stella was grateful. She was expected back in London soon, which gave Stella another reason for gratitude since the season was not doing too well and she was pressed financially; Letty would see her through, she hoped.

She was fussing round the kitchen, opening cupboard doors and then closing them again. 'Oh, you've fed the animals.'

Coffin said he had.

'What sort of a day?' she asked.

'Oh, this and that. What about you?'

'Trouble with *Twelfth Night*. Martin came in with a black eye, nothing much, just a mark under one eye, but someone gave it to him – the love of his life, I suppose – and a bruise right down the side of his face. That wouldn't matter, make-up could deal with it, but his wits seem to have gone too. The rehearsal was bad, very bad, and mostly due to

Malvolio – the part is quite as crucial as Sir Toby, you know, and he buggered the whole thing up ... I don't think I can get away tomorrow. Must stay around and steady their nerves.'

'You're not directing though?'

'No, I brought Archie Tree in for three productions of which this is the first. It's his nerves I must steady.'

'Won't it be a pity not to see the boy in Edinburgh or wherever?' asked Coffin, thinking of his dinner with Phoebe.

'St Andrews ... no, I've seen a tape he sent me, and I saw him at Chichester in a Pinter play. I'll get him, I think. He's not a name.' So she would get him cheap. He would be a name, and she would have got in early, and that was all to the good. 'You know, I'm beginning to wish you hadn't got into this weird hunt for a dead woman. There's something odd about it. I don't like it.'

'I feel the same, but I think I have to do it. Not in person – I've put Phoebe Astley in charge.'

'Oh.'

'She's good,' said Coffin defensively.

'I wish she dressed better, but among all you men it's probably as well not to.'

'We're not that bad.'

'Yes, you are, a lot of chauvinist pigs.' Stella had had a role recently in a police series on TV and said she had learnt a lot, not from her fellow performers but from the police expert checking the show.

'It's not all like television,' protested her husband. 'I'm changing things. Anyway, Phoebe dresses to suit herself.'

Beneath the words they were throwing at each other there was amusement and affection. It was an argument, not even a discussion, they were enjoying each other's company.

One of your better moments, Coffin decided as he got out a bottle of wine.

They ate the casserole in companionable ease at the kitchen table.

They had finished when the bell rang below.

'I'm not going to look out of the window,' said Stella, covering her eyes, although she knew that she could not see their front door from the kitchen, 'but something tells me that it is Martin.'

'I'm afraid you are right,' said Coffin, going over to the window. 'He is invisible . . . although still ringing the bell . . . but there is the old bike you say he goes about on propped up against the wall.' He looked at the TV viewer fixed on his porch as a security aid. Yes, there was Martin; no one was really invisible.

He went down the stairs.

'I'm terribly sorry,' said Martin, as he came into the kitchen. 'I came to apologize for my behaviour today.' The bruise under his left eye was a dark evil streak, while on the other side of his face a long bruise stretched from cheekbone to jaw. He looked pale and thin.

'Sit down and have a glass of wine.'

'I let you all down, one of my worst goes, but I'll –' he stopped.

'You'll be all right on the night?' supplied Stella. She said it with some humour, but with intent. Then she went on, more gently: 'We all have emotional crises, performers more than most. Maybe they power the machine, I don't know, but your best work has to come through, or you are nothing.'

'Discipline,' said Martin, as if he had heard that word before in his life.

'Discipline – stay with us and you will get it.'

'I can't always control what I do, I have to admit it.'

'All performers have a devil inside them,' said Stella, 'or they wouldn't be what they are or be able to act. You have to have something strong and hard pushing you forward or you wouldn't stay in a tough, competitive craft. No easy answers for actors, Martin, and it never gets easier. If you win any laurels you can't rest on them, they turn into thorns and prickles. You might not win any laurels, probably will not, most of us don't, but you won't give up. The devil inside will see you don't.'

Except professionally and when speaking the author's lines, Coffin had never heard such a long speech from his wife. He got up and refilled her glass.

'Jaimie has got her own devil too, and that makes things

difficult. I admire her very much, she has such tenacity when she follows up a story, she's a good writer, too, but when she gets aggressive so do I. Or the other way round, either one of us can start it. Last night it was her fault, I think, but I did my bit.'

'Go round and make it up with . . . flowers, a book, chocolates,' suggested Coffin, anxious for the lad to finish talking and go away.

Martin was silent. 'I don't think she's there, not in our flat. I went round to look and it's empty. She's gone.'

'Left, you mean? Taken all her things with her.'

'No, not that I could see.'

'She'll be back,' said Stella.

'Yes, you are right, of course. She's working, I expect, she's very keen on one story she has in hand . . .'

'Does she have more than one?' asked Coffin.

'I think so,' Martin said slowly. 'She hasn't said much but she's been using the libraries a good deal, looking at old newspapers.' He looked at Stella. 'I think she also just might be doing a bit of research on me and my sister . . . I don't know how you would feel about that, Stella . . . Publicity, I mean, perhaps bad publicity.'

'Oh, no publicity is bad,' said Stella, rising to her feet. She too felt a hint might not be a bad idea. 'I wouldn't mind. It's past. Your past. But can't you ask her to leave it?'

'You don't ask Jaimie,' said Martin. 'She wouldn't take interference in her work. Anyway, I'm not sure. I may be imagining it and it's the other story that is what she is really keen on.'

He too had risen. 'Thanks for letting me talk. I won't let you down, Stella.'

'Better not.'

She walked down the staircase with him, halfway down they were joined by Tiddles, who stood waiting by the front door, ready to depart.

'She's got another place,' said Martin, as he stepped through the door, 'a little flat near the Tower, a workplace; she's probably there. I'll take a look.'

Stella marched up the stairs, talking as she went. 'Let's

have some coffee ... What a pig that girl must be, if she's really going to exploit Martin and his sister. He loves her.'

'It seems a very explosive relationship.' Coffin came down the stairs and they met by the kitchen door. 'He's had a fight, you know, those were real bruises.'

Stella was tolerant. 'The young are like that. Didn't you ever have a fight when you were young?' She was already measuring the coffee into the pot and wondering why Max had not sent a Thermos of his own coffee. The cat had decided not to leave but to return to the source of food which smelt pleasantly tasty to him.

'Only when I was working,' said Coffin. 'And not with a woman.'

Stella paused with the coffee pot in her hand. 'I did once, threw a bottle at my producer ... hit him right on the nose.'

'Did it break?'

'The bottle did, not the nose. He had a nose like Cyrano de Bergerac, that one. The bottle had red wine in it, ruined his suit.'

'You could have killed him,' said Coffin, accepting the cup she held out.

'Not that one, he's alive to this day, one of my best friends ...' She looked at Coffin and laughed.

'I think you are making it all up.'

'Perhaps a bit.'

'And all that stuff to Martin. About performers having the devil inside them. Did you mean it?'

'Half and half,' she said. 'We do show off a bit, but I was really trying to cheer him up. All the same, we aren't easy people.'

Rogues and vagabonds once, outcasts, if not working in a company, thought Coffin, looking at her lovingly, not easy people.

'In any case, I think it is another history that engages her more.'

Stella raised an eyebrow.

'Yes, I think she must be the young woman journalist who is researching Dick Lavender. If she is, then Phoebe Astley will be following in her footsteps.'

'Let's hope they don't collide.'

'Phoebe's not a bad sort,' said Coffin, going to his window to look out at the old churchyard. 'I suppose we had better dig it up over there. Just to take a look. As asked.'

He had a sudden picture of a dark night, with little street-lighting and no moon, when a boy and his mother pushed a dead woman through the streets to bury her in hallowed ground.

The past touched him with a cold hand.

Martin took the Dockland Light Railway out to near the Tower of London, then walked to where Jaimie had her little workplace.

She had the top flat above a flower shop. The shop was closed but the staircase at the right had a bell and an entryphone.

He pressed the bell. M. Flower, the name card said. It was one of her working names. He had no idea which, if any, really were hers. Probably there was yet another identity out in Berkshire or Surrey which was the real Jaimie. She said that investigative journalists needed pseudonyms. He wished he had brought his key, but he had thrown it at her in their last fight.

Always at the back of his mind was the memory of how they had met. He had been wandering round the public library near his rooms; he was new in the Second City and knew no one much except his fellow performers, and Stella Pinero. There was always his sister, but he was chary of bothering her, he was never sure she wanted to be reminded of him. So he was lonely and read a lot. The John Evelyn Library was a very good one, one of those libraries that the Scottish industrialist Andrew Carnegie had founded with money made in the steel mills of Pennsylvania.

The building itself was an old manor house, early seventeenth century, modified inside but still beautiful. A little parkland remained around it. Jaimie had picked him up in the Reading Room there where he was reading *The Times*. He realized she had made a set at him but he was young enough and sufficiently aware of his good looks to know his own attractions. Jaimie was so pretty, so intelligent (an Oxford graduate, child of stuffy parents in Berkshire – not in favour of education, she had said, so she did not see them often now – who made her own way in the world), so sexy, that their affair began at once.

It seemed all so spontaneous and natural that he never questioned it, never wondered how much of it was lies, but now he asked himself if she hadn't sought him out on purpose to get her story. She was going to write him up, and Clara as well.

Cold, scheming bitch, he thought. But he loved her. Or had loved her. How much could love survive?

'Jaimie,' he called. 'Jaimie, can I come up?'

There was no answer. He had expected none, he knew he was like a child, calling through the letter box of an empty house.

It was not death, for I stood up,
And all the dead lie down.
    Emily Dickinson, 1830–1886

4

As November the fifth approached, figures of Guy Fawkes began to appear on the streets. The shopping centre in Spinnergate was particularly well provided with small groups who had put together a guy, dressed in borrowed clothes, and propped up in a pushchair or an old pram, if they could find one, or if not sitting up in a cart made from a wooden box with wheels. Some guys looked smarter than others.

Jimmy Barlow and Tom Fisher were aided by Tom's sister, who was ignored by the boys and apparently nameless. Occasionally she would mutter to herself: I do have a name, I am Louise. Every so often she spoke, but she usually got no answer.

The trio were standing at the corner of Edward Street, which was not far away from their school, and led to Fisher Street, a row of shops with several large stores. Not far away was a car park. They had chosen this site on purpose, chasing away at least two rival Guy Fawkes shows.

Louise said: 'Watch your pockets, boys, crime corner, this is.' She was walking up and down, shouting out to remember the guy, remember the guy.

'Tell her to go home,' Jimmy muttered to Tom. 'Better without her. It's getting late.' It was a dark November evening.

'She won't go. She knows we have permission to stay out late, that's when the money is good, and we are collecting for charity.' Sort of, he added honestly to himself.

Louise said loudly: 'I want to stay. I am going to stay. It's quite safe, the police station is just round the corner.' She moved forward down the street and rattled the box she was carrying. 'Remember the guy, please, remember the guy.'

A woman who was coming out of Boots the Chemists tried to pass her, but Louise waved the box and called out again: 'Please remember the guy.'

'Here you are then,' said the woman, dropping a silver coin into her box. After all, she had pushed a guy around herself as a child. She looked at the guy. 'Not bad. Did you make it?'

'Helped,' said Louise. She hopped back to the two boys. 'There you are, I am collecting better than you are.' She rattled her box.

The woman who had made her donation to Louise turned back; she said: 'Is that your guy too, the one in the car park?'

'No, Mrs,' said Tom.

'Someone has left one there. Been there all the morning. Might have come last night.'

'Someone has lost it,' said Tom.

'Is that likely? Dumped, yes, lost, no. You don't lose a guy. I have been young myself.'

'I will go and have a look,' said Tom. They could have two guys and Louise could have one all to herself. Lucky Louise.

His sister was there before him.

The guy was in a big box, propped up against the fence of the car park. He was wearing a big hat, very old and battered, made of black felt, underneath was fixed one of the usual Guy Fawkes masks, this one looked particularly unpleasant because it had shifted sideways slightly. A jacket covered the top of the body, and the hands wore gloves which rested on an old blanket. You could just see the tip of a shoe.

Louise went up to look, she walked round the back, pulling the guy away from the wall. 'Jolly heavy.'

Then she screamed.

5

Coffin and Phoebe Astley had their dinner together as arranged. The table in the corner of the big room (Max had expanded over the last two years, creating two rooms where the kitchens had once been, separated by an arch) was the one where you could observe all, be seen yourself if you so desired – although there was a row of little shrubs in brown pots that could be dragged forward to shield you – and yet not be overheard.

If the Chief Commander had known that the performers in the Stella Pinero Theatre, and picking it up from them, his own officers, called it Lovers' Corner, he would have avoided it. In unusual innocence, he thought of it as a private spot to talk. He was often there with Stella but not tonight. After a difficult day full of dull routine and irritating interviews, he would have been glad to see her, but she had decided, after all, to fly to Scotland to interview the young actor in whom she was interested.

Phoebe had got to Max's before him, studying the notes she had made.

'I started with two lives of him written about the time he retired from office. He lost an election and bowed out. Both the books are lightweight: *The Lavender Years* and *Life of a Prime Minister*. He didn't like the boring official life, apparently.'

'Not then.' Coffin poured her some wine. 'He does now. Or anyway, one over which he has control.'

'Yes, that side of him comes across: he had to be in charge. I got the books from the local library. You know it, I expect, the John Evelyn? I haven't used it much, but I knew the librarian, she belongs to my Women's Group –'

'Good heavens.'

'I shall ignore that, and as it happens, we don't just discuss women's issues, but we are a support group. And if you think I didn't need one when I joined the Second City Force, then you are wrong.'

Women had so many ways of making you feel humble, Coffin thought; this was not Stella's style, she went for the straightforward stinging comment, but Phoebe's was just as powerful. Also, in Phoebe's case, it annoyed him because he knew that in the background of her life there was always a man giving her support in one way or another.

'I'll look into it,' he said. 'You weren't harried in any way, were you?'

'Nothing overt, or I'd have cut their balls off.'

Coffin winced. He was old-fashioned about words.

'They knew I was under your protection.'

Coffin winced again; he wondered if Phoebe was doing this on purpose. She and Stella could circle around each other like suspicious cats, and this might be a circling.

He moved the conversation back to the library. 'What did you find?'

'The two lives, as I have said, but then I started in on the files of newspapers. They keep *The Times*, and all the local papers back to the Boer War as far as I could see. Possibly further. Probably got the obituary of John Evelyn in the *London Gazette* for 1600 or so. When did he die?'

Coffin shook his head. 'After the Great Fire of London, I think. He had Peter the Great of Russia to stay with him to learn shipbuilding.'

'It's all interesting reading ... they had a female serial killer there in the 1920s.'

Coffin raised an eyebrow.

'No, not a Mrs Lavender. She was a nurse, she suffocated her victims ... I suppose her craft made that easy for her. Seven, she did in, and three more suspected. All old men who left her what they had. Not a lot, they were not rich, but their families took it badly and that was what got her in the end. She was hanged, of course, they did use the rope and the drop then.' Phoebe spoke with a certain gusto.

I needn't worry about her having a soft heart, decided Coffin. 'Don't waste your time reading papers of the twenties, these deaths were just before the 1914–1918 war.'

'I am getting the feel of the area, though, and that counts. When I started I must own I could not believe the tale, somehow it sounds more credible now. You get the feeling that it was a place where anything could happen.'

'Still is,' said Coffin.

'One woman produced four babies at a birth – sensation. They all died, of course, one after the other, but she was so upset that she would not admit the last one, a boy, was dead and pushed him around in a pram for days and days until she was stopped. And then a man claimed he had a talking dog, people queued up to hear the dog talk. They knew it couldn't and didn't and that it was him, but it made them laugh to see him struggle to get the voice out and move the dog's jaws. The interesting thing was the man–dog voice used to predict the future if you paid enough, and it seems often got it right. Odd, isn't it?'

'Don't believe a word of it.'

'Yes, I have to admit that I did think that the dog was a bright reporter trying to get a good story. Especially when it was by-lined E. Wallace.'

It could have been the young Edgar Wallace, Coffin thought, he was a Londoner and knew the Docklands. Greenwich and Deptford was where he grew up. Also, a Ripper murder was just what would attract him. 'He was an established writer at the time,' he said. 'He'd been a war correspondent in South Africa. I think he might have been short of money, he had family responsibilities ... he was writing anything he could turn his hand to ... ghostwrote the life of Evelyn Thaw whose husband murdered her lover in New York, and any number of articles and short stories.'

'When I have tracked down the names of women found murdered in Spinnergate or Swinehouse, then I will try to find out all the details I can. I will also be going through the police records. Unfortunately, the Records Room, which was in the old Headquarters, was bombed by a zeppelin in the First World War and in the Blitz in the Second. Fire bombs did most damage, there are great gaps. If you take my advice . . .'

'Go on.'

'You won't expect too much.'

'I don't.'

'And you might get one of those keen young archivists from Oxford or Cambridge to go over the early records and see what they can salvage.'

'Can't afford it,' said Coffin in a detached voice. Across the room, he could see Martin sitting with a group from the theatre. Although with them, he was apart.

'Excuse me a moment.' He went across to Martin, who was staring into a cup of coffee. The lad looked up as he came over. He looked surprised, then he smiled.

'How did the rehearsal go?' asked Coffin, although Stella had spoken about Martin on her mobile from the airport, and had already reported that the boy was steadier.

'Better.' Again that charming smile. 'I just pushed everything aside and got on with it.'

Coffin nodded. The boy must have had plenty of practice at that sort of thing. Pushing the horrors aside and getting on with it. But the trouble was that they festered inside.

'And Jaimie?' He wanted to know about her, because she touched his life and this matter of Dick Lavender. Where she had gone, he might send Phoebe.

Martin looked at his coffee, he shook his head. 'Not back with me. I went to her flat in the City where she works. I don't know if she was there, but she did not answer. I don't believe she was there. I know she is angry with me, but she has never kept it up, always comes back.' He added slowly: 'It may be this other story she was working on – I don't mean me and Clara. It excited her, she is very ambitious.'

'Let me know what happens.' Coffin patted him on the shoulder, then returned to his table.

'What's up with that young man?' Phoebe had been watching. 'He looks hag ridden.'

'You think it's serious?'

'I do.'

'So do I.'

The first course of their meal, one of Max's famous cold fish mousses, was waiting for them. Phoebe picked up her fork. 'I know who he is, of course.'

'Sure you do.' Coffin tasted the mousse. 'I had better tell you, he has had a row with his girlfriend, she's cleared out.'

'He's looking for her, I suppose.'

'She is a journalist, it seems likely that under her pseudonym she is the young woman working on the Lavender story.'

Phoebe nodded. 'I may have met her then. One of my best friends works for the *Daily Shout*' – this being the name given by all to a bestselling daily – 'and I went to a party there. Is she fair, pretty and tall? Well, perhaps there are a lot of them around, but this one was a bit drunk and talking about the story she was going to sell.'

She added: 'I believe she wears a dark wig sometimes.'

'She is also working on a story about Martin and his sister Clara,' said Coffin in a level voice.

Phoebe blinked. 'Loyalty to a lover doesn't come into it, does it?'

'The boy has come to the conclusion that he was only her lover so she could get the full details.'

'I think it wise of her to go missing; if I was her I think I'd stay away permanently,' said Phoebe, turning to look at Martin. 'He's lovely, isn't he? But perhaps not too safe to know.'

'He didn't kill his father, he helped his sister but he was only a child. He remembers, of course.'

'A bad memory to grow up with.'

'For them both, I think.'

Neither of them were eating very much, the fish mousse had been replaced by a chicken dish. Presently, Phoebe produced a file of papers. 'I have more to show you than I said: I got a print-out of some of the pages in the local newspaper. There were some articles on three deaths. I did go back to 1912 and 1913, almost up to the beginning of the war, in fact.'

She produced a selection of print-outs. 'Look, three articles. Not signed, probably was not allowed, but initialled as by E.W., and there is a photograph.'

It was a thin, young face, with dark hair sleeked back and shining. As yet you did not see the familiar heavy spectacles of the adult and famous Edgar Wallace. He had probably needed the spectacles even then but perhaps had not wanted to be photographed in them. We all have our vanities.

She pointed. 'He did one article on the first murder, that terrible photograph is of the dead woman Mildred Bailey, but two on the second – I suppose it was more sensational. The first was in January 1913, and the second, Mary Jane Armour, in April of that year. There was a third, a woman called Eliza Jones, in May 1913. There may have been at least one other death, Isobel Haved, who just disappeared, probably dead – he mentions her. Made it more of a story, I suppose, but she may have been one of a series of murders by one man.'

Coffin reached out for the papers to study them. 'You've done well, I think you are on to something.'

'Now I have got a start, I shall go backwards through the newspapers to see what details I can find . . . Pity the police records went up with the bombs, but I will poke around and ask questions. There might be a response.' Especially when they know you are involved, she told herself.

Coffin was reading what she had already. 'All three strangled, but savaged in other ways . . . two of them, anyway. Not too much detail there, he doesn't give too much about it, wouldn't do at the time, I suppose . . . All the bodies found tucked away, one in an alley, another in a gutter and one in a park . . . Killed elsewhere, though, it was thought.' In the Lavenders' family home or thereabouts, if Dick Lavender had it right.

And soon after the first Great War in Europe had started and the young journalist, as well as the rest of England, had had other deaths to think about.

'If I go through the newspapers, I will probably get more on the killings. Also, I may read that the murderer of these women was found, in which case, it cannot be the deaths that worried Mrs Lavender and son.'

'Unless he is having a fantasy,' said Coffin thoughtfully. 'And he and his mother never got up to any high jinks at all. Just an imagining of an old man.'

'Worth thinking about.' Phoebe frowned. 'But I don't believe it, though. Did he give you that impression?'

'No.' Coffin drank some wine. 'Something hard to understand in that household, though. It puzzled me. Didn't seem natural.'

'Old age can be like that,' said Phoebe tolerantly. 'My grandmother used to tell me how she fought, in uniform, in the Great War. In fact, she had still been at school. In a way, she knew it, but she just managed to live on two streams . . . Lavender may be doing the same.'

'Giving me some work,' grunted Coffin.

'He's a former Prime Minister. There's the ghost of power still there.'

'No need to remind me.' He was looking across the room. There was someone pushing through the glass doors of Max's restaurant. 'There's Dr Bradshaw. What's he doing here?'

Phoebe looked across, she also looked pleased, and it struck Coffin again that Jack Bradshaw did please women.

'He's looking for you, of course.'

Jack Bradshaw was weaving his way through the tables to where they sat. With unashamed lack of style, which somehow became him, he was carrying a bag from a well-known grocery store. 'Chief Commander, there you are . . . your wife said you would be here.'

'She's back, is she?'

'She drove me here.' He looked at Phoebe. 'Now, we have met, haven't we? Forgive me if I don't know your name.'

'Phoebe Astley,' she said, holding out her hand and smiling. If Jack Bradshaw pleased women, then in Phoebe he had met an experienced connoisseur. 'I came to one of your lectures.'

'You sat in the front row, and asked a question. I knew I had seen you before.' Then he turned back to Coffin, placing his carrier bag on the table; he drew out some papers.

71

'I thought these might interest and might even be of use.'

Coffin reached out to take them. 'I should tell you that Chief Inspector Astley is helping me with this enquiry.'

Across the room, he saw that Stella had just entered. She was wearing a pale-pink pleated skirt with a darker pink shirt, all new to him, and he had a good memory for Stella's clothes, while being grateful that she paid for them herself. She smiled at him and gave him a little wave before going to speak to Max. A rush of happiness rushed through Coffin at the sight of her.

'I think I guessed,' said Jack Bradshaw. 'I am glad. I think a woman might see through more than a man would.'

Coffin put the contents of the carrier in front of him on the table. 'Have a drink, Bradshaw, while I look at these.' He motioned to their waiter, who was studying them with interest anyway. He had every intention of writing a crime novel and meant to put Coffin in it. (Max's staff were almost entirely recruited from out-of-work actors and hopeful writers.)

On the table in front of him were three photographs, one in a silver frame, the other two loose, all yellowing with age.

He picked up the one in the frame first to see a fine-looking young woman in bustle and feathery toque. 'Mrs Lavender?'

Bradshaw nodded. 'In her Sunday best, so her son assures me, he just remembers her dressed like it. Probably the same hat and skirt and jacket; I doubt if she had many choices, they were poor enough by all accounts. May even have been her wedding clothes.'

The unframed photographs were of a young boy and a man. Lavender and son, Coffin guessed.

He picked up the boy's photograph first. An earnest, intelligent face stared out at him. Not handsome, the older Lavender had grown into good looks. No, he corrected himself, life had made him look distinguished. History had made his face: this was the man who had worked through two wars, managed the British army, created an export drive, been Chancellor of the Exchequer, and finally Prime Minister. A man who had retired at the height of his powers.

Dick Lavender must have taken after his mother, or possibly an earlier forbear, because he did not look like his father. Edward Lavender senior had a pinched, nervous face, lined and thin as if no one had ever fed him enough. He was photographed wearing a jacket and tie and cloth cap. Perhaps he had been on a works day out. What had he worked at, Coffin wondered, looking at this slice of Docklands history.

'What did he do?' he asked. 'He doesn't look strong enough to be a docker.'

'He wasn't. No, he was a tally man, sold goods by instalments. Never a popular figure, of course, since people fell into debt so easily. Brought him in touch with the women, which he must have enjoyed.'

You don't like him, yet you have a touch of him yourself, thought Coffin as he pulled more papers out of the carrier bag. Some very old newspapers fell out before him. The first was the original of which Phoebe had a copy, the second was from another local paper, the *East Hythe Chronicle*, with a story about the murders in Spinnergate. Possibly by the young Edgar Wallace too, decided Coffin, but no photograph and no by-line.

'I've got a copy of the first of those articles,' Phoebe, who had been watching, told them. 'Not the second, but I would have found it in time.'

'I thought they might help,' said Bradshaw. 'Send you in the right direction.'

'They will . . .' Phoebe smiled. 'I'm just finding my feet. Historical research has not been my thing.'

Stella arrived at their table. 'I've ordered some more wine . . . No, no food, darling. I ate on the plane . . . the usual sort of wooden food, but it stops hunger pretty effectually.' She sounded cheerful. 'I got my man and I think he will be a winner as Jerry in Albee's *Zoo Story*, and I got him cheap.' She nodded. 'Well, cheapish; when he thinks it over he will be cross.' She smiled. 'Only two characters, too.'

'But will people come?' asked Phoebe, who admired Stella, but felt a little brush at times did no harm.

Stella ignored her and waved to the waiter to pour the wine. They drank a glass while Phoebe and Jack talked over what they were doing, and Coffin sat thoughtfully looking at his wife. She was up to something and he would like to know what. Max came over and murmured quietly in Coffin's ear that he was wanted on the telephone.

When the Chief Commander came back, he apologized, but he had to call in on his office. Nothing important, foreign affairs, but he must go.

Phoebe said: 'I've got some stuff in my office that might interest you, Jack. Let's go too.'

'We'll all go.' Stella stood up. 'I will drive and then sit and wait for you, John.'

As they drove through the streets the short distance to the Headquarters of the Second City Police, they passed a boy running towards a constable on the beat. The boy clutched at the policeman and started to talk. Words were pouring out and the policeman was trying to calm him down.

'Stop please, Stella,' said Coffin. 'I want to see what is going on.' He got out of the car.

'He can't keep his hands off,' observed Stella sadly to Phoebe, 'but I expect you know that.'

'I'm not allowed to notice,' said Phoebe.

The boy, his face blotched with red and white patches, was shouting at the constable: 'I'm not playing a game, and I am not being silly. We've got a body, it's dressed up as a guy, but it's a person.' As Coffin came up, he said, almost in despair: 'It's in the car park round the corner.'

Coffin put a steadying hand on the boy while acknowledging the constable's salute. 'You're out late with your guy.'

'We've got permission.' Tom controlled himself; he realized he had been on the point of tears. He was glad to talk about something else other than a deader in a box. 'It's for charity, see. Leukaemia research. We do it for them. Just keep back our expenses,' he explained.

'Of course,' said Coffin. 'Well, let's go and look and see what you've got.' He had a son once, long ago and long since dead.

'Don't say anything,' said Stella, as Coffin came back with the boy. 'Wherever it is, we will all go.'

*   *   *

In the car park Louise and Jimmy stood solemnly together, their own guy parked by the railing, while they stood guard over the guy in the wooden box. Louise was wide eyed at the approach of the party. 'Thought you were getting a copper,' she accused.

'I have.' Tom was now proud of himself, having picked up the picture of whom he had with him. 'This is the boss man.' He turned to Coffin. 'Here you are, sir, here you are.'

Phoebe was by his side, while Stella and Jack Bradshaw were a few paces behind. Jack had made an attempt to stay behind but had been dragged along by Stella Pinero. Even Phoebe had looked over her shoulder to say: 'Come on, Jack, it might interest you.'

The guy was leaning against the wire fence, which supported the lolling head. He had sagged after Louise had touched him as if he could bear no more. The mask still hid the face but the hair was falling down from underneath the hat.

It was a mass of hair, thick and gleaming, beautiful once, now ragged and stained with blood.

Coffin gently took off the hat and peeled off the mask. A livid bruised face stared back at him, the skin swollen about the eyes, the mouth a blue slit. But it was recognizable.

'Oh, my god.' Stella put her hand over her mouth.

Jack Bradshaw, moving as if he could not stop himself, came up closer to observe the face. There was a moment of silence, then he paused, swallowed and turned away to stare at nothing. As he turned, he muttered: 'I think I know her, I think it is Marjorie Wardy.'

'It is Jaimie Layard,' said Coffin.

6

The group of them waited, Tom, Jimmy and Louise as well, until the first police cars, followed very quickly by an ambulance, arrived. It was a dark night, but the car park was lit by a harsh yellow light which crept into every hole, and which made them all look sick. Jack Bradshaw leaned against the metal fence, his face turned away. Coffin and Phoebe talked in low voices.

Stella, it is true, removed herself a little, taking Louise with her – she could see the child was shivering in her lightweight jacket. 'Don't feel too warm myself,' she said, deliberately cheerful, as she put a rug round the girl's shoulders.

'I touched her, I wish I hadn't.'

'I know, it was a horrid thing to happen. I won't say don't think about it, but just try to keep in your mind that it was a good thing you did, because now she can be properly looked after.'

'Dead though,' whispered Louise.

'You still need looking after,' said Stella firmly. 'It's not good to sit around in a car park, dead or not.' She wound the car window down, air seemed necessary; she was not without imagination herself. Make a good scene, though, she thought, a bit out of Beckett?

A slight smile curved Louise's lips as the wind blew through the window; she was a pretty child. 'Yes, that's true . . . I know you are being jokey but I feel better.'

'Good.' Stella looked out of the window. She saw the police cars arrive, and then the ambulance. 'We can leave soon. I will take you home.'

Louise was a long-time addict of many a police series on

television. 'Will we have to go to the police station to make a statement?'

Stella was saved answering because her husband put his head through the car window. 'The police surgeon has arrived and the SOCO, so we can be off. The boys want to go in a police car and Phoebe and Jack will go too. I will come with you.' He smiled at Louise. 'Have you home soon.'

Louise received this platitude with the contempt it deserved. 'What about our guy?'

'That is safe. One of the police cars is bringing it along.'

'In its pusher?' demanded Louise. 'There'll be trouble if we lose that. We hired it, and we would have to pay.'

'I assure you that they have transported more difficult things than that pushchair.'

Louise's sweet smile showed. He's not so bad, she thought, quite handsome really, if he wasn't so old. She's lovely even if she is old too. Louise was ten, sophistication was thick upon her now, had been hers since birth. She had an older sister and a much younger brother. And they had not hired the pushchair but borrowed it, without permission, from the young brother. But it was always better, as Louise knew, to say you were in danger of losing money.

'It's all for charity,' she said, still smiling.

Of course it is, thought Stella, as she started the car, and charity begins at home.

Coffin sat beside Stella as she drove, but he did not speak.

'You're thinking.' The traffic lights at the turn towards the Central Police Station were red.

'Plenty to think about.' He looked over his shoulder at Louise who was staring out of the window. 'I will tell you some of my thoughts later.'

'I can guess at some of them. You didn't expect to see that girl, Jaimie there . . . and Jack did not expect to see Marjorie Wardy . . . Same person.'

'I knew she used the name of Marjorie Wardy.'

'As which person did she get killed?'

Coffin said absently: 'I don't think you can separate the two out like that.'

'I'm worried about Martin. Someone will have to tell him.'

77

Coffin did not answer, so Stella turned to look at him. 'I know what you are thinking: Unless he knows. He loved her, he didn't do this.'

'Keep your eyes on the road.'

'I am not saying he might not have killed her; he's got a record, hasn't he?'

'He's done it before. As you remind me.'

'But no man could dress up a woman he loved like that and leave her where she was found.'

'He is an actor, used to costume, make-up and setting the scene. There was a bit of theatre in all that.'

'Thanks.'

Coffin reached out an apologetic hand. 'Sorry, forgive me. It hasn't been a good scene, finding her there. You there too, and the children.' He looked back at Louise, still staring out of the window. Heard every word, he thought.

'It's this, darling . . . if Martin killed Jaimie, it would have been a serious killing, done out of love and anger . . . and there is a horrible, mocking, jokey side to this that is not Martin.'

'Clever of you to notice that,' said Coffin.

They had arrived at the police building, behind them two police cars were drawing up.

'You drive on home, I'll come back soon, there will be no need for me to stay long, the usual team will take over. The children will be driven home with a policewoman.'

'With our guy,' said Louise. She smiled at him and then let the smile fade, gently.

'With your guy.' He got out of the car. 'Come on, Louise.' What are you going to grow up like, Louise? He could just see an adult Louise, sharp, poised, well made-up, a businesswoman, selling something, driving a hard bargain, but fair and kind of heart. Damn you, Louise, already you know how to charm.

The other cars were near now, and he could see Phoebe and Jack Bradshaw. The ambulance turned left towards the police mortuary. Jimmy and Tom approached in the charge of a uniformed policewoman; they had got their nerve back and were looking cheerful. They waved. 'We are going to have a cup of tea and a biscuit.'

Coffin handed Louise over. 'Your parents will be here soon, Louise, and after you and the boys have answered a few questions, you will be off home.'

He went in through the main entrance, not his usual habit, since he had his own staircase and lift. Here he waited for Phoebe and Jack.

'We can leave them to it,' he said. 'The children will have to make their statements when the parents arrive but we need not hang about.'

'I was going to take Jack up to my office and give him a drink,' said Phoebe.

'Yes, he will have to make a statement sooner or later, but I don't know if it need be tonight in his case.' He looked at Jack Bradshaw. 'I think you need that drink.'

'It was a shock finding her there . . .' He shook his head, as if trying to drive away the memory. 'Poor girl, poor girl.'

'You recognized her at once,' said Coffin, not without interest. The face had been distorted and swollen.

'Yes.' Bradshaw got the word out as if speech was still difficult. 'It was instantaneous. In spite of the swelling and the bruising, I knew it was her.' He said with difficulty: 'Do you think this was just a random killing?'

She was a girl who could make enemies, Coffin thought, and to him it looked like a death and dressing-up specially devised for Jaimie or Marjorie. 'I think it was personal,' he said, 'but we don't know which of her personalities it was devised for.'

'I wonder how many people knew her as Marjorie Wardy?' asked Phoebe.

'I believe she had done a fair amount of work under that name,' said Jack Bradshaw. 'I looked into her a bit when she wanted to work on Dick Lavender. He asked me to.' He passed his hand over his face. 'Oh hell, I shall have to tell him.'

'You can tell him it's a good team on the job.' Coffin had run his eyes quickly over the CID officers who had turned up – he knew them by name and reputation.

In fact, Chief Inspector Darcy, having heard that the top man himself was on this case, had come hurrying forward, having spotted the Chief Commander from the staircase. He had been working late on a robbery with violence, but for the moment this body must take precedence. Inspector Upton and Sergeant Foster and the SOCO were down at the car park already.

'Just on my way, sir.' He halted by John Coffin. 'I wanted to take a look at the body. I understand it's on the way to the mortuary?'

'Be there by now.'

'I'd like Mr Garden to do the postmortem, if that's all right by you, sir.'

'Good idea.' Dennis Garden. 'He will probably want to do it in his own laboratory in the university.'

'He can, sir, once I've had a look. Like to do that first.' As he spoke, the chief inspector was unobtrusively observing who was with the Chief Commander. It paid to assess that sort of thing. Phoebe, he knew, but not the man.

Coffin introduced Bradshaw. 'Dr Bradshaw was with us when we were led to the body by the boy – I take it you know this happened? Right, well, Dr Bradshaw was able to identify the woman under one of the names she used.'

Chief Inspector Darcy absorbed all this without expression. 'I shall have to talk to you, sir,' he said to Bradshaw. 'One of the inconveniences of knowing a murder victim means people like me talking to you.' And even more so if you were there when the victim was found, he said to himself. But be polite, Darcy, and remember where you are, this chap knows top brass. And the mighty and mysterious Astley. Phoebe's activities and friendship with the Chief Commander had been noticed.

'Dr Bradshaw is writing the life of Richard Lavender,' Coffin told him. It wouldn't do to let Darcy fall into a hole he could miss.

'The Grand Old Man. That must be interesting.' Darcy looked at Coffin. 'He's on our list of people we look out for.'

'I know.' Not guarded, exactly, but offered a special awareness.

'Most people think he's dead,' said Jack Bradshaw.

'Not me, no, my grandfather used to vote for him.' He began to move away, trying to display that tact which his wife told him he did not have. I got them all smiling anyway, he said to himself, and it was a lie: Grandpa was a conservative from the day he was born, and he called old Lavender: 'That bloody red, who hangs around duchesses.' Not many duchesses in Spinnergate. And if you heard of a duchess in East Hythe you knew where his sexual appetites lay.

He saw his own boss giving him a wry look and decided it was time to go. And he did want to see the body. There was a lot to think about in this case of the woman with two names. Writers did have pseudonyms, he knew that, but life and his work had taught him that motives for two names were always worth looking at.

He turned to go, when the swing doors were thrust open. It might be the wind, a strong wind had got up which would blow away the mist. A dishevelled, frantic figure pushed through, came up to the group with a rush and then stopped dead.

He was a young man, wearing jeans, no jacket, in spite of the cold, dark night, his fair hair was tumbled by the wind; his face was bruised and scratched as if he had been in a fight, but the scratches were drying. The tears, though, were new, and still wet on his cheeks. He had cried on his way here and he was crying still. Trembling.

He held out in front of him a small bundle wrapped in a towel.

Coffin came forward. 'Martin, what's the matter? What is this in the towel?'

Darcy drew back a pace, watching. Another friend of the Chief Commander?

He took the bundle from Martin's hands and unwrapped it. The towel had been used and was wet from the rain. Inside was a brown paper parcel, not addressed to anyone. Still keeping his eyes on Martin, he unwrapped it slowly.

There was a stain of blood on the brown paper. Coffin was about to unfold the paper when Martin snatched it from him. 'It's Jaimie, it's her hair.'

81

Inside, resting on the paper, was a long tress of blonde hair which had been bundled in upon itself; it was stained with blood at the roots, and the roots were there, as if a strong grip had pulled the hair from the scalp.

'It's Jaimie's hair.' Martin shuddered.

Coffin took the hair from Martin. 'Calm down, Martin. How did you get this?'

'Came to me,' Martin whispered.

'How?'

'Pushed through the door.' Martin was talking in gasps. 'Just now, this evening. I opened it, Jaimie's hair. Where is she?'

He got hold of Coffin and began to shake him, crying out that he wanted help.

Darcy stepped forward and hauled Martin off. Coffin shook himself, like a dog that had been rubbed the wrong way. 'It's all right, Darcy, no harm done.'

Martin stood between them, head down, he was quiet now, but Darcy hung on.

The swing doors opened again. This time a woman came through. She had a raincoat flung over her shoulders, her hair was the same colour as Martin's, her eyes the same shape and just as blue. She stood there for a moment, without speaking.

Coffin moved away from Martin. 'What do you want?'

Then and only then, she spoke. 'Let go of my brother. Martin, are you all right?'

Martin muttered: 'What are you doing here, Clara? Go away.'

'I followed you.' Without looking at them, still staring at Martin, she said: 'I am Dr Clara Henley, Martin is my brother.'

Coffin acknowledged her silently: Yes, I heard that you, if not Martin, had changed your name and no doubt in medicine this is wise. He saw George Darcy's face, he too knew who Clara Henley was, part of his job, after all, and Darcy did his job well.

'I am John Coffin. Martin has been working with my wife, Stella Pinero.' Some instinct told him that if you did not oil the wheels with this woman they did not move. 'Martin came here to show us this packet . . . I was here by chance . . . he says it is the hair of Jaimie Layard.'

Clara did not answer, but she nodded.

Jack Bradshaw said in a clear voice: 'She had black hair when I knew her.'

'She had wigs,' said Clara. 'She's dead, isn't she? I saw the hair. I would call that hair from a dead woman.' She put her arm round Martin.

Coffin looked at George Darcy. 'Let's go into an interview room down here. Lead the way.' He looked at Clara and Martin.

Clara stood still, holding on to Martin, who was white but quiet. 'You've answered me: she's dead.'

'I told you so. I knew it. She's dead,' said Martin. 'I won't move a step till you tell me what you know.'

Coffin answered him. 'I am afraid so.'

He led the way into the small interview room on the ground floor. It was chill and damp with not enough chairs for them all, as one by one they filed in: Martin and his sister, Phoebe and Jack, and the two policemen.

Outside a rocket sailed through the air, Coffin heard the explosion. Then another and one more.

What kind of person, he asked himself, dressed up a dead woman as a guy? Someone full of dislike, someone who wanted to mock and belittle. A killer with hate inside. Love could turn to hate, of course.

'You have found her.' Martin looked from Coffin to Darcy and then to Phoebe and Jack Bradshaw. 'That's what this is all about. Where is she?'

Coffin did not answer. Not for you to see yet, he thought.

Martin stared at Phoebe and Jack. 'What are they doing here? Did he kill her? Did she?'

Bradshaw muttered, a wordless growl.

'Jaimie has been found,' admitted Coffin.

'Where? Where?'

'Not far away. I think that's all I can tell you at the moment.' He looked at Clara Henley, who was standing close to her brother, her eyes on the floor. She's been through this before, he told himself, she remembers. 'Dr Henley?' He

83

made it a question so he could get an answer. Any answer to start her off.

In a low voice, Clara said: 'I knew her sister Teresa at medical school.'

'There is a sister?' asked Coffin.

'Oh yes, any number, five, I think. That is how Jaimie got on to Martin. Teresa introduced them in the library. So it is my fault.' She bowed her head, accepting blame. 'Except she was a selfish little bitch, Teresa said so.' She put her hand on Martin's arm.

'Oh, shut up, Clara,' said Martin, turning his head away. 'You don't talk much but you always say too much. I am a grown-up now, and what I do is up to me.'

Coffin stood up. 'Martin, Dr Henley, Jaimie is dead and her body was found this evening in a car park. It is a case of murder and the rules have to be followed. An investigation has already started, with Chief Inspector Darcy in charge. He will want to talk to you both.'

He found he was still holding the parcel with Jaimie's lock of hair in it. He held it out and Darcy took it from him.

'He will want to talk to you about that as well, Martin.'

Coffin walked to the door. 'Darcy, this is for you now; I would like to see you when you have a chance to get on top of things. Tomorrow, sometime.'

Darcy was brisk. 'Right, sir.'

Coffin turned to Phoebe Astley. 'Chief Inspector, I would like a word now.'

Phoebe followed him to the door, and Jack Bradshaw moved after her.

But Darcy checked him. 'No, Dr Bradshaw, don't go, you stay. I need to ask you some questions too.'

Jack Bradshaw, Clara Henley and Martin Marlowe watched the door close behind Coffin. Bradshaw, who was not without humour, told himself that this was how the sheep felt when the sheepdog rounded them up.

Clara had been here before, and knew that now the questioning began. She looked at her brother, who did not look back.

*   *   *

Coffin faced Phoebe in the corridor. 'Up to my room, I want to talk.'

'Sure.' She followed him to the lift.

In his office, Coffin poured them both a drink. 'You realize what has happened, don't you? Two have become one: your digging into Richard Lavender's serial-killer father and the investigation into the death of Jaimie are now joined at the hip. Like twins. You understand the implications of what I am saying?'

Phoebe took her drink. 'I certainly do: I saw Jack Bradshaw's face when he saw Jaimie and again when he said she had black hair: he was in love with her.'

'Yes, I think so. Strong emotion there, anyway. Well, George Darcy will get it out of him.'

'He saw. He took it in. Martin Marlowe and Dr Clara Henley too, he'd heard of them. I saw it in his face.'

Coffin picked up his telephone. 'I must tell Stella I am on my way home.'

Phoebe finished her drink. 'And what do I do about my digging into the past of the Lavender family? Do I go on with it?'

'Yes, carry on with it. But remember, this young woman may have been killed because of her investigation, so look after yourself.'

'I can look after myself,' said Phoebe.

'Phoebe was not pleased that I recommended care,' said Coffin to his wife, when he got home not long afterwards. Stella was in bed, reading, with the cat looking out of the window and the dog on the bed with her. She was wearing big horn-rimmed spectacles as she read a script.

'You are taking this business seriously.'

'I am. You realize what this murder means, don't you?'

Stella took off her spectacles, she knew her husband, he was about to walk up and down the room, talking to her, clearing his own mind while throwing ideas at her. If she followed his movements while he paced she would become dizzy, so she had developed a technique of listening while not looking.

'No, tell me,' she said. You are going to do so, anyway.

'Two investigations have joined, not exactly become one, but twinned. Siamese twins, joined at the hip.'

'Has anyone told Dick Lavender yet?' Stella asked the question that interested her.

'No. Jack Bradshaw will do that, but George Darcy will be calling on him, I suppose. I shall go myself.'

'Is the old man mobile? I suppose he couldn't have nipped out and killed Marjorie–Jaimie?'

Coffin stopped walking to look at his wife, he gave a small laugh. 'You saw that guy.'

'All dressed up and nowhere to go? No, he could not have done that, but someone might have helped him out.' She laughed herself. 'No, life isn't like that, is it? It might happen on the stage but not elsewhere.'

'I think the same person killed Jaimie as dressed her up . . . let's settle on that name for her, shall we? It was her real name and we might allow her that dignity . . . the person who killed her, also turned her into a guy and wheeled her into that car park. There is real, personal hate.'

'I wonder what she did to deserve it?' Stella saw with relief that Coffin had ceased his walk up and down to stand looking at her. Perhaps she really served a useful function, lying here, asking questions. She looked at him with sympathy and respect.

We will stay together, she thought, in spite of all my sinful behaviour of which he is too clever not to know, but far too clever to show me he knows. There are his occasional fancies towards people like Phoebe Astley, but I forgive him for those.

She looked down at her hands, stretching the fingers. She had to accept that she did feel jealous of Phoebe. Quite strongly on occasion. Jealousy was a powerful emotion, irrational, too.

'What about jealousy as a motive?' she asked. She patted the bed. 'Come and sit down.'

Coffin sat on the end of the bed. 'She had charm, I admit it . . . Jealousy is such an unfair motive.'

'Charm is unfair.' The cat sprang down from the window to leap on the bed, giving the dog a cuff on the ear as he passed. 'What about Martin?'

'Darcy will have put him through it and sent him home. You had better keep him busy tomorrow.'

'I will do that.'

'I was glad you turned up today with Jack Bradshaw.' He was undoing his tie and taking off his jacket. 'Oh God, I am tired . . . Funny how it all happened, everything and everyone all rolled together to find the girl. Fate. It happens sometimes. And then I feel that there is someone or something sitting up there pulling strings and maybe laughing. Smiling, anyway.'

'That's called irony. You get a lot of it in the theatre. Although,' she added thoughtfully, 'not as much as you used to, writers being against what they call contrivance. But I like a bit of it myself.'

'You're talking for the sake of talking, aren't you?'

'Well, sort of.'

'Calming the old man down . . . I do love you, Stella. So you did get your actor? Good.'

'I did. He's joining us tomorrow.' She smiled reminiscently. 'Now, he has charm, his own peculiar unusual charm.' She laughed. 'He'll make an impact, I think.'

'I'm coming to bed.' Coffin took up his jacket and disappeared through the door.

'Take a shower,' called Stella after him. 'You smell of the police station.'

But I work there all the time, he thought as he plodded away, so I must smell of it all the time.

He went back to the bedroom door. 'That smell, Stella . . .'

She raised her head from the play script. 'It's an emotional smell, love, nothing more. You are emotional tonight, don't let it worry you.'

He went away, wondering what an emotional smell smelt like: sharp and lemony, he decided. Better than vanilla and custard.

*   *   *

In the morning, he came down to the kitchen to make them both some tea. Briefly, he wondered what he smelt like now. Love had its own smell, he knew that.

The tea was just made, in the special Herend pot that Stella liked so much, when the telephone rang. It was Chief Inspector Darcy.

'This is early.'

'Been up most of the night. Dennis Garden did the post-mortem on the girl in the small hours. He's off to a medico-legal conference in Toronto tomorrow for twenty-four hours and he wanted to get this done before he went off. She died from a blow to the back of the head. A blow in the posterior parietal region, he says. Produced diffuse neural injury, followed by oedema and massive haemorrhage. Stabbed as well, more blood.'

'Right.'

'Caused by a heavy object but a smooth one. Could be a stone wrapped in a cloth. We'd be lucky to find that, but we will go on looking. When we know where to look. We made a start on her own flat in the City. And I sent a man round to Marlowe's place in Spinnerwick. Signs of a bust-up there, but he said they had had a quarrel.'

'Where is he now?'

'Staying with his sister in his own flat. Not charging him, but he knows he is under suspicion.'

'Right,' said Coffin again.

'No evidence yet, but there will be some circumstantial evidence in due course ... And that guy business and the hair ... theatrical, isn't it, sir?'

In the middle of the night, Darcy had stood looking at the clothes removed from the body for forensic examination. The tweed jacket which had covered the top of the body, the soft felt hat and the old blanket tucked around her. Old clothes all, they had belonged to someone once and might yield a clue. He stared with particular interest at the jacket.

'Something about the jacket,' he said to Coffin.

Coffin did not answer. Outside, the early sun was reddening the sky and casting long shadows on the old churchyard across the road. I have an obligation there, he told himself. To look for another dead woman. How strangely events wove in and out of each other. Would Jaimie have died, but for the earlier death?

Supposed death, he said to himself. You don't know for sure as yet that there was such a death. Perhaps old Lavender was being theatrical in his old age.

George Darcy was talking on: 'There is something, sir, that came out of the postmortem.'

Coffin listened. 'Really? I am surprised.'

'I'm never surprised at that sort of thing,' said George Darcy.

'Keep me in touch.'

'I will, of course, sir. I'll be seeing Marlowe, hear what he has to say on it.'

Coffin put his hand on the teapot, it was still hot. He carried the tray up to Stella. She was awake, lying looking at the ceiling.

'I heard the phone.'

'Yes, it was Darcy.' Coffin poured the tea into the matching cup which he handed to her. 'Garden has done a postmortem . . . She was killed by a blow to the head.'

Stella nodded.

'He also discovered that she was pregnant. Very early. About six weeks.' He stirred his own tea. 'She must have known, though. Damn, and damn and damn.'

7

The old churchyard across the road from St Luke's was shrouded in the mist with the hint of a feeble sun. It was early morning, light had only just appeared across the sky and was struggling to break through the thick haze.

'Almost a good old-fashioned peasouper,' Coffin said aloud as he drank his morning mug of tea, staring out of the kitchen window. Stella was still in bed, although she had politely welcomed the hot tea he had taken in to her.

The news that had come with it about the pregnancy of the dead girl was less welcome. She did not say anything but he could see by the troubled look on her face that she was thinking of Martin. Whether he was the father or not, it didn't look good for him. In her experience, and Coffin's too, for that matter, the lovers of pregnant murdered women were in for a rough ride.

'May not be Martin's child,' Coffin had said to her. 'We shall have to find out.'

'You can ask him.'

'He may not know . . . but either way . . .' He paused.

'Oh, go and walk it off,' said Stella, turning her face into the pillow. 'Take the dog.'

He put the dog on the leash, walked down the stairs into the churchyard. He still thought of it as that, as did most of the neighbourhood, although officially it was now a small park with a swing and a roundabout for children, with seats for their parents. In fact, few children ventured in, whether they had their parents with them or not, but the seats were popular with pensioners on their way back from collecting their pensions at the post office round the corner.

90

Coffin walked towards the park, remembering how, when the church itself was turned over to secular use, the old churchyard had known neglect, and how as a result of pleas from Stella Pinero and Coffin himself, as well as his powerful sister Letty Bingham, it had been given a new life; a special dispensation from the Archbishop of Canterbury himself had allowed all the dead to be disinterred and buried in a new cemetery, lying in one great companionable grave, friends and enemies alike.

And now he thought: And maybe they left one behind. An unshriven soul, murdered by a man long dead himself.

On this cold November morning, Coffin and his dog were alone. Keeping Augustus close beside him, Coffin stepped off the narrow path to walk through the wet grass towards the area to the west which had been left with thick, uncut grass, dotted with aged shrubs and trees. It was a little crescent of rough ground that might go back to ancient woodland.

The ground under his feet was bumpy. He walked on, dragging a reluctant Augustus (who found the trees inviting) after him. A trio of bushes had grown together so that they formed a little thicket. Behind them was a plane tree, up whose trunk ivy was growing.

It was its own little world here, he thought, stepping carefully, keeping his eyes on the ground. The ground was particularly irregular under the tree, and to his imaginative eyes, the grass looked ranker.

No, he wasn't wrong there: the grass was taller, and thicker. He prodded the soil with his toe, not frozen but stiff and hard where it had been left untouched for years. He thought he saw signs – a grass thicket trampled down, a branch hanging loose on a bush – of other feet having pushed in here. The ground was too hard for a footprint but the frosty grass had been pressed down.

He could see where the feet had gone: round the tree, up towards the stone wall which was hidden by a belt of bushes and shrubs. Vegetation was triumphant here.

He could imagine what it must have been like here when the streetlamps of the early twentieth century had been lit by flickering gas jets, and when terraces of small houses had filled the streets. It would have been dark and quiet here among the trees. People probably minded their own business around here. A police constable would have walked the beat, but nothing would take him into the churchyard. If any noises or any movement was noticed then a pair coupling would be shrugged off as the answer. No one except a Peeping Tom would go to look.

Dick Lavender said he and his mother had buried the body in the autumn of 1913; a year later in 1914, there was war. Fighting in Flanders, and streets darkened against zeppelin raids. This would have been a dark and private place.

There were always animals, of course, he thought, looking at Augustus. Animals scrabbled and dug, but that did not seem to have happened here.

As if picking up his thoughts, Augustus sat down, raised his head and howled.

Coffin took the hint, he was cold himself, and turned back towards the road. As he walked forward, he heard a car draw up.

He thought he had found what he wanted in any case.

George Darcy was just getting out of his car. He saluted Coffin.

'I suppose 1914 was a pretty bloody year,' Coffin said, staring into the thicket.

''Morning, sir. Yes, pretty bloody.' Darcy walked towards the Chief Commander. 'The casualty lists soon started. Wiped out the old, professional British army. I see what you are getting at.' Darcy came up the path. 'You're out early, sir.'

'1914 . . . a terrible war, the victims of murder might get overlooked.' Missed but forgotten, he thought, not important when the slaughter in Flanders was racing on.

'There was a chap called Ball, hung in 1914,' said Darcy. He was a student of crime. 'So murders were investigated.'

Coffin said: 'I guessed it was you arriving.'

'Been up all night, as I said. I was driving past when I thought I saw you.'

Don't believe a word of it, thought Coffin, you were looking for me.

'I have been talking to Phoebe Astley . . . she's been around most of the night too, the work she is doing . . .' He did not look at the Chief Commander, tactfully looking into the distance. 'Kind of secret.'

'Confidential,' said Coffin. 'If she hasn't told you, then I will fill you in.'

'She mapped it out,' admitted Darcy. 'Anyway, word had got around, you know how things are . . . the upshot is that we agreed to keep in touch, if that's all right with you, sir.'

Coffin nodded. 'I agree . . .'

'She's got her line of enquiry and I've got mine, but that dead girl comes into both.' Darcy took another step into the churchyard. 'Phoebe wants to dig up here.'

'Someone has been in here already, trampling down.'

'Might have been Phoebe Astley.'

'Looks like bigger feet,' said Coffin thoughtfully. Phoebe was a tall woman but her feet were elegant and slender, whereas the feet that had left marks on the ground in the shrubbery had been big: boot-sized was how Coffin put it.

'She needs my help here with the digging. If you agree we will start digging today.'

'You don't need my permission: do it.'

The two men were pacing the path, side by side. Coffin was dragging Augustus, who would have preferred to go home.

'Come and have a look round,' said Coffin, leading the way into the rough ground. 'Tell me what you make of it.'

'Is this where Phoebe plans to dig?'

'It will be, I think. I have walked over the ground, and I think these' – he searched for the right words – 'either of these humps might be worth a look.'

'Could be anything.' George Darcy's natural reaction to almost everything was scepticism. It made him a good and cautious police officer, but a wearing colleague. He looked around. 'No cover, but I suppose you wouldn't be seen from the road.'

'I don't know what it was like over eighty years ago,' said

Coffin. 'But I guess it was dark enough. Lavender says they came here.'

'Does he really remember all this?' asked the sceptic.

'God knows.' Coffin shrugged. 'He believes it himself, I was sure of that. I wasn't sure if Jack Bradshaw believed him, or if Janet Neptune did. Have you interviewed her yet?'

'No, she has been seen by Sergeant Belle Dixon. Dixon said she seemed vague, she didn't have much to say about Marjorie Wardy ... she knew the girl as that, but Dixon thought she might know more than she was saying. I shall see her myself.'

'I got the impression she would be jealous of anyone getting at all close to Dick Lavender. I wasn't sure how she felt about Bradshaw.'

'Tricky customer, himself,' said Darcy.

'Oh, you think so? You could be right.'

'He had no reason to like Marjorie Wardy, who was encroaching on his own work and probably about to make more of a splash, not to mention more money.'

'Not going to be easy to find out if she was killed as Marjorie Wardy or Jaimie Layard.'

'Or both.'

'The pregnancy must be important. We ought to be able to find out who is the father ... who she was close to, the blood groupings, opportunity.'

'There is always opportunity,' said Coffin.

'She was only six weeks gone. I wonder if she knew herself.'

'Sex comes into it, must do,' said Coffin. 'I saw her with Martin Marlowe and she was highly sexed and difficult with it. Did she know she was pregnant? Did he know?'

'I haven't asked him yet, he may say yes and he may say no, I am not relying on him telling the truth,' said Darcy. 'I'm not telling anyone. Holding it in reserve. I like to have a shock or two in hand, it can loosen things up.'

The fog was lifting but it was as cold as ever.

'It'll get out,' said Coffin, 'always does.' He pulled Augustus forward. 'Is that what you came to talk about?'

Darcy shivered. 'Cold here, isn't it? Is it much of a success as a park?'

'Don't think so,' said Coffin, 'the kids avoid it.'

'Not surprised. I don't like the feel of it.'

I suppose the dead haven't quite walked away, thought Coffin. Not to mention that there might be another still here.

'It will be crowded once the digging starts. Press as well, TV cameras, the lot,' Darcy said. 'But Phoebe Astley will be masterminding that exercise. And what we are looking for and why is something else that will get out. Do you think Lavender took that into account?'

'No. He's a bit out of the world, just sees what he wants to see now.'

'He could not have killed the girl?'

'No,' said Coffin. 'Not without a lot of help. Is that what you came to ask?'

'No. I came to talk about the jacket that the girl was wearing. She was wearing an old felt hat that could have come from anywhere, a stall in the market, a charity shop, anywhere. It was old but in good condition.' He considered: 'I think a charity shop, it had that smell somehow; we might identify the shop and be no further forward. But the jacket . . .' He paused. 'I would like you to look at it.'

'Now?'

'If you could. I would really value your opinion, sir.'

Coffin looked down at Augustus. 'I'll just take him in. I will join you in the car.'

George Darcy sat waiting in his car for the Chief Commander to come back. He put the radio on as he waited. There was music, then the news, no mention of the murder in Spinnergate. Only a little, ordinary, unoriginal murder, after all.

Coffin planted Augustus in his basket, hurriedly fed the cat, and went to say goodbye to Stella, who was still in bed. He opened the window curtains to wake her up. She would be cross but grateful.

'Thanks for nothing . . . Thought you'd gone,' she said, stirring. 'Will Martin be into work today?'

'Yes, but keep an eye on him.'

'Why?'

Coffin paused at the door. 'You saw those cuts and scars on him. I am not sure what they mean now we know Jaimie was murdered, but I don't like them.'

Stella sat up in bed and watched him go. She too was troubled about Martin Marlowe.

The two men went into the long low building which housed the forensic laboratories.

George Darcy led the way down the corridor to room F3. All the clothes that Jaimie had worn were spread on tables awaiting the attention of the scientists.

She had worn very few underclothes, but they were silky and expensive: a brassiere, white pants and tights. On top she had worn cotton jeans, and a thick cashmere sweater.

On a table by itself was the jacket: it was dark-brown tweed, it had a roundish collar and a belt and big pockets.

'Worn originally by a big man,' said Darcy.

Coffin studied the jacket. 'He wore it hard, it's threadbare. And stained.' There were darker patches on the cloth, you could call them stains, almost of vegetable growth.

'Something else too, sir.' Darcy was watching his face.

Coffin looked at it thoughtfully. 'It's not new, and it was bought a long time ago. Jackets haven't been made for men like that for a very long time.'

'Old-fashioned,' said Darcy. 'Very. But that's not all . . . smell it, sir.'

Coffin gave Darcy a sharp look, then bent down to smell. Slowly he straightened himself. 'Smells . . .' He hesitated. 'It smells of damp earth. As if it had been buried.'

Buried a long age in the deep delved earth.

'Would anyone bury a jacket?' asked Darcy.

'It might be on someone,' said Coffin. Someone dead. Dead and then dug up. Or at least, uncovered. He could see Darcy frowning.

Mustn't get into fantasy land. 'The forensic report will be helpful,' Coffin said. Scientists were not always helpful, while sometimes being prone to their own little fantasies, but you had to listen to them. 'It's odd, but all cases have oddities.'

'Sometimes they are useful, they can be useful,' said Darcy in a dogged way.

'But sometimes you never discover what lies behind them.' Coffin knew something of the ironies of life. He put his hand on the jacket. 'It could have been bought anywhere, I suppose, and just draped over the body. If it leads us anywhere, I shall be grateful but surprised.'

The puzzle about the jacket on Jaimie's body was passed on to Phoebe Astley, who was now preparing to dig up the rough ground in the old churchyard.

'Take a chance,' the Chief Commander had said. 'I have walked over it and there could be an unofficial grave.'

'I too have looked it over. I thought someone else had been there too, someone with heavy feet.'

So she had noticed as well, Coffin thought.

'Could have been someone sleeping rough,' he said. 'Anyway, good luck. I will tell Richard Lavender. Ask him to keep quiet, of course. He knows about the dead girl. Darcy and his men have been to him. He's confused, I think. It's a mix-up, Phoebe.'

Good phrase, Phoebe thought. In her head she carried a litany of the women murdered in 1913: Mildred Bailey, Mary Jane Armour and Eliza Jones. There was a fourth woman, Isobel Haved, who had disappeared. There was not much mention of Haved, but she might have been a victim.

If the three women were victims of Father Lavender (as Phoebe had taken to calling him) then she might find the body of Isobel Haved, the missing woman.

If she existed, Phoebe thought, and if Father Lavender really was a killer. She found it hard to believe in him. As a parent, yes. Richard Lavender existed to prove this. A husband, and apparently an unhappy one, she had to accept that too. But as a serial killer . . . He seemed to melt into the shadows as he had done in real life.

His son thought he had joined up in the army in 1914 and been killed. Or missing.

He seemed a man bent on being missing. What on earth's

it really all about, Phoebe asked herself, trying to be practical. And if I find anyone what does it matter?

Wicked thought, really, since all human life was valuable, wasn't it? An old man's conscience had to be assuaged, that was it.

A shame that Edgar Wallace was dead because he might have been able to help her. Among the journalists working on the local papers in Spinnergate and East Hythe there must have been stories and speculation.

It took time to set up the digging, because as well as the diggers there would be men needed to guard the ground and keep out onlookers, journalists and TV cameras.

Perhaps it should be done at night. There was a streak of drama in Phoebe that made her like the idea of a night dig. Stella Pinero would have understood.

And, in fact, administrative difficulties slowed her down so the night looked like being the time after all.

'It gets dark so early now,' she told John Coffin on the telephone. (It was November the second.) 'But we shall make a start. I thought you would want to know. Will you be there?'

The answer had been: Yes, of course. It was a strange case, with a former Prime Minister at one end and a dead girl dressed as Guy Fawkes at the other. It made him feel out of normal space and time.

'Do you ever read Edgar Wallace?'

'No, not much – *Sanders of the River* when I was a boy.'

'Pity, it might have helped. I think he knew a few answers.'

Coffin's working day was long and boring – he found himself looking forward to the excavations. He came back from heading a tiresome committee to find a message from Dr Jack Bradshaw: Would he call on Richard Lavender at home?

Dick Lavender was seated in a big armchair by a blazing fire; he was wearing a dressing gown with a plaid wrapped round his knees. He looked frail but bright eyed. Could it be that he was enjoying the excitement?

Jack Bradshaw followed Coffin into the room where Janet

Neptune was pouring out tea with a bottle of whisky on the table beside her; she handed a cup to Coffin. 'You'll need a drink, it's cold out. And himself will,' she nodded at Dick Lavender. 'Helps him to keep his mind on the track.'

'Mind your tongue, woman. And take your big feet away.'

She took no notice; she did have big feet, she knew it. 'Now, Jack, have a cup too, you haven't eaten or drunk all day . . . Nerves takes him that way,' she said to Coffin.

Having provided this insight into the two men, she left the room, not without satisfaction. 'Just getting some more hot water for the pot. Now drink up.'

Coffin sipped his tea. More whisky than tea here, he decided. 'How are you, sir?'

Dick Lavender ignored this question. 'I don't suppose you are surprised that I should want to see you about this poor girl. I wasn't questioned myself but Jack was, he's under some suspicion, I understand. He's a stupid fellow for not letting me know he had been seeing her. He's had to admit to it.'

Coffin looked at Bradshaw. 'I was in love with her,' said Bradshaw. 'Still am, I think. Can you be in love with someone who is dead?'

'I think you need that drink with whisky in it,' Coffin said kindly.

'Janet has been telling me that all day.'

Dick Lavender said from his chair: 'She came in for a few questions herself.'

'Hardly knew the girl.' Janet came through the door with the teapot. 'But I could tell she was a little trollop. It was in her eyes.'

Dick Lavender ignored her. 'Jack, you had better tell the Chief Commander about the girl. Do we call her Marjorie Wardy or Jessamond Layard?'

'Either will do. Wardy was her writing name, but she was born Layard and christened Jessamond: her chosen name was Jaimie.'

Dick Lavender's hands were shaking as he held his cup, he spilled some tea on his knees. He caught Coffin's gaze and shrugged. I am old, his eyes said, I shake and spill my tea, I have to be helped to walk, but I still have a mind. 'Go and get me some hot water and a towel for the stain, Janet.'

'Messy thing,' said Janet, but she departed. 'I know you will talk about her when I'm out of the room . . . whatever you call her.'

Jack Bradshaw put his own cup down on a table. 'She was Marjorie to me. I see now that she made up to me because of my friendship with Dick.' He avoided looking at Richard Lavender, turning his face towards the window so that he presented a bony profile to Coffin.

Not a handsome man, Coffin thought, but certainly attractive, noticing too that both he and the former PM had noses like the Duke of Wellington: strong and arched. Roman noses, were they not called? If a woman inherited such a nose, it was no benefaction, but a man could be proud of it. Bradshaw probably was.

'I found her very charming, interesting, she seemed interested in me.'

'You were in love with her,' said Dick Lavender, sipping some tea and whisky. He sounded amused.

'I suppose I was. I thought she returned my feelings. I had every reason to think so.'

'You mean you went to bed with her.' Dick Lavender spoke with gusto, his hand might shake, but he still took a keen interest in the living.

Bradshaw did not answer.

Coffin looked at him. 'Did you?'

'Just once. In her flat near the Tower . . . I thought it was where she lived as well as worked. You may think we quarrelled when I found out she was working on Dick and meant to make a splash. But we didn't quarrel. And if you can believe me, I didn't kill her. I know I am under suspicion. But if I had killed her, do you think I am the sort of person who would dress her up as a guy and leave her in a car park?' He looked at Coffin. 'Oh, don't answer, I know you can't.'

Dick Lavender leaned forward. 'Go and help Janet in the kitchen . . . I want to talk to the Chief Commander.'

Bradshaw took a deep breath, hesitated, but went without a word.

It's interesting, Coffin thought, watching his silent departure, how the habit of power remains. Because men and women jumped to perform his wishes, Lavender still retains the power. I am obeying him, I came when he called. I ought to learn the trick myself.

'I want to tell you something in confidence. It is about Jack Bradshaw. Have you noticed anything about him?'

'What sort of thing,' said Coffin cautiously.

'A resemblance to anyone . . .'

'He has your nose.'

'Good, you have the eye. Yes, he is my son. I knew his mother.'

'In the biblical sense, I suppose?' said Coffin.

Lavender laughed and slapped his thigh. 'Good, good. Yes, just so. Not for long, but she had this child. It was a secret but I always kept in touch until she died. I helped with money, and it is why I chose him to write my life . . . It's not the first one, of course, there have been several, including what people call the official autobiography . . . the Party paid for that to be published and very boring it was too.'

He added quickly: 'Jack does not know, of course.'

'Are you sure?'

'Sure,' said the old man into the silence of the room.

Coffin sat thinking; he wondered if he believed this story, and whether the old man was having a fantasy.

'What about the girl?'

Lavender smiled. 'You are quick . . . Yes, I knew her family once. She was named Layard, a very well-known lot . . . And yes, I had a relationship with the girl's grandmother. It would be interesting, wouldn't it, if there was incest as well as murder.' He gave a little laugh. 'But no, no offspring from that union!'

I believe you would enjoy it, Coffin thought. 'Tell me,' he said. 'Have you missed an old tweed jacket?'

Dick Lavender sat in silence, and his heavy brows drew together. 'No.'

'You might not have seen it for some time,' suggested Coffin.

Lavender shook his head. 'No. You can ask Janet.' He leaned back in his chair, closing his eyes. 'You can go now, I am tired.'

The royal dismissal, the congé, Coffin thought, rising. Perhaps he sometimes thought he was Louis XIV of France, or Queen Victoria.

Obediently he left the room. No one was to be seen, not even Jack Bradshaw. Gone away to shoot himself, Coffin thought, and who to blame him? Might do the same myself in his position.

A row of coats hung on pegs in the hall by the door. He was quietly examining them, when he was aware that Janet Neptune was observing him.

'Just looking,' he said.

He opened the door. 'Tell them that Chief Inspector Darcy will be back again to interview them. Or his sergeant.'

He took some satisfaction in the remark.

He drove straight back to St Luke's and to his own home. He felt he needed to touch solid ground, and for him, these days that meant Stella. Maddening, elusive, loving, kind, Stella was always real.

He had hoped to find her in the living room, or the kitchen or even in her bedroom, changing for the evening, but she was nowhere to be seen. Augustus was gone as well, which he thought meant she was in the theatre, in her office or prowling round observing and thinking. She was not performing at the moment, a long TV series had just finished and she was 'resting'. Not that she ever did rest.

He looked at his watch. Too early for any performance to have started. He knew his way round backstage and so he crossed to the theatre and climbed the stairs to Stella's office. She was there, he heard her voice, clear and carrying as he advanced.

She had a youngish man with her, he had a crop of dark-brown hair and a compact, well-muscled body. He was not handsome but Coffin recognized that he had an actor's face and could assume good looks when the part demanded.

Stella waved at him from her desk: 'This is Ric Rivers, who is joining us.' She flashed him a radiant smile, her usual smile on the job, and got one back in return. 'Our new recruit. Ric, this is my husband, John Coffin.'

Ric held up a hand in greeting. 'Hi, I have heard of you, sir.'

Stella stood up. 'That's it then, Ric, we have done all the business part and you know your way around ... I told Martin Marlowe you would be coming along ... he's in dressing room B12, he shares that with Aelred Cooper and you will be the third ... you don't mind sharing? We are a bit cramped here, but when money permits we plan to do some more building. This is a listed building, believe it or believe it not, so we are a bit constrained.' It was her usual speech of explanation and Coffin had heard it many times before. It was more or less true; St Luke's was listed as being of some historical interest to the district, but architecturally it was not valuable, few objections were raised to any expansion but Stella found it sounded more impressive than saying: Darling, we haven't got a bean.

'I'll find my way around.' Ric gave them both the smile that made him seem a tremendously sincere and straightforward fellow (with just a clever hint that maybe he wasn't and wouldn't it be fun to find out, both of us together, you know) and moved gracefully to the door.

'He's clever,' said Coffin with conviction. 'Bet he always knows his way.'

'Always. He's well known for it. But he is also a good actor with a wide range, very handy.' She stood up, collecting her bag, gathering her coat over her shoulders. 'Not a great actor, of course, although he has pretensions, but I often think a handy actor is the best sort to have around. He's had rather a dry patch, poor love, so I was able to get my hands on him. Happens to all of us.' Got him cheap on that account ... Coffin could be puritanical about that sort of thing, he had not been liberated by a university education, or the rough and tumble of street life, she thought, half amused.

She was talking on, wondering what had brought Coffin round to see her.

Augustus emerged from under the desk where he had been asleep, and began to make his presence felt by jumping up and down at Coffin's feet.

'Get away, you devil,' said Coffin. 'Train this creature, Stella.'

'No, that's man's work ... lovely to be collected in this way.' She put her head on one side. 'But what's up?'

He put his arm round her, lately he had found just touching Stella gave him comfort. 'Come on home, and I will tell you.'

They passed down the corridor together, Stella, Coffin and Augustus.

From behind a half-closed door, they heard Ric's voice: 'What's the policy here? Do we all sleep with anyone who asks, to keep the company happy?'

'Listen, it's a personal matter.' This was Martin. 'No policy.'

'Oh, if you say so. Not like my last company.'

'Where was that then?'

'That would be telling, but it was in Scotland.'

'You do surprise me ...' Another voice chimed in: Alison Summers.

'What's she doing in there?' whispered Stella.

Ric was going on: 'There's no accounting for taste, we had an old spaniel who wouldn't drink from a bowl of clean water but lapped up a dirty puddle on a walk.'

'What's that got to do with it?' Alison again.

'Just making a comparison.'

Coffin drew Stella on. 'You've caught a corker there.'

She bent down to pick up the dog. 'Home or a drink at Max's?'

'Home.'

Serious talk, Stella thought. 'Right. Well, it's not a champagne evening, that's clear, but I would enjoy a cup of tea. Strong and Indian and with cream.'

Stella made the tea herself in a brown earthenware pot. 'Tastes better that way.' She carried the tray up to their sitting room where she poured a cup for each of them. 'So, what is it?'

Coffin took his cup of tea to the window from which he could see the old churchyard. Light shone through the trees. So Phoebe and her team were at work.

'It's old Lavender ... I don't know whether to believe what he says or not. He seems to spin stories out of his own mind. Today he said that Jack Bradshaw was his son, the result of a love affair that was kept secret.'

'I can believe that,' said Stella thoughtfully. 'Richard Lavender was quite a lover of women, everyone knows that, seems to come to some men with power.'

'How do you know so much about him?'

'Read about it. I do read, you know. Well, let's be honest, someone sent me a script once.'

Coffin was walking up and down. 'It didn't end there: he claims he was a lover of Jaimie Layard's grandmother and her mother or father perhaps was his child too. He denied it first time round.'

'Was he joking?'

'God knows. I think he is fond of Jack Bradshaw, he may believe he did kill the girl, and he is putting all this up as a kind of smokescreen.'

'Does he know about Martin and his sister ... who they are, and Martin's affair with Jaimie?'

'I am sure he does. I am beginning to believe that in spite of his air of withdrawing from the world, he maintains an efficient information service ... probably run by his niece. If Janet *is* his niece,' Coffin added. 'I don't know what to believe. He claims that Bradshaw is his son, but is not aware of it. I don't know if that is true either.' And there is also the fact that the dead girl was pregnant. They would have to take specimens from Bradshaw and Marlowe to see if either was the father. But he did not say this aloud to Stella.

Stella said it sounded a bit mad.

'I have thought that myself,' said Coffin with bitter conviction. 'He speaks with such an air of telling the truth, telling it to me and me only. Isn't that what politicians always do?

I don't know if he believes all this is true. I am beginning to think I sent Phoebe Astley off on a goose chase.'

Stella joined him at the window. 'What are all those lights?' she asked.

Coffin did not answer. Digging up nothing, he said to himself. What a fool I am.

She's dead, sir, long ago.
The Bailiff's Daughter of Islington

8

The room was quiet but they were both conscious of the lights across the road. Coffin, who had good distance vision, could see a line of police cars plus a dark van parked along the kerb.

He couldn't be sure, but he thought a few interested watchers had also turned up.

Already, he thought.

The telephone rang. Stella, who was nearest, picked it up and handed it to Coffin. 'It's bound to be for you.'

Coffin listened. 'Phoebe here. We have something. Do you want to see?'

'I am coming across at once.' He stood up. 'I won't be long.'

Stella stood up and said: 'I am coming too.'

Coffin hesitated. 'I'm not sure . . .'

'Augustus needs a walk.'

'Don't bring the dog,' said Coffin sharply, before he could stop himself.

Stella stared at him. 'It's a body then. Another one.'

'Stella, I don't know. Not yet.'

'I think I will come. You can order me not too, of course, you are the Chief Commander.'

'It's police business, Stella, darling, not fun.'

'Did you imagine that I thought it was?'

'No.' He didn't know what to say. 'Why do you want to come?'

'I want to be a part of your life. You join in mine, I let you into the theatre, you never let me into yours.'

'It's totally different.' Anyway, she often crashed in.

They stood looking at each other, very close to a quarrel then.

'I want to help.'

'You do help, Stella, just by being there.' The conviction in his voice got through to her. 'It's a bloody awful job I do most of the time, and it's getting worse.' He was speaking from the heart: political pressures, shortage of money, the loss of good men from the Second City Force, all added to his burdens. 'I was happier as a CID officer in South London in the old days. Except for having you, Stella. That makes all the difference.'

Stella gave a sudden smile. 'Thank you for saying that, my darling. All right . . . I won't push. Tell you what: I will put a coat on, put Augustus on the leash and walk across the road with you, then I will take Augustus round the block.'

At the bottom of the stairs, as he opened the front door, Stella looked up at him, her face circled with the fur collar of her coat: 'It's difficult being a wife.'

'It's difficult being a husband,' said Coffin with feeling.

Stella laughed. 'I knew you would say that; I can always provide the cues for you.'

They walked towards the old churchyard in companionable silence, with Augustus pulling at his lead ahead of them. Around the cars, a trio of uniformed police were standing by the black van, and beyond them a small gathering of onlookers. Coffin recognized a local journalist.

'It's beginning to rain,' said Stella. Faithful to her word, Stella and the dog drew away. She did not look back, but walked briskly on. She did spare a thought for wet diggers in the sad, sodden grave. Mud seemed to make everything worse.

Coffin was saluted by the uniformed officers, and was then attended by a silent sergeant who showed him the way through.

Phoebe Astley came forward; she was wearing a raincoat but her hair was wet.

'We're putting up covers to protect the digging area. I'm afraid it's muddy.' She was walking ahead of him down the

110

track already beaten out on the grass. 'We've made a bit of a mess putting up lights and everything. We had to get the local council's garden department to give us permission, but we got it, on the promise to restore everything as we found it . . . It wasn't so great, actually, might look better if we left it tidy.'

'Meant to be a wilderness, I think,' said Coffin, slithering on the wet grass.

'Watch your step . . . it gets worse where we've been digging.'

Ahead was a large canvas tent which in turn was protected by canvas barriers. A wet figure shrouded in a white uniform already earth-stained stood by the entrance.

'Was that Stella I saw with you?' Phoebe asked as they came close enough to the shrouded figure to see his wet red face and recognize one Sergeant Appletone.

'Yes, she was taking the dog for a walk.'

'You should have let her come in and bring the dog. He could have done some digging.' Said straight-faced, this was typical of Phoebe's bleak humour. She went on:

'This may be a surprise to you. Of course, we know this was a graveyard, but we didn't expect a spare coffin.'

'What?'

Phoebe did not answer, instead waved him forward for a look. There was a spread of canvas to his right and straight ahead was where they had been digging. In the light of big lamps, Coffin saw that they had been digging where one of the mounds had been beneath the trees.

No very deep excavation had been necessary to reveal a wooden coffin.

It was open and empty. A width of disintegrating wood still partly covered with earth was close by.

'Nobody in it,' said Phoebe with grim satisfaction. 'Just an empty casket.'

Coffin stared down into it. 'Not quite empty, a lot of earth and leaves.'

'Know what I think?' asked Phoebe. 'I think it got dumped here when the bombs fell and gradually covered up. Perhaps it was booked for a body and just didn't get it.'

'Amazing the things you find when you start digging,' said one of the white-clad figures.

'It's a little bit of past history.' Coffin studied it. 'But I would like to know what that history is.'

Phoebe was assured. 'We'll find out.'

'It hasn't been there since 1914.' This was from another of the diggers.

'I agree.' Coffin nodded. 'The layer of leaves and earth and debris is not thick enough.'

'The last war,' said Phoebe again.

'Probably . . .' He turned to her. 'But this isn't why you brought me over here.'

'You guessed?' She allowed herself a touch of irony. 'No, have a look over here.' Phoebe nodded to the diggers. 'Open up, lads.'

The stretch of canvas to his right was rolled back so that Coffin could see what was underneath. Not much earth had been removed so all he saw was a shallow pit. He moved forward to take a closer look.

From the earth, a bone protruded, sticking straight up. A small slender finger.

'I suppose that is a finger,' he said thoughtfully.

'I don't know, a finger-shaped piece of bone . . . but it means we have to go carefully now, spoon the earth up. It's going to be a slow business . . . Do you want to stay around?'

'Can't even be sure this is a human bone.' Coffin was studying what he could see of the yellowing piece of bone. 'Could be anything.'

Phoebe did not answer, but knelt down to get a better look. Then she shook her head. 'I am no anatomist, but I'd guess it's human.' She stood up. 'Of course, we could cover it up and go home.'

There was a faint, hopeful murmur from the three diggers, but they knew it was a joke.

'This deserves the Edgar Wallace touch; pity we haven't got him here,' said Phoebe.

'I don't think Edgar Wallace would be much good to you.'

'Oh, he would: he would write a short story called *The Finger of Mr Bones*.'

'Or Mrs Bones.'

'You staying to watch?'

Coffin said: 'I will just go and tell Stella what is happening and then I will come back.'

He found Stella in the kitchen drying Augustus, who was growling softly with displeasure. 'I didn't mind getting wet myself, but apparently Augustus hates it.'

'He smells, of course,' pointed out Coffin. 'The wet brings it out. Doggy but strong. And you don't: at least, only of your own special scent and soap.'

Stella laughed. 'Miss Dior today, thank you.' She threw the towel from her and planted Augustus in his basket. 'I walked past all the police cars and the van, and concluded it was real business.'

'I think so. I am going back.'

Stella hesitated. 'I saw something when I was out . . . I saw Clara Henley. Augustus and I walked down the road to the big shopping centre near Edward Street and Fisher Street. It's not far from the hospital where she works and not far from the car park where Jaimie's body was found . . . the shopping centre has its own parking, of course.'

'Of course,' said Coffin, wondering where Stella was going.

'I saw her parking her car; Augustus had stopped for a sniff, he likes the wall there, it's kind of a newspaper for him, tells him the day's news and who's around . . . She didn't recognize me, but I knew her . . . she drives what used to be called an estate car . . . you don't see so many of them around now . . . the back lets down.' Stella looked at Coffin. 'You could get a pram in and out easily.'

'So you could.'

'It's not likely that pram could have gone far through the streets. And, of course, she'd be used to handling bodies.'

'I don't know if surgeons do much of that,' said Coffin.

'Then Augustus and I walked on to the Spinnergate tube, it's not so very far from there, and had a talk with Mimsie Marker – she was just packing up.'

'And what did she have to say?' Mimsie Marker sold newspapers and magazines from a stall near the tube station. She always wore a smart hat with flowers in summer and fur on in winter. She heard everything and knew everything. She was willing to talk to those she trusted: Stella was one, she admired Stella. 'A marvellous performer,' she said.

'She was wearing a mink hat, a new one, so trade must be good ... Isn't she supposed to be a rich woman with a house in the country as well as a luxury flat overlooking the river? She said she had seen Martin and his sister around the car park several times ... she knows who they are.'

'She would do.'

'They were just walking around talking, but she thought it strange ... there must be better places to walk.'

'I am sure she had more to say than that.' Coffin knew his Mimsie.

'She said that there are at least three ways out of the car park, so it's easy to get out. One way towards the hospital, one to the theatre, or more or less ... Another to Spinnergate underground station. A way out for each ... She didn't say that but I could see what she meant.'

'She seems to have thought it all out.'

'You know Mimsie ... It's interesting. She says she's seen Clara park her car there too. She did not draw any conclusions but you could see what she was thinking.' Stella added: 'Never saw Jaimie there, she says.'

'She knew Jaimie too?'

'Oh yes, knew her other pen name too. Said you can't trust a woman with two names.'

'Phoebe thinks we need the pen of the late Edgar Wallace, but who needs him when we've got Mimsie Marker.'

Stella looked at her face in the looking glass opposite the door; she sighed deeply – 'What a wreck.'

'That was a long walk for you and Augustus,' said Coffin.

'Oh, I took a cab back, that's why I went towards Spinnergate and Mimsie. She rang up for me.'

Coffin laughed and shook his head. That was his Stella.

'You are going back to the dig, I suppose?'

'Must do.'

'What about food? You haven't eaten anything.'

'Save me something.'

Stella and the dog watched him go across the road, and as Coffin went out, the cat came in. Stella called after him, cheerfully, he thought:

'Mimsie said she likes Dr Bradshaw but doesn't like the housekeeper.'

That would be Janet Neptune. No doubt, Coffin decided as he walked to the churchyard, whom it was Mimsie and probably the neighbourhood thought guilty of killing the girl: Martin with or without his sister. And that was without knowing the girl was pregnant. He knew that both Bradshaw and Marlowe had given body samples, but neither had been told the very special reason.

– I don't think I like cases which join in the middle with another case, especially if that one is eighty-odd years old and involves, or so some say, the spirit of Edgar Wallace.

Phoebe Astley came forward to meet him. 'The bones are human, but we are going slow. Dr Marriot has turned up.' Henry Marriot was one of the police surgeons in Spinnergate. Coffin could see him through the trees. 'We haven't given him much to work on at the moment.'

Marriot nodded to Coffin. 'Been dead a long time.' He was a deeply moralistic man who was made gloomy and depressed at some of the sights he saw. He usually identified with the victim. 'Not sure if I need have come so soon.'

'Sorry to have brought you out on a wet night,' said Coffin politely. He had met Henry Marriot before, with whom he sympathized because he occasionally suffered from the same depression himself. He had never got used to the bodies of those dead by violence, fractured, raped, mutilated, and although he saw less of them now he was Chief Commander, those he did see were just as hard to take.

Bones, however, were easier to bear. Far away and long ago, yes, that did make it less painful. If you picked up a bone on the battlefield of Waterloo or Agincourt you were respectful and interested but not pained.

Sixty to eighty years were, however, marginal. Empathy was alive still.

They were moving the earth away, spoonful by spoonful,

sieving it, studying it carefully, then moving on. By careful degrees the surface was being lowered, exposing the bones.

The bones of the upper arm and the hand were exposed. Nothing else.

'Moved by an animal, probably,' said Phoebe. 'It happens.'

'Perhaps there is only the arm,' said one of the diggers.

'No, we will find the rest.' She was confident.

'What made you start digging here?' asked Marriot.

'I heard there might be a body.'

Marriot looked at him curiously. 'Someone with a long memory.'

'You could say that.'

'Found a plague pit, once,' said Marriot. 'By the Tower. Nasty. Even the rats didn't get inside there.'

'How long do plague germs hang around?' asked Coffin absently, watching the veil of earth thinning . . . here were bones, he could see the brown and yellow gleam.

Marriot shrugged. 'Not as long as believed, but we didn't risk it – I wore a mask . . . Men, women and children all jumbled together in that pit . . . just thrown in. Not nice.'

He produced a flask and offered a medicinal draught to Coffin and Phoebe, both of whom refused; he took one himself. 'Damned cold out here.' He walked around stamping his feet.

Phoebe produced a flask of a different sort of her own. 'Want some coffee, sir?'

Coffin accepted a mug; they stood side by side, drinking. The cold wet work was really being done in the pit at their feet, but the smell of damp earth was chilling. Coffin moved restlessly, wandering into the trees, from where he could see the lights of his own home – they went out as he watched. So Stella had gone to bed.

Things moved faster once the skull was uncovered. The neck, the vertebrae of the spine, and the legs were exposed. The legs were drawn up, one arm rested across the ribcage, the other had been buried with the arm extended. The hand on this arm had been the one whose fingers had protruded.

Marriot looked at what he saw appraisingly: 'Buried with

the left arm sticking up. No animal interference here. Rigor must have already set in when the body was buried.'

He continued with his survey while the others – Coffin, Phoebe and the diggers – stood in a group watching. Marriot was on his knees, looking but not touching.

Then he stood up. 'Well, that's it. Can't tell what the cause of death was for sure, but I think strangulation, the hyoid bone was broken. There's injury to the skull as well.'

'Is that all?' asked Coffin, who was beginning to have his own ideas.

'Well, it's a man, probably not young. Were you expecting a man?'

'Wasn't expecting anything,' said Coffin into the pause that followed.

He looked at Phoebe, and nodded. They moved aside into the trees to talk; the diggers and Dr Marriot watched them. Marriot had another drink and considered a cigarette. Mustn't drop ash and contaminate the murder scene. If it was a murder scene. Still, a chap didn't bury himself. Especially if he was already stiff.

Phoebe raised her eyebrows in query. 'Who?'

Coffin shook his head: 'The dear Lord knows who he is. And shall we ever find out? There were signs of clothes here and there, I thought, possibly something will come out of it. I'm not hopeful.'

'Edgar Wallace would find a train ticket or a diary underneath the bones, buried in the soil but still readable.'

'Oh come on, Phoebe, we will be lucky if those poor scraps of cloth even give us much of a date.'

'The bones can probably be dated,' said Phoebe.

'To a decade or two. I doubt if anything will ever be established about this one.'

'Have to try, of course.' She gave Coffin a hard look. 'What do you mean about this one?'

Coffin said, in a thoughtful, abstracted voice: 'Let Marriot go, I think, don't you?'

'If he has much more whisky he won't be able to stand up. Not his first drink he had here with us.'

'I noticed that myself.'

'And, sir?' Because there was an 'and', she knew him well enough to be sure of it.

The Chief Commander looked across the open grave to where the diggers were standing. One of them was sitting down and the other two leaning against trees; all three had the air of men who had had enough and would be glad to go home. He felt a certain sympathy for them.

Beyond the group was another patch of rough uneven ground that interested him.

'Over there, Phoebe . . . I think a dig there must be next. There may be nothing there, but I don't feel like leaving it.'

'Tonight?'

'I think so, don't you?'

Only one answer to that, Phoebe knew, and that was: Yes, sir. She moved towards the diggers, aware that they would not be pleased.

'Would you like to tell them, sir?' she asked over her shoulder.

'Go ahead, Phoebe.'

'Oh, thank you,' she said under her breath as she plodded through the mud, 'thank you, thank you, sir.'

Coffin walked out to the road where the police cars lined the kerb. The small crowd who had been observing had long since departed to their dry beds, but the journalist remained. She was sitting under the tree, a raincoat over her and a waterproof hat on her head. Clutched protectively to her chest was her telephone on which she spoke at intervals. No one was at the other end at this hour but it looked more professional if she spoke. She stood up when she saw the Chief Commander.

'Have you got anything for me, sir?'

He frowned. 'Still here? You ought to have gone off long ago.'

'Not while there is something going on that will interest my editor.' She looked over her shoulder. 'Still going on. Lights, noises, people coming and going. You there, now that's a sign of how big it is . . . I know who you are, sir.'

'I don't know you.'

'Elaine Spring. *Spinnergate and East Hythe News*.' She was

very young, no more than eighteen or nineteen, with long yellow hair and soft brown eyes. It was probably her first job.

'Well, Elaine, there's nothing to say now. If there is anything, then a statement will be made tomorrow.'

'It is tomorrow already,' said Elaine, not a girl without spirit. 'Well into it, too.' She showed her steel: 'All those lights, all those policemen, all the coming and going, show it's important . . . There has to be a body.'

Coffin was silent. A body or two, he thought. 'Hang on, and I'll see that if there is anything to report, then you get told.'

'Will I be able to photograph?'

'I am afraid not.'

A light flashed in his face. 'Well, I have got you, sir,' she said with spirit. 'And that will please my editor. I might get a by-line out of it yet, Chief Commander.'

Coffin laughed and walked away. Pretty girl.

Elaine adjusted her camera, which was not the newest, smartest gadget – she couldn't afford that – but a touch old-fashioned. She adjusted her thoughts as well: I like him and he liked me, I've heard he is just a touch susceptible. Good.

She ran after him. 'Sir, is there anything on the Guy Fawkes murder?'

Coffin shook his head and walked on. So that was what they were calling it? Poor Jaimie, no dignity in her death.

Phoebe Astley was waiting for the Chief Commander as he walked back through the old churchyard. 'I think we may have something.'

'Already?'

'Not too deep . . . Nothing to see as yet, but one of the men clearing the soil says he felt something underneath.'

The first two digs were already covered with canvas to await more attention tomorrow. Dr Marriot had already departed, Phoebe said. 'Wanted to be off before we found something else for him.'

We wouldn't be doing this, Coffin reflected, if it wasn't for the moral and spiritual force of a very old man. Was it worth it? Or should the dead be left in peace?

So far tonight, they had an empty coffin, the bones of an unknown dead man who might be a casualty of one of the Great Wars when bombs fell on London, and now . . . well, what was coming?

'Here we go,' said Phoebe, pointing forward to where once again the gentle quiet removal of the topsoil was going on. 'Keep your fingers crossed.'

When Phoebe spoke in platitudes like that, then Coffin knew she expected results.

He stood in silence, watching.

With late dawn, when it was still raining, Coffin came home; he entered quietly, climbed the stairs to the kitchen where he made a pot of coffee; he arranged a tray with toast and honey, then carried it up, still being quiet, to the bedroom.

Stella was asleep, her cheek on her folded hands – she looked calm and happy. The cat was on her feet, he too was peacefully asleep; he woke up, looked at Coffin out of one wary eye, then went back to sleep.

Coffin touched his wife on her shoulder. 'Wake up, Stella, love.'

Stella opened her eyes and yawned. 'Heard you come in.'

'Did you now?' He smiled his disbelief.

'But I was so comfortable . . .'

Coffin poured the coffee, a cup each, and pulled up a chair. Stella sat up, drew a pale-blue silk bedjacket over her shoulders, and took her cup. 'Still raining, is it?'

'Still raining . . . drink your coffee.'

She looked at him over the rim of her cup. 'So what has happened? Tell me.'

Coffin told her. He told her about the first two early discoveries: the empty box, and the man's skeleton.

Then he told her that in another site, not so far away from the other two, there had been found bones.

The bones of a woman, fragments of clothing, a necklace and a brooch. Not valuable.

And between her hips, the shadowy remains of the bones of a foetus. She had been with child when she died. Not easily recognizable by the lay eye since the bones of a developing embryo do not come head and feet first, but the police surgeon knew what they were. Seen them before, no doubt.

'How hideous,' said Stella, calling up a picture. 'How pitiful. How hideously pitiful.'

The telephone by her bedside rang. For a moment, they both ignored it, but it rang and rang again.

9

A dark figure had flitted through the streets of Spinnergate that night while the police team still worked in the old churchyard. The quiet figure watched until they packed up. They were gone now, home to warm houses. A heavy November mist hung over the river with fingers spreading all over the area; it was patchy, some streets obscured while others were almost free of it. Around St Luke's the air was relatively clear.

The figure looked at the lights in the tower where Coffin and Stella lived, saw that someone was at home, was actually seen by the family cat but not recognized, and passed on. You couldn't break into that tower easily even if you wanted to, and this figure did not. Just checking.

A brief look was accorded the churchyard because the dead here had been dead a long time. It was interesting and worthwhile, however, to know what the police were doing. The figure stayed under a tree across the road to stare for a while and then moved on.

A person who kills because of love can never be blamed, the dark wanderer said quietly. Love gives licence. It must do. Think of Shakespeare and what goes on there with lovers. No one condemns Romeo or Juliet, nor do Cleopatra and Antony come in for too much criticism.

Pass over Othello.

'Jealousy has a human face'. So William Blake said, and he was a great poet too.

The dark figure flitted on, unnoticed, hurrying towards the now famous car park. Or infamous.

It was still cordoned off, much to the annoyance of those

motorists who used it either to go to the hospital or the large store.

The dark figure slipped underneath the tape, noticing with scorn that there was no police officer to be seen. Of what use was a length of tape?

The killer had enjoyed the tour.

Gut ist der Schlaf, der Tod ist besser.
Sleep is good, death is better.

Heinrich Heine

10

Coffin answered the telephone, his coffee cup in his hand, which he was proud to see was steady even after his second rough night.

'Sorry to ring so early, sir.'

'Darcy, have you had any sleep these last two nights?'

'Some, sir, but you know how it goes when a case starts . . . everyone moves as fast as they can. And as a matter of fact, I think we are going into one of those times when no one sleeps much.'

Coffin drank his coffee, while keeping one eye on Stella and thinking that Darcy was talking too much. Strain. It did tell, however professional you were. To oblige him with confirmation, his own left hand set up a tremor.

Damn – he controlled the muscles. 'Darcy . . . I missed that.'

'I was just saying that I was surprised when forensics came up with something so quickly; they usually take their time down there.'

Up there, Coffin thought, the Forensic Department of the Police Scientific Bureau of the Second City was on the top floor. The Flies in the Sky, they were called when working coppers were angry with what they felt were delays and procrastination and which the scientists called checking the facts.

'However, what they came up with on the jacket was so interesting, I thought you would want to know as soon as possible. In the circumstances . . . It's so strange, isn't it, sir, when just the name you do not expect comes up? Although the connection was known, the name was there . . .'

'Come on, man,' said Coffin into his cup of coffee. Stella was moving around the room now, she was listening, trying to make out what was going on. So am I, Coffin thought.

He put the coffee cup down. 'Yes?' he said hopefully.

'It's a very old jacket, old in style, old in years, very well worn . . . Stained, as you know. In dealing with the stains, which seem to be mildew and Thames clay, they brought up the faint remains of a name written inside. Old-fashioned marking ink: the name is Edward Lavender.'

Silence. He let the name sink into Coffin's mind.

'Edward Lavender was Richard Lavender's father,' said Coffin.

'I checked.'

'Thought you would.' Coffin was thinking. 'Have to question the Grand Old Man himself . . . It might be a good idea to have the jacket checked by the Museum of Fashion in the university . . . Could be a modern jacket, faked.'

'Could be. Doesn't look it, and the faker would have a funny sense of humour.'

'It wouldn't be a joke,' said Coffin. 'I don't think we have a joker here.'

'Not joking here, either, sir.'

'Never thought you were.'

'I will go to the museum myself . . . as soon as forensics release it.' Darcy considered aloud: 'Lavender's father, eh? Well, the coat's been around a long time . . . If genuine, we always have to remember that . . . Unless we see the old man coming back to life wearing it; don't believe in revenants myself, sir.'

'Grab it, tell them you want it, I want to see it myself,' said Coffin. 'Might be important . . . I will call on Richard Lavender myself.'

'Tips suspicion the way of Bradshaw.'

'It's more complicated than that, Darcy. Remember the name was not visible, we hadn't seen it, it had been obscured by the years.'

'He wouldn't have used it if he had known the name was there. He wouldn't have used it if he had known there was a name there we could bring up,' said Darcy obstinately. 'But

Bradshaw is in and out of Lavender's place – he could have used it not knowing it would point to him.'

'I can't believe that a clever man like Dr Jack Bradshaw would choose to use a jacket like that.'

'We don't know what choice he had, sir. We don't know the circumstances of the killing.'

'The dressing-up of the body is bizarre enough,' said Coffin.

'Just camouflage to get the body out from where she was killed and into the street.'

Coffin was sceptical: 'And what did he wear while he pushed it along?'

'Went in the car; he's got one of those big old-fashioned shooting-brake affairs. He used that for most of the way, and did it in the dark, of course.'

'You've got it all worked out.'

'I think I have, sir.'

'I am trying to imagine Jack Bradshaw doing all that; it doesn't seem in character.'

'He's in love, sir, crazy, maddened.'

'Do you think so?'

'I have questioned him, sir, and he admits it. You know how it is, if passion comes late to a man like that, he can find it hard to handle.' Darcy said quickly: 'I've had to ask him to turn in his car so we can look it over.'

'I don't suppose he liked that.'

'No, he said he needed it to get to his own home near Oxford ... Apparently, although he often stays in Spinnergate with Richard Lavender while he is doing the book, he has his own home in Oxford, and also a small flat in Greenwich.'

'Of course. He is a serious figure, Darcy, a well-known man in his own academic circles.'

'I know that, sir, but I don't think it rules out a crime of passion.' Darcy added: 'He was not the father of the child, by the way. Marlowe could be; he hasn't been told. But Bradshaw could have done it out of a kind of anger. It's how I see it. He asked to see you. I think he sees you as a protector, sir.'

'I can't be that,' said Coffin in a decisive voice. 'I am neutral.'

'You are coming over, are you, sir?'

'Yes, straight away. I want to see that jacket again for myself.'

Stella said: 'Neutral, eh? You have never been neutral in your life, thank God. You always take sides. It's why I love you.'

'It's nice to know.'

You have to pay for that sort of knowledge, he thought, and he wondered what price Stella would exact. He looked at her now, dishevelled and pink from sleep, but inwardly totally composed. He couldn't be so, he wanted her too much, and this was not the time to attempt possession. It was always 'attempt', he knew that, had learned early in their relationship – Stella was the free one and he was the captive.

Fortunately, he liked it. But better not dwell on that thought.

'And whose side am I taking here?'

Stella frowned. 'I am not sure, but judging by the last conversation, it is Jack Bradshaw.'

Coffin said seriously: 'Darcy's a good man, a clever detective. I have to listen to what he says.'

'Even if you don't believe it; he knows that, of course. Couldn't miss it, could he? I admire him for sticking to his idea that Bradshaw is the man, even though you don't take that line.' She was brushing her hair. 'Mind you, I think you are wrong.'

'Do you?' He had some faith in Stella's powers of observation and understanding; often she saw more than he did.

She swung round on the chair at the dressing table to face him. 'Yes, I think Bradshaw could kill.'

'And I think I know whom you are backing as innocent victim,' said Coffin. 'Martin.'

Stella said: 'Well, I do need him in my cast, but you can have his sister. For my mind she could kill anyone.'

And hasn't she already? thought Coffin, but did not say

so aloud. It was there though, that thought, and both of them knew it.

As he made his way to meet George Darcy, Coffin knew that his investigation was made more difficult by the way in which the two cases ran together. A kind of twinning.

The join was Jaimie Layard.

Was she an innocent victim or had she brought her death on herself? All he had heard about her suggested she was a violent woman herself. He had only met her once but she had made an impact as a strong, even aggressive woman. Perhaps that was unfair, clearly at that time her relationship with Martin was under strain.

Was it physical passion that lay behind her death? She was certainly the sort of woman that could provoke a fierce, killing anger in a man.

But there was something else: it now seemed that she had cultivated Martin because she was going to put him in a book. She was also investigating the murky depths of Dick Lavender's youth.

Dick Lavender had asked for help from Coffin to find his father's last victim: the old man might not welcome publicity of the wrong sort, but he was anxious to make belated amends. An old man, with a distinguished past, who now wanted to die having cleared his conscience. Not likely to murder.

On the other hand, Martin and his sister had a stronger motive; Clara Henley had served her sentence, and was building a fine career, but she was very protective of her younger brother. Martin might easily have killed the woman he loved, Darcy liked the idea of a crime of passion, and Darcy had a good record for being right in murder cases.

If Martin had done the killing, then Clara might set up the charade of Jaimie dressed as a guy in the car park. She might even have enjoyed it.

Martin was a good actor, possibly she was one too.

He had a picture of Clara, dressed perhaps as an adolescent in jeans, pushing the pram through the street.

It was a foggy, cold morning; he had a chance as he drove

past to stare into the old churchyard which was cordoned off and guarded. No one seemed to be taking much interest, even the young journalist must have packed up and gone home. Unless she was the sleeping figure in the little red Metro. He thought she was; she would get the whole story of the bodies in the churchyard, she was game. The spirit of Edgar Wallace stirred again. Rivalry between the police and investigative journalist could operate here; she might get the true facts before he, the Chief Commander, did, but he felt no jealousy, he was glad to say – he always liked pretty young women.

An empty coffin, the bones of a hastily buried man, and the skeleton of a woman with child.

They might never discover who either of the dead were. But if Dick Lavender was telling the truth there was a chance that the dead woman was Isobel Haved, who had been a missing woman in 1913 and believed to be a Spinnergate Ripper victim.

Or killed by Edward Lavender, if you believed his son.

The same Edward Lavender whose jacket had now been wrapped round the body of another murdered woman.

He liked the idea of a revenant coming back to wreak revenge on a biographer. Or possibly go in for one last murder.

He was laughing as he arrived; parked his car in his own marked parking space (which he knew was regularly monitored to check if WALKER – his code name – had arrived).

CI George Darcy was waiting for him: he was a punctual and reliable man who was always where he had said he would be and at the time appointed. 'I have warned them we are coming, you have to with that lot, a law unto themselves.' There was a war between the CID and the police scientists, the scenario made up of accusations from both sides of delays, loss of vital material, and obfuscation. Darcy found them particularly irritating.

'Nature of their work, I suppose.'

'So they say.'

Darcy led the way in through the swing door, checked their arrival as he would check them out (Darcy knew the rules), since no one, not even the Chief Commander, was allowed in without a pass. Too many confidential, and sometimes dangerous and even highly contagious, materials came into this building.

Coffin followed him politely (he also knew the rules and had long since known how to circumvent them, this being one of the reasons for his rise and on occasion fall); he knew there was a back door that was regularly left open.

'Hello, Dr Miller.' He knew Daisy Miller from an earlier visit; she had helped him catch a man who was threatening Stella, and writing obscene letters. Daisy specialized in writings, although probably not on aged jackets.

She had a charming smile and a polite way of talking, although the burden of what she said was often sharp. Coffin thought that her parents must have been reading Henry James when she was christened.

'You've come about this fucking jacket,' she said in her ladylike voice.

'You don't like the jacket?'

'I don't usually feel one way or the other about the artefacts I work on, but this gives me the creeps.' She stared down at it. 'Where did it come from? Whose tomb?'

She saw Darcy staring at her rubber-gloved hands. 'I always wear gloves when I'm working and you ought to do the same. You could pick up anything in here . . . this jacket, straight from the Plague Year?'

'Not quite that old,' said Coffin. 'Say eighty years.'

Dr Miller looked at the jacket with assessing eyes. 'I'm not a fashion expert, but the fabric and the cotton lining could bear analysis. I bet they contain dyes and stiffening no longer in use. You might be able to date it that way . . . if that matters.'

'It could matter. The name matters.'

He stared down at the jacket which was pegged open so that he could see the lining. It had been marked just below the collar.

Not much to be seen, just a blur, a shadow.

'Comes up better in the photograph.' Dr Miller handed over an enlarged print.

In a cursive hand, with flowing curves, at once ornate and yet unsophisticated, the typical copperplate handwriting of a London Board School in late-Victorian England. It was the handwriting of someone who followed the rules but did not write much.

Edward Lavender.

That was all that could be read easily. There was some writing underneath, but very blurred.

Daisy Miller appraised it. 'I might be able to bring that up.'

'Be useful if you could.'

She looked at Coffin. 'Yes,' he said. 'Probably the address. And addresses are always useful.'

'Get lucky and you might get a date and a confession as well.'

'That would be even more useful.' Had she heard about the hunt for a serial killer of long ago?

'Of course, he would be long dead.' She had heard. The whole Second City Police Force knew and was talking about it, seeing their Chief Commander as a lunatic pursuing the unfindable.

Coffin's eyes traced some faint shadows on the photograph; he turned back to the jacket to look there. Yes, there was discolouration. 'Stains? Is it blood?'

'I don't know why you lot are always so keen on blood . . . Stains are not my speciality but the word is not blood, but earth . . . clay probably, dear old London clay as laid down in the Ice Age or earlier.'

Coffin bent down to study the jacket. 'Are you saying the jacket has been buried?'

Dr Miller shrugged. 'I don't know, more your job than mine . . . perhaps the chap was a gardener.'

Coffin traced his finger along a line across the breast of the jacket.

'Is that the sign of a fold . . . where the jacket was folded up?'

'Mind how you touch,' said Daisy Miller. 'Mustn't pollute or contaminate the evidence. Yes, could be where it was folded.' She pointed to the photograph. 'See it better there.

A set of lines where it was folded. Folded for a long time, too.'

As the Chief Commander and CI Darcy left together, she held the door open for them and then called after them: 'Wish you luck.' Her tone and manner suggested she hoped for the opposite.

'I think we stepped on a mine with her,' said Darcy as they walked away.

'You always step on a mine with Daisy.' Coffin accepted it as a fact of life. 'I always do. It's known as having a short fuse, I think.'

'She doesn't like men.'

'So I have heard.'

No more was said, but a bridge had been built between them, gratifying to Darcy who was a career man and allowing Coffin to go back to his own thoughts.

A jacket that might have been worn by a murderer while at his killing, a jacket wrapped round another murdered woman some eighty years later.

How long can a man live? Surely he couldn't be killing at the age of a hundred and twenty or so?

Or had he stepped out of the past, out of the fourth dimension . . . No, people didn't talk like that now. Time was indivisible but we could not walk through time where and how we liked.

Or so Coffin had always piously supposed. He looked at George Darcy and saw he knew no such doubts, secular or religious, rational or the opposite.

'I shall have to question Bradshaw again, inspect his rooms and have his car gone over.' His voice was practical. 'There was no trace of him in her rooms but we shall see. There is her workplace – it was looked at, of course, but we might have another go.'

'I doubt if she was killed in either of those places. Still, I would like to see them too, I will come with you.' He looked at his watch. 'I will have to consult the diary, work out when.' Darcy nodded, not pleased, he would have preferred

135

to have been on his own. 'And I shall talk to Dick Lavender myself.'

Suddenly he realized he was both desperately tired and very hungry. Darcy seemed to read his face.

'What about some breakfast, sir? I have been on the go all night.' And so have you from what I have heard, but he did not say this aloud. 'The canteen does a good breakfast, and we have our own room.'

'I'd put the rest off their food.'

'I don't think so, sir,' said Darcy, who had seen his colleagues eating.

'Right. Lead me in.'

The Senior Officers' Mess was not crowded, as Coffin reckoned Darcy had counted on. Most officers took breakfast at home or didn't eat it. It was a pleasant room, even on a foggy November morning, warm and cheerful with pale oak-panelled walls and a nut-brown carpet. At the beginning, the Chief Commander, feeling the push of political correctness, had experimented with one big, all-ranks eating hall, but it was soon clear that people liked to sit in groups with whom they felt at ease. Segregation was natural, it appeared, so the Chief Commander had bowed to wishes that were apparent but not expressed, and created a separate room for the most senior officers.

The two men sat at a table by the window. Darcy went across the room to pour them orange juice and bring cups of coffee. He also picked up the local newspaper and *The Times*. 'Bacon and eggs on the way. Fried bread too, sir.' He gave the Chief Commander *The Times*, as his due, and read the local himself.

Across the room, Coffin saw that his old friend Chief Superintendent Archie Young had arrived. Archie was one who often breakfasted because his wife was a high-performing career lady who did not eat breakfast.

There was one long table down the centre of the room with several smaller tables ranged along the wall by the door and by the window. Coffin had noticed that most people avoided the middle table to take one of the small ones. Whatever happened lower down the ranks, top brass liked to eat on their own. You didn't have to be a solitary to succeed, but it didn't hurt either.

Archie Young was not by nature one who liked to be on his own, but life had thrust it upon him, since his so successful wife and his own promotions had removed him from his own kind. But he still maintained a friendly relationship with John Coffin, their pasts ran together for such a long way.

All three men read the newspapers, eating without much talk. Coffin noticed that Darcy seemed more interested in his local newspaper than he himself was with *The Times*, even muttering with what sounded like pain at one point. Then he folded the *Sentinel* to get on with his breakfast.

When he had finished eating and reading the latest scandal about a member of the House of Commons, and there always seemed to be one, Coffin looked up, met Archie Young's eye and smiled. 'Come over, Archie.'

The chief superintendent gathered up the scattered pages of his paper and came over.

'See you've got the *Sentinel* too.'

'Not me. Darcy here.' Darcy being named, nodded in a slow, reluctant way and without offering the paper.

'You ought to read it.'

Coffin dragged the paper towards him. 'Oh? Any special reason?'

'You'll see.'

George Darcy said, but sadly and as if he would rather not: 'Page two, sir, and then again on the editorial page, that's six.'

Coffin turned the page. The headline stared out at him. With it was a photograph: big-eyed, pretty, winsome even, there was Jaimie Layard.

Or, as the *Sentinel* had it: Marjorie Wardy.

MURDERED WRITER'S LAST STORY.

She told our interviewer how she is researching the story of a killer, in Spinnergate.

She names no names, but says there will be a sensation

when her work is complete. Her book will link the past and the present.

This study she planned to follow up by the story of a contemporary murder that will stagger all who read it.

But Marjorie says that her flat was broken into and her work attacked: her word processor was broken; some of her research destroyed.

She herself was followed and attacked but she managed to escape. She felt under a threat.

She reported all this to the police in Spinnergate, one night, late in October, about a week before she died.

SOMEONE IS OUT TO GET ME, she said,
AND I THINK I KNOW WHO.

WAS THIS WHY SHE WAS KILLED?

The rest of the article was just padding, making hints but giving no details of any importance.

Coffin turned to the editorial page.

WHAT WERE THE POLICE DOING?

He knew what to expect after that beginning.

'Lovely,' he said to Darcy and Young, looking from one to the other. 'Is this true?'

George Darcy said: 'It's one of those Our Reporter Learnt jobs. Can't tell how much of it is true and what she really did say, but I'll look into it, sir.'

'You mean you don't know?'

Archie Young said: 'I think it's probably true, sir. I know the editor of the *Sentinel*, and though he is not a lover of the police, he is very professional and I don't think he would run this story without having something solid.'

Darcy stood up. 'I'll get off, sir, and investigate. I don't know what's true and what's not true, but I will find out. You can be sure of that.'

His back was expressive as he marched off.

He went off bearing his own burden of anger to spread around.

The other two men watched him go. Coffin was still wrathful. 'It's his job to know what's going on and not to let stories like this get around.' He looked at Archie Young. 'You knew.'

'I just happened to hear something going around.' He could see the Chief Commander's anger. 'Information gaps do happen sometimes, I have had them myself.' He did not add: And so have you, in the past. 'I gather one officer was ill, away.'

Coffin got the message. 'Well, yes, I've dug a few holes for myself in the past, and fallen into them.'

He stopped being angry and finished drinking his coffee. 'The fact is, Archie, as you probably know, I am close to two cases at once ... not a good thing at all in my position.' Especially as one of them was an investigation eighty years too late.

The anger felt by the Chief Commander was carried down by George Darcy to the inspector beneath him and the CID unit dealing with the death of Jaimie Layard. By the time he had finished, about a dozen men and women had felt the lash of his tongue.

George Darcy made to feel a fool was nobody's friend.

Eventually, in company with Detective Inspector Upton and Sergeant Foster, he was talking to a uniformed constable who had been on duty at Blake Street Police Station when Jaimie Layard had called about the break-in and about the attack on her. He was Constable Eric Casey. They were not being rough with him.

The reason they were handling Eric Casey gently was because the night that Jaimie came in to talk to him at his desk was the night that his wife was hit by a stolen car and plunged into a coma. She stayed on a life-support machine for ten hours, after which she died.

Eric Casey was not seen around Blake Street during that time and not for some days after it. When he did return to work, although he had, at the time, made all the necessary signs on paper to record Jaimie's visit, he remembered nothing. He went on remembering nothing, and having been transferred to quiet duties in the Register and Library at

Central, he may have been the one man in Spinnergate who was not taking much notice of Jaimie's murder.

Professional opinion from the police psychologist treating Casey was that the memory was there all right and they would get it out if they handled him the right way.

The right way?

Quiet talk.

George Darcy rang the Chief Commander and told him what the situation was, how things had come about, and that they had a very short written record of Jaimie's call at the desk but nothing more. As yet.

Coffin said: 'Find out, if you can, how it was that when there was this great black hole at Blake Street, yet the *Sentinel* knew the facts.'

'She told them herself, sir.'

'But they knew to ask.'

It was strange and uncomfortable, thought Coffin, how one person's tragedy, in this case Eric Casey's, melded into a murder investigation.

Eric Casey himself, interviewed in George Darcy's office, was quiet and willing to be helpful. If he could be. 'The doc says I had a transient ischaemic shock . . . to the brain . . . knocked it out for a bit. A kind of line in the mind goes . . . I knew who I was and about Margaret but before . . . gone.'

'Could you try to remember?'

'I expect it's all there inside.' He was dignified but sad. 'I suppose I don't want to remember, sir.'

'It might be important.'

'Yes.' He understood all that. 'I am willing to try.'

Don't give him another shock, the doctor had said, there's always a chance, when under stress.

Darcy wondered whether to ring the Chief Commander again, thus transferring ultimate responsibility for anything that might happen to the top. But he looked in Casey's eyes and wondered if it wasn't better, maybe, to get it out, that memories left inside festered and poisoned a life.

And he did want this memory himself, very much. He was honest about that.

He looked at Eric Casey and he studied the faces of his

two subordinates, and because he was English, he knew what to do next.

'Jim,' he said to Sergeant Foster, 'pop down to the canteen and ask them to bring up a pot of tea.'

Very quietly, over the first cup of tea, hot and strong but with no sugar, he began his questioning. It had been bad weather the night that Jaimie came in, had it not? He knew that from his own checkings . . . wet and windy. Did Eric remember that?

He saw a flicker in Eric's eyes: the wet-weather road had been partly the cause of the rolling, rollicking car that had hit Margaret. That and the poor brakes and the drunken driver.

'Yes, I remember the rain.'

Darcy laid off the weather. 'You were on duty in the evening?'

A dangerous corner here too because it had been late evening when the car crash happened.

Eric was silent for a space. Then he said, in a slow voice: 'I believe so.'

'It was a quiet evening.' George Darcy made it a statement.

'I believe so . . . bit of a blur.' Then he said: 'Yes, it was quiet and I was glad of it.' He frowned and Darcy waited. 'Now why was I glad of it? I like working . . . I like to be hard at it, still do.'

George Darcy kept quiet.

'I think I had a headache . . . No, no I never have a headache, not even now. No, I was worried about my eyes . . .' He looked straight at Darcy and then at Sergeant Foster. 'I was frightened I wasn't seeing as well as I might.'

That explains why your notes on the arrival of Jaimie Layard and her complaints look more like bird scratching and are no help to us at all.

'Do you know, there's no trouble with them now, it's funny how stress can work on you . . . I was anxious because my wife hadn't been at all well that day, she died later.' He smiled at Darcy. 'Don't worry, I can talk about her, that's official, but they had to kind of train me to do it . . . I'm

141

supposed to let it all out, but it isn't easy. The people who tell you that don't know what it's like.'

'Can't all just be strain with the eyes,' said Darcy cautiously, more to push things along than because he knew one way or another.

'No, I reckon I am a bit short-sighted. Managed to cover it up.'

There are layers here, thought Darcy. 'A quiet night with you not seeing well, or thinking you didn't, but there was a bit of business, wasn't there, Eric?'

'I think a woman came in with her dog . . .'

Darcy shook his head.

'No? That's the blank bit then, I did tell you.'

'It's all there though, hang on to the woman and forget the dog.'

Eric looked very serious. He opened his mouth to speak while Darcy waited. Eric shut it again. Then he said: 'I think I'll have another cup of tea.'

'He is trying, sir,' said Sergeant Foster in a low voice, as he poured the tea.

'If I thought he wasn't trying I'd shoot him,' said Darcy in a gruff whisper.

'A cup for you, sir? He heard that.'

But Eric had his head down, staring into the cup of tea. 'Peter Pennyman subbed for me; I went down to the canteen for a quick cup of tea . . . Then I came back up and Peter went away. A girl came in, no dog, she said she'd been attacked . . . someone had followed her, grabbed her and hit her. You could see the bruise on her throat . . . he'd had a go . . . I think I took the details down, sir.'

So you did: in a way. Darcy nodded: 'Go on.'

Eric picked up his cup and drained the tea. 'I hope I've given you all you want, sir. I'm surprised that came out. It's true though, she was a pretty young woman. Class.'

'But she didn't stay and speak to a CID officer?' said Darcy carefully.

Eric took a deep breath. 'No, I didn't take it seriously, I remember that now . . . Of course, I put it to her, but she said: "No, leave it there, no charge." I thought to myself:

her boyfriend's done it to her. It was what she thought too.'

'Yeah.' He looked down at his empty cup. 'How funny I should forget all that.' He frowned as if he knew that now the two halves of his memory had joined up, that there was no black hole, nowhere left to hide.

Darcy had one more question: 'Did anyone else come in while she was telling you about the attack on her?'

Eric stared into the distance as if there he could see tiny figures acting out the scene on that baleful night. 'There might have been . . . I seem to think . . . a young chap.' He asked himself a question: 'Could he have been a stringer from the local paper?'

'He could indeed,' said Darcy.

Coffin, who had waited patiently in his office, was told the news on the telephone.

'It was the boyfriend, sir,' said George Darcy. 'Or she thought so, and she wasn't charging him. I reckon they had a quarrel and he beat her up. That was then, and the next time, there always is a next time, he went too far and killed her.'

Coffin reflected. 'She was violent, too.' He remembered the deep scratches he had seen on Martin's wrists and arms.

'Makes it all the more likely, sir.'

Coffin had to admit that it did.

'What about dressing her up as a guy and wheeling the body through the streets?'

'He's an actor, used to putting on a performance, it would come easy to him.'

'And the name on the jacket?'

'Perhaps it's a stage prop and he added the name. Faked it.'

Coffin shrugged. 'Could be, I will ask my wife if it could have come from the theatre.' He shook his head. 'He would have to be skilful indeed to get the name in position. And remember it was sort of hidden, had to be brought up by photography.'

'He's clever, very clever, I'd say. And there's the sister,

she's a scientist. She wouldn't want him charged with murder, she knows what that means.'

'It's thin, very thin.' It was clear to him that Darcy was casting around for a solution. 'See if you can get anything concrete.'

When George Darcy had rung off, Coffin sat looking at the papers on his desk: he was behind with them, that was one thing. He was tired from his disturbed night, and that was another. There had been an explosion down at the Nelson Docks, the exact origin of which was not yet clear, and a woman was being held hostage in a block of flats in East Hythe. In addition, he had to read the reports of several committees and must still chair one on staffing problems.

What he had wanted to do this day had been to call on Dick Lavender in order to see if he had an answer to the name written in the jacket used by the murderer of Jaimie Layard.

Now another question had arisen.

Absently he drew a scheme on the blotter in front of him: two arrows, one pointing one way and one the other.

11

Coffin went in search of his wife. He found Stella in her own office in the theatre. She looked well groomed, except for her hair which was fashionably confused and wild. It was a new style, done that day.

'Doesn't suit you,' he said bluntly.

'Thanks.'

'You always look lovely, of course,' he added in a hurry. 'Nothing could touch that.' This was true and belatedly he realized he was being the traditional male, admiring in his wife only what he had seen before. He didn't like to tell her that the same style was sprouting in the ladies of the street who plied their trade in Beswick Square and thereabouts.

'What is it you want? This has not been a good day.' She turned to Eden who had just come through, bearing a pile of scripts. 'Oh Apollo!' Stella, who could swear with the best after her long years in the theatre, had lately decided that the Greek gods would serve her best to swear by. Naturally she relied on Apollo a lot. Sometimes she called him Phoebus but Apollo was easier and quicker to say. 'Eden, have you got those scripts photocopied now?'

'Yes, Miss Pinero.'

Eden was obliged to turn her hand to everything as needed, as the theatre was always understaffed and short of money. Nominally, she helped in the wardrobe, but in fact she could be found working anywhere, even in the box office. She had put on weight since the days she had managed a dress shop, the short period when she had been Phoebe's landlady and when murder had touched her life. She was happy. Theatre turned out to be her real world. She was never going to be important, or a great figure, but she knew she would prove valuable. If that was an ambition, then she had it.

'The photocopier wasn't working as it should but I got it fixed.'

'Oh, clever – how did you do that?' The photocopier had been bought at a bargain price from a firm that was closing down, but it gave constant trouble.

'Well, I'm a pal of the man delivering the paint for the designer, used to deliver for me when I had the shop and he has a friend who knows about photocopiers and he came round to see what he could do.'

'That was good of him.'

'Glad to do it. He's an electronic engineer but he's redundant.'

'Can I talk?' asked Coffin. He observed that Eden had the other current version of hairstyling: very, very short with little fronds falling down her ears. He had to admit it suited her, but Eden seemed to flourish on theatre street.

'Of course you can talk.' Stella was still concentrating on the papers on her desk, but she managed to look up and smile as she spoke.

'Oh, thanks . . . well, what I want to know is: could a garment go missing from your wardrobe here?'

Both women burst into laughter. 'Could it!' said Eden, and it was not a question. 'We lose things all the time, but they come back . . . people borrow what they fancy for a ball or a publicity shot or even a wedding.'

'Not those sort of clothes.' Coffin's voice was sombre.

Stella frowned. 'What's this all about? What sort of clothes are you talking about?'

Coffin ignored the question. 'Do you keep a catalogue of what you have in the wardrobe? Check things in and out?'

Stella and Eden looked at each other with guilty amusement. 'Sort of,' said Stella. 'it may not be quite up to date.'

'Oh, baby, baby.' Eden kept a straight face.

Stella emerged from behind her desk. 'If you are asking about a garment from our wardrobe here, about which I may say you are very vague, be more precise. It's your professional voice. Of which I have been hearing rather a lot lately.'

'Oh, surely not.'

Stella took no notice. 'I know you when you won't give a direct answer. There is one murder that we are all concerned with just now, the murder of Jaimie Layard, and we are anxious because of Martin. Somehow you are trying to tie in this jacket with Martin.'

'Just asking.'

'I cannot say with my hand on my heart that it did not come from here, but I don't believe it did.'

'Thank you,' said Coffin humbly. 'I will take your faith into account.'

Stella threw a script at him, which he caught. 'I meant it, Stella, what you think does carry weight with me . . . but the fact is . . .'

'Oh, you and your facts.'

Coffin laughed, and dropped the script on her table. 'I am accepting your No. The jacket probably came from another home.' Stella had planted her hand on the script but Coffin had seen the title. '*The Case of the Frightened Lady* . . . You going to put that on?'

'Just thinking about it.'

'Out of date, isn't it?'

'It's a very good melodrama and might be just the thing to run after the Christmas pantomime; this is Edgar Wallace territory, you know . . . I'll edit it a bit.'

'Tart it up, you mean.'

'I'll ignore that . . . I can't afford to be experimental here, you know. Not with your sister Letty on my back.'

'I'd like to see Letty's face if you take her to it.'

'She might enjoy it.'

'With Martin as the neurotic, mad young peer, I suppose.' He knew Letty's weakness for a beautiful male face.

'No, I would not ask him to play it,' said Stella with dignity. 'And you know why.'

Eden said, 'Oh, he's a lovely man, I've got my eye on him.'

Their sparring put aside, Coffin and Stella looked at each other with sadness. Eden was never lucky and who knew what the future for Martin was?

Stella gave a sigh. 'I admire him, looks and talent all there, but his life might be a bit of a wreck.'

'I know what you are thinking, but I don't believe he is a killer.'

Coffin said nothing and Stella looked down at her hands. 'He was a child when his father was killed, we know that, but it happened. He touched blood then, Eden.'

'I blame his sister. Perhaps she killed Jaimie; I reckon she could be jealous.'

Stella looked at Coffin, in his eyes and saw he shared that thought.

'It's too early to speculate.'

'But everyone is in the frame? Of course, don't bother to answer.'

'It has to be so,' he said softly.

Stella stood, tidied her desk, locked the drawers and announced she was going home.

'Keep your feet on the ground,' she advised Eden.

'Oh trust me, Stella, remember the little creatures that crawled around the feet of the dinosaurs, who saw them die, and whose descendants are us . . . I am that little creature, I will crawl out from the wreck of Martin's life and flourish.'

On the way home, Stella said: 'She means it, you know. Determined woman is Eden. Unluckily, as far as I know she has always been determined about the wrong things and the wrong people.'

'You like her, don't you?'

'Yes, and so does Phoebe, that's how she got the job here. Why?'

'I trust your judgement, Stella. When you say you like someone, then I look at them and think: there has to be something good there.'

At their front door in St Luke's Tower, Stella paused: 'I like Martin,' she said.

The fire in the big upstairs living room was warm and comforting, outside another fog was assembling its forces, putting itself together in little strands which wove out of the trees and the damp gutters to join up in clouds which came even lower. Across the road in the old churchyard, all was shrouded and dark. But it was cordoned off from the road still and one cold, solitary constable was on duty.

There was a smell of chicken casserole, which they ate in the kitchen attended by both animals.

'I miss the old dog, don't you?' Coffin had felt sympathy with the old mongrel, a street dog if there ever was one.

'He had a happy death.' He had been a self-appointed guardian of Stella, whom he had once saved from death.

'That's true, he did.' The old dog had been chasing an enemy down Spinnergate High Street when out shopping with Stella (who had not asked for his company, one never did, but found herself with it), he had caught his foe when his heart gave way and he died. Just like that.

Stella had made the chicken casserole, but Coffin made the coffee, between them they dealt with the domestic details. Occasionally, Stella longed for a cook and a chauffeur and a maid but those days were over. (Except that Letty Bingham, her much married and clever sister-in-law, seemed to maintain a high standard of living. A Rolls, last time, wasn't it?)

'I have to go back to the theatre,' she said. 'I am needed there tonight. Keep the fire in.'

'I will.'

'But you are going out yourself.'

'How did you know?'

'Telepathy ... No, you didn't hang your topcoat up, you threw it on the chair by the front door. Also, you didn't lock the door behind you ... So I knew you were not having an at-home evening.' She smiled at him. 'Don't forget I am an actress, I look for those signs of intention. It might come in useful in building a character.'

Coffin watched her preparations for departure: the touch of lipstick, the hand through the hair, although to his eye it was dishevelled enough, the quick spray of that new scent.

I am not an actor, he thought sadly, but I am a detective and I too observe behaviour. And he did not think she was going back to the theatre to work. Not entirely.

Was it Martin? Or that new actor she had brought down from the north?

Damn, jealousy was an ignoble emotion, destructive to the spirit. Dangerous, too. Would he kill for Stella? No. Would she kill for him? Laughable.

You could be angry and miserable, however, and watchful. He allowed himself that much.

He went downstairs, put on his coat, and walked out into the night. The white Pekingese did not try to follow him, unlike the previous incumbent, who, always game for a walk, would have been at the door before he was. He turned towards the river and then took the long, bleak road that led through the tower blocks of Spinnergate towards where Dick Lavender lived.

It was dark, foggy, a London winter night, the Second City was not rich London – here was no Knightsbridge, no Mayfair; Buckingham Palace and the House of Commons were the other side of the river, but the shop windows were bright, and the big supermarket in the High Street was lit up and its car park was busy.

Coffin walked on. St Luke's, created by Stella, out of enthusiasm, professionalism and hard words and hard work, was the only theatre in the Second City, but there were cinemas and a public house called the Lion at Bay where rock groups played. There was life and mirth here as there always had been through the centuries, native British, Roman, Anglo-Saxon and now the polyglot population that would have interested Shakespeare. What an audience to play for, he would have said.

When he got near the river, close to Lavender's flat, he stood looking out at Jericho Docks where ships had once loaded for the East Indies. Quiet now, with berths for private yachts.

Two crimes to be investigated, divided by eighty-odd years, but strangely linked. A coat with a dead man's name in it, a man whom his son called a multiple murderer of women, his coat wrapped round another murdered woman. A grave with an empty coffin, a woman with a child inside her, and the bones of another man, shallow in the earth.

He sighed. It would need the dark voice of John Webster to write this up. Shakespeare was too humane.

The lights were on in Lavender's flat, and the old white van was parked outside among a cluster of smarter vehicles. Perhaps the bicycle padlocked to the railings belonged to Janet Neptune.

He took the lift, rang the doorbell and waited. He had to wait, then the door was opened by Jack Bradshaw, who looked surprised to see him. He hesitated, then: 'Do come in, Chief Commander.'

Coffin could see Dick Lavender himself in the room beyond, supported by pillows in his big armchair. He gave a small dignified wave of the hand. Sitting beside him, sewing in her lap, was Janet Neptune. On the floor beside her was a workbox full of cottons, silks and scraps of materials, she was obviously an accomplished seamstress. She looked bright and cheerful but Dick Lavender seemed tired. Well, that was his privilege, Coffin thought.

Jack Bradshaw hesitated at the door.

'Do come in, Jack,' said Janet. 'And shut the door, you are making us all cold.'

The room, in fact, was very hot, but the very old do feel the cold and Dick Lavender was wearing a thick dressing gown with a rug over his knees. Coffin had thought him immaculate and well groomed on his last visit, not so today: his hair was ruffled, he could have done with a shave and there were food spots on his dressing gown.

Old age has its degradations, Coffin thought. Didn't even the fierce old man Bernard Shaw have marks on his jacket and trousers in extreme old age?

She stood up. 'I expect you want to talk to these two alone.'

'No need to go.'

'Oh, we always have a cup of tea or coffee about this time.' She walked to the door. 'Jack, I will give you a shout when I want help with the tray.'

'She's a good girl,' said Dick Lavender, 'but a mite bossy.' He sounded tired.

Jack Bradshaw sighed. 'She's what she always was, only more so. You need her though, sir.' He turned to Coffin. 'I told all I knew about Marjorie to your colleague Chief

Inspector Darcy. He saw me more than once. I don't think he was satisfied with what I told him. Suspects me, I suppose. Poor Marjorie . . . I think of her as that still, but I know now it was only a name she used for writing.'

Dick Lavender reached out to pat his hand. 'She was a liar, that girl, but we all fall in love with a wrong 'un sometimes. Don't blame yourself.'

'Thanks, Dick, but I do, of course. And don't be hard on her, she was trying to do a job. Maybe it killed her, I hope not, I would like to think her death was nothing to do with me.' He turned to Coffin. 'Is there any news? Anything you can tell me?'

'I am not always up to date with the news myself,' said Coffin evasively. 'I do get the reports, of course, but sometimes they are slow to filter through.'

From the tilt of the old Prime Minister's left eyebrow, Coffin saw that he knew an evasion when he heard one.

'So, is there anything for me, if you prefer not to talk about the other business . . . You came here for something.' Old age had not taken away his sharpness.

'The skeleton of a woman has been found.'

'I told you it would be,' said Dick Lavender, his voice testy. 'I sent you there. So what now?'

'Nothing for the moment. Forensic tests, that sort of thing.'

Evasion again, said Dick Lavender's eloquent eyebrow. In the old days, his cabinet must have got to know that look and prepared to take cover.

'You are not telling me everything.'

'No,' said Coffin in a level voice. 'No.'

'Will you ever?'

Coffin considered: how much power and influence did the old man still wield? 'Probably not.' Then he added: 'But I have told you what I can at the moment; I thought you had a right to know about the skeleton.'

'You have told me something else already: that there is more to tell.'

Round one to you, old fellow, on points, thought Coffin. But I know what I know: the woman had a baby inside her and next to her, in his shallow grave, lay a man. And by them both, an empty box.

Connected, those two bodies, or not? If he is an air-raid victim, we will find out.

He and Dick Lavender exchanged glances of mutual respect. He is my real protagonist, thought Coffin, age or not, and he too knows more than he is saying. I will have to consider that, I am not being his servant.

He saw the old man's hands, plaiting and weaving the rug on his lap. Yes, something there all right.

A call from the kitchen summoned Bradshaw to carry the tray. He seemed to have shrunk in stature since the discovery of Jaimie's body, and probably ranked lowest of all in pecking order in this household.

Janet poured coffee. 'Here you are, Uncle.'

'I am not your uncle,' he growled.

'Great Unke, cousin, be what you like.' She handed a cup to Coffin.

The coffee was good. Angry, tough lady, as he was beginning to see her, she made a good cup of coffee. As they sat drinking he looked at her sewing basket from which a fold of soft pink chiffon spilled.

'Lovely silk,' he said. 'I like the silk, lovely colour.' Soft, very pretty, expensive, it would suit Stella. Or a bride.

She sipped her coffee and gave the basket a little push with her foot. 'Yes ... I was making myself some undies, but I couldn't seem to get on ... I expect I'll finish it one day.'

'Pity to waste it.'

'Oh, there's always waste, isn't there?' She stood up. 'Like Uncle with his coffee there. Now look out, Nunky, you're slopping it.'

Jack Bradshaw went across to Dick Lavender. 'Had enough, sir?'

'Yes, take the cup away.' Command came back into his voice. 'Sit down, girl, and stop fussing.' He turned to Coffin. 'So why are you here today? What is it you want?'

'I thought you had asked once already, Uncle,' said Janet.

'I always knew you listened at the door, woman.'

153

Coffin produced a photograph which he passed across to the former Prime Minister. 'Do you recognize this jacket.'

The jacket was pinned against a sheet on a table, arms wide, unbuttoned. It was in colour, the dusty mid-brown tweed clearly to be seen.

A card covered the spot where the name Edward Lavender showed up.

Dick Lavender studied it without picking the photograph up. He shook his head. 'No. Where did you get it?'

Coffin ignored the question and looked towards Janet. She picked it up, giving it a long careful consideration.

'Take a look,' he said in a quiet voice.

'That's police talk . . . I watch the soaps . . . take a look, they say.'

'I could say something else,' he said, his voice mild, but anyone who had worked with Coffin, and knew him, would have walked carefully.

Janet turned to stare. 'I know you, I'm local, you see. So's he, sitting in his big chair, but he lives in a rarefied atmosphere. I know you are straight, that you sometimes play friends.'

Coffin drew his breath in.

'Nothing dishonest but you have your favourites, but on the whole, I say on the whole, you are trusted to be clean.'

'Thank you.'

'I thought you would say that. Well, don't flash photographs at us.' She subsided, sinking into her chair.

'Have you ever seen this jacket?'

'Not that I know.'

Coffin looked at Jack Bradshaw who said: 'Just a jacket.' He paused: 'The dead girl was wearing it, I think – is that it?'

'It might be useful evidence.'

'That's saying nothing again,' put in Janet. 'Police talk, police talk . . . it might be this or it might be that . . . never mind it helps us cut your throat.'

Dick Lavender sat up. 'Hold your tongue, woman.'

'Someone's got to have one.'

Coffin took the photograph back, giving it another look himself.

'So it was never in this house, anyway?'

Dick Lavender said, 'Not as far as I know.'

'It looks the sort of jacket you might pick up at a charity shop or a church fete,' said Jack Bradshaw.

'I went to enough of those in my time,' said the old man, 'and bought stuff, you had to, and came home and threw it in the attic. I had a row of old trunks. Full of papers, books, old clothes.'

'Still got them,' said Janet. She shook the coffee pot and then poured herself another cup.

'You've been taking an interest in them, haven't you, Jack? Digging around for archive material?'

'Yes, you have two trunks full of paper – letters, drafts of documents and speeches . . .'

'Some Cabinet papers, I daresay, which I ought not to have' – the old man gave a laugh – 'but I doubt they'll put me in the Tower now, although in my time many would have liked to.'

Janet was chewing a biscuit. 'You took a trunk of old clothes and books down to the church sale, Jack, didn't you? I suppose the jacket could have come from them.'

'Yes, I remember that trip, the church down by the tube station, St George's, I don't know what was in them, though.'

Janet bit into the biscuit with decision. 'No, you wouldn't.'

'If the jacket came from here at all,' said Dick Lavender, turning upon Coffin. 'But I suppose you have reason for thinking it did.'

'Yes, I have reason.'

Dick Lavender struggled to stand up, failed and fell back into his chair. 'I would like to look into your face, I can't see it clearly from here. Come over.'

Coffin obeyed the command without a word. He stood before the old man to be studied.

Lavender drew back and sighed, 'You are a good man, I think. I used to be able to tell, to trust my judgement, but people have changed. Or I have. Tell me, is this jacket anything to do with the story I have asked you to investigate?'

'I can't answer that now. There may be connections.' He hesitated, then said: 'Do you have any knowledge of any other body there?'

Lavender breathed deeply. 'No. Is that what you have found? No, I know nothing.'

The old man closed his eyes. 'You had better go now, I am tired. Call again when you can tell me more. Stuff I can believe. Remember you are talking to a politician, even if an old one. I learnt to listen what lay underneath words . . . I don't like what I hear underneath yours.'

Janet led the way out, with Coffin carrying the loaded tray into the kitchen while Jack Bradshaw tended to the old man.

'He needs some looking after, I can tell you . . . but Jack is a help, there are some things you need a man for . . . Put the tray down here.'

The kitchen was clearly her province, and a door leading off it was her sitting room and bedroom too. Through the open door, he could see photographs on the wall above the bed. She liked photographs, there were even photographs on one wall in the kitchen.

It was a kind of picturama of the former Prime Minister. She saw him looking. 'Well, I am proud of the connection; I think he is a great-great-uncle, but I don't dig into it too much because not everyone married who they should and some of the children don't quite fit into the family tree . . . We were that sort of family.'

She pointed: 'That's Uncle when he first got into the House of Commons . . . handsome, wasn't he? You can tell how young he was by his ears, young men always seem to have bigger ears. There he is later, and much later, that's when he resigned. Far away and long ago; I don't remember it myself.'

There were groups on the wall. Richard Lavender with a group of political figures, Richard Lavender with King George, Richard Lavender with his wife. A recent snap of Lavender with Jack Bradshaw and Janet. Janet and Jack Bradshaw.

There was a wedding party on the top of the small refrigerator. She saw him looking at it. 'Friend of mine – a lovely dress, isn't it?'

'Beautiful.' Although, in fact, he thought it fussy and frilly. 'So is the bride.' As she was, lovely.

The telephone fixed on the wall rang and he took his chance to go. 'I'll be off.' He observed that she was one of those who scribbled their telephone numbers on a pad stuck on the wall. She saw him looking. 'I do have a life outside of Uncle, you know. I belong to a few local organizations. Chair of two. I have got Lavender blood.'

'Take care, Miss Neptune,' Coffin said soberly.

She laughed. 'I am not in any danger.'

'We are all in danger sometimes, Miss Neptune,' Coffin said. He ran down the stairs, ignoring the lift. Outside, the fog seemed to be clearing, he could see the sky; he stood there breathing in the air and assembling his thoughts. Plenty to think about.

Jack Bradshaw came out. 'Just off home. Don't stay here all the time. I have a place across the river, just a room, I live in Oxford when I can. Your lot have my address. I suppose they will be back to see us here, Darcy and Co?'

'I am afraid so, yes. They will want to talk to you all again, you and Janet and Lavender himself. It's the way it goes with an investigation of this type.'

'I didn't kill her . . . I loved her. Even if I had killed her, I couldn't dress her body like that. Only a special sort of killer could do that. A mad person or someone who hated her.'

'Sometimes love can turn to hate,' said Coffin.

Jack Bradshaw took this for what it was: a show of scepticism. 'And what about the old man's gadget . . . Dad the Ripper?'

'Don't you believe it?'

Bradshaw shrugged. 'Half and half.'

'There might be something in it,' Coffin offered cautiously.

'My, you do give a lot away.' Bradshaw turned his head. 'I have to get off.'

Coffin nodded. 'Quite a ride home for you.'

'Not too bad. I go through the Greenwich tunnel. I like the ride.'

'Easier than a car?' An accident vehicle, as he recalled.

'Not better than the Rolls,' he smiled. 'That's Dick Lavender's. Yes, a bike can be quicker. A bit dangerous though.'

Coffin looked round the parking area. 'That old white van is nothing to do with you then?'

'No. Janet drives that. All over the place, she's a good driver.' He began to wheel his bike away. Both men turned to look at the lighted windows on the top floor. One light went out.

Bradshaw shrugged. 'I'm off duty now.'

'Will they be all right up there?'

'They won't kill each other, if that's what you mean. Janet is a bit of a bully but it's more for show. I think they are better on their own.' He got on his bike. 'He's been a great man . . . just lived too long, that's his tragedy.'

And Janet's too? Coffin asked himself.

He walked home through the fog, now reduced to wisps by a light wind.

What to make of a house with pink chiffon and pictures of brides where a distinguished old man sat in a dressing gown spotted with spilt food?

Stella was not in, so he sat in the kitchen and drank some wine. Must be careful about what he drank, he had gone that way once before and it was to be avoided. The cat jumped on the table to study his face. 'Want something to drink?' Apparently not. 'What do you make of pink chiffon, puss?' Pink chiffon and that square solid little figure – there was sadness in the thought. Puss had no answer to give, which meant there might not be one.

When Stella came in, lateish but looking happy and unruffled – he was glad about the unruffled bit, surely a woman who had been made love to by someone other than her husband would look ruffled – he said: 'What do you make of pink chiffon lingerie?'

'A love affair, and a first one,' said Stella promptly. 'With a bit of experience you forget about the pink chiffon.' She met his eyes and began to laugh.

'You are a devil, Stella,' he said fondly.

12

The new day was a kind of celebration day for the Second City Force.

After months, no years, of committees, discussions, representations and despairs, the new police baton was to be issued. Displacing the old copper's truncheon, which had been in use more or less since Sir Robert Peel invented the Peelers and with them the modern police force, there was now to be the Asp, a friction-lock, expandable baton. Coffin was told it was well thought of in the sergeants' room, a crucial judgement.

Coffin himself had seen one first in operation in one of the tougher areas of New York, the Upper West Side of Manhattan, where a police lieutenant had showed him the speed and force with which it worked. Later, Coffin had tried one out himself, and now, on this special day, presented one to the first man to use one. He was the uniformed officer with the longest service. He was due to retire within the month so his use of the expandable baton was likely to be limited.

The presentation involved a certain amount of dressing up and speechmaking and formality, none of which was really to the Chief Commander's taste, but all were expected of him. At such times, he felt he understood and sympathized with his sovereign who faced such affairs almost daily. Stella said when he expressed this once that she thought that perhaps wearing a couture dress and beautiful jewels might help one, but even this comfort was denied the Chief Commander, who was instead laced into a uniform of military smartness and stiffness.

The function over, he disappeared into his office, to loosen the collar and find something to drink.

Phoebe was waiting for him. 'You can give me one too,' she said, eyeing the bottle. Phoebe allowed herself a certain liberty with Coffin when no one was listening. The habit had been noted, however, in the eagle-eyed world in which they lived, and produced some speculation.

'I thought you would like to hear the latest about the bodies . . . bones, really, in the old churchyard.'

Coffin nodded. 'Go on.'

'The latest scientific and medical judgement . . . and this is from Dennis Garden, back from his rapid trip, his judgement is that the female bones are that of a young woman probably between twenty and thirty, he declines to be more precise than that. The child, the foetus more accurately, was probably in the fourth month of its development . . . it seems the bones develop in patches in the uterus, not a straightforward strengthening all round.' She handed Coffin a photograph. 'You can just about make out what he means there – he's marked it with white arrows. Told me which bones . . . arms and chest, I think.' She held the photograph before her. 'You'd think it would be skull, wouldn't you, but I suppose that was to stay soft so the brain can develop.'

'How did she die?'

Phoebe threw up her hands. 'Can't say, no flesh to show stab wounds or strangulation and no broken bones . . . Not naturally, we have to believe, since she hardly buried herself.'

'And how long has she been there?'

'He's just guessing, says soil, leaf deposit, insect remains and so on come in here, which are not strictly his line . . . over half a century . . . probably about eighty years . . .'

'It fits in with what Dick Lavender said.' Father Lavender killed the woman and his wife and son buried her.

'We might be able to identify her positively with Isobel Haved, the missing woman, but I doubt it.'

'And what about the other remains?'

'Ah, more evidence of violent death there . . . skull broken and the neck as well . . . interestingly the chap had a badly broken leg as well but that had healed. He would have limped though.'

'And how long had he been dead?'

'A few scraps of clothing have gone away to be analysed . . . but a coin was found close to the body . . . dated 1914. Not long after that, he thinks.'

Coffin assessed this information. 'Might have been a zeppelin victim, killed by a German bomb.'

'And then buried himself?'

'I suppose he might have been buried by the bomb.'

'By the way, the coin was French.'

'Don't say he was a Frenchman?'

'I am not saying anything, not just yet.'

They stood for a moment, in silence. '1914,' Coffin said. 'A French coin . . . a man with a badly damaged leg, still limping. A soldier?'

'Could be . . . another unknown dead.'

Coffin sighed; he walked away to look out of the window where a pale sun was shining in an almost white sky. 'What a gathering of the unburied dead in that place.'

'The empty box might have been for him . . . a burial disrupted by an air raid.'

'Do you believe that?'

'No.'

'Neither do I. The zeppelin raids didn't get going till 1917 as far as I know.'

'Is this as far as you want me to go? I mean, we can tell the Grand Old Man that yes, we have one of his father's victims and what does he want us to do about it.'

Coffin thought about it. 'No, carry on for a while, see if you can tie this skeleton in with Isobel Haved. I don't know, I don't feel this is the end of it.'

'Right.' Phoebe prepared to depart. 'Could this have anything to do with the jacket that was on Jaimie Layard's body with the name of the GOM's father in it?'

'Oh, you know about that?'

'Of course.'

Of course. There were no secrets. He had a momentary

picture of the gossip in the canteen or the locker room. He'd been there himself, knew the way it went.

'I am not at all sure about that jacket. It may not be genuine and if it isn't, then it is either a joke or an attempt to incriminate Jack Bradshaw.'

'He's in there from what I hear, isn't he?' said Phoebe. 'Darcy thinks so . . . He wants to talk to you, by the way.'

Coffin was protected from casual callers in his office by several secretaries and assistants in the outer office and the office beyond them, but people like Chief Inspector Darcy could get through. The outer office was staffed by two young women officers of acknowledged charms combined with sternness. In the inner office his two secretaries, Gillian and Sylvia, used their word processors and operated the fax machine with quiet skill. Coffin stuck to a pen and paper. In a small, hutch-like office of his own, Inspector Paul Masters, Coffin's personal assistant, worked away in silence interrupted only by his telephone. He too was part of the barricade to protect John Coffin, who did not always wish to be protected.

Darcy was well drilled in getting through to the Chief Commander, but even he was only allowed to do so on the telephone.

'The jacket, sir? I understand you saw Richard Lavender . . . any joy?'

Coffin admitted that no one in the Lavender household had owned up to recognizing or ever having seen the jacket. 'But there was a suggestion from Janet Neptune that it might have been among a trunk of old clothes passed along to a stall at the local church's sale.'

'It could be enquired into,' said Darcy gloomily. 'See if anyone remembers taking it in or selling it.'

'Yes. You will have to do that, but don't be surprised if you get nothing. I am not sure if I know what to make of the jacket.'

'The Department of Fashion and Costume in the university is examining it, and I hope they will come up with a date. May not be helpful, but at the moment anything helps . . . But I am still looking at Martin Marlowe, especially since the dead girl herself said he had attacked her once at least. I think they had a violent relationship – he might well have killed her. There's his sister too.'

'You aren't suggesting that she killed the girl?'

'No, sir, but she is very close to her brother and might well connive at anything to keep him out of trouble.'

He never forgets the past history of those two, Coffin thought. Perhaps he himself never did. It was always there. A shadow at the back of his mind.

But Darcy had more to tell. 'One of my detectives was coming out of the hospital where Dr Henley works – it was late evening . . . his wife had just had a baby and he had been with her – when he saw the brother and sister talking outside in the hospital car park. He thought they were arguing so he stayed watching. I had told the team to keep an eye on Marlowe but we weren't watching him. After a bit Marlowe got into his car and drove off fast . . . my man decided to follow to see what he did. Marlowe drove to the nearest station of the Light Railway.'

'So?'

'By the time my man had parked his car, the train had left and taken Marlowe with it . . . he was travelling towards the City. He has a friend in the City of London Police and he rang ahead and asked if one of their cars would meet the train at the Tower and see where Marlowe went.'

'And?'

'A car did get to the terminus . . . but no Marlowe, so either he got off at an earlier station or he was not recognized.'

'You aren't suggesting he put on a wig and a false beard?'

'He is an actor, sir.'

'What are you suggesting, Darcy?'

There was a pause. 'Jaimie Layard's flat in the City, where she operated as Marjorie Wardy, was the scene of an attempted break-in last night.'

'Are you suggesting it was Martin Marlowe?'

'Could be, it's a possibility.'

'Might he not have had a key?'

'Yes, quite likely, but we had changed the locks after searching the place. There was an attempt to break the lock.'

'He didn't get in, apparently, so whatever he wanted, he didn't get. If it was him.'

'I shall be talking to him today as well as Bradshaw. If I can find him. Bradshaw has agreed to come in to see me today, but Marlowe is not answering his telephone or his door. In fact, at this moment, I don't know where he is.'

Coffin made his decision. 'Keep the flat under observation . . . set it up with the City of London men . . . it's their area.'

'We usually mix well there,' observed Darcy.

A tacit, unofficial quid pro quo arrangement, Coffin meditated: you scratch my back and I scratch yours. Bills no doubt appeared in some shape or form and were settled.

'And I shall want to take a look round the flat myself.'

'Of course, sir. I'll come with you.' On his own telephone, Darcy ordered the car to pick them both up, and as he put the receiver down, he heard a faint, jovial whisper about the CC's dead dolly in the car park. So that was the word that was going round? Darcy frowned but decided against reproof. Perhaps it wasn't a bad description for Marjorie–Jaimie as seen in her Guy Fawkes dress. But on an impulse he strolled down to the CID sergeants' room where the men sat at their desks. The CID room at Central was large but not large enough for the men who usually crowded it; today it was almost empty and he knew why: as well as the investigation into the dead dolly, there was an arson case down by the tube station and a dead man in the loading bay at a supermarket in the High Street.

He looked around, then went out to meet the Chief Commander. Making good terms with him, he decided, and that never did a man's career any harm.

A uniformed constable stood outside the front door of Jaimie's workplace above the flower shop. The flower shop was open for business, as was the coffee shop next door.

The door showed the signs of the attack on it where an attempt had been made to chisel away at the lock, but failing to do so or to break down the door.

'An amateur attempt,' Darcy said appraisingly. 'We had

changed the lock and in any case there is a sheet of steel backing the wood put on after the first break-in.'

'What about the back . . . windows and so on?'

'No attempt, you'd need wings, and anyway, access from the back is difficult.'

'And no one heard anything?'

'Half the offices below are empty.'

Darcy acknowledged the constable, and let the two of them in.

Marjorie–Jaimie, as well as sharing an apartment with Martin, kept this set of two rooms as her working address. She had a word processor with a big printer, a photocopier and telephone and fax.

George Darcy led the way in. 'We've had a good look round, checked the messages on the answerphone . . . all business, and only a couple, both saying why hadn't she answered a previous call.'

'And the previous call?' asked Coffin, moving quietly around the room.

'Wiped. I reckon she came in regularly.'

'Where she worked, I suppose.' Coffin was examining a file of typed pages on the desk. It appeared to be the rough outlines for an article on Richard Lavender, Man of the Past. There was no direct mention of a murderous father but a few cryptic notes suggested that she would be dealing with this.

Wonder how she got on to it? he asked himself once again. Jack Bradshaw seemed the likely answer, although he would certainly deny it. He might not even have known that he had given anything away, he was in love with her after all.

How much had he known himself? It was possible that Jaimie had picked up hints from someone else. The old man himself, garrulous and free of speech without realizing it in his old age. Although he had not said so, he certainly still liked a pretty face.

Then there was Janet Neptune, she probably knew as much as anyone about events in the past. Or could make a good guess. She was part of his family and families often knew more than they were willing to tell.

But this had been a clever girl who might have come across evidence on her own, evidence which Phoebe might track down in her turn in a local newspaper or even in an article by Edgar Wallace.

'Do you ever read Edgar Wallace?' he asked Darcy absently.

'No. Did as a boy: *Sanders of the River* and that sort of thing. Found them in my grandfather's bookshelves.'

'That would be it,' said Coffin. 'My wife is putting on one of his plays: *The Case of the Frightened Lady* ... bringing it up to date a bit, I gather.' Tarting it up, Stella had said, and you had to rely on her own natural good taste to make it something more. 'Be on after Christmas.'

He went on walking round the room, which was well furnished in a businesslike, unfussy way. 'She wasn't short of money.'

Darcy agreed. 'No. I got her sister, or one of them, they are a big family, to come in and have a look round, to see if anything suggested itself to her; she said that Jaimie had a small private income, and that she earned well too.'

'And no idea what lies behind the attempt to get in?'

'Might just be vandals, or a chancer who knew the place was empty.'

Coffin went into the kitchen which was neat and clean with some smart but unused-looking kitchen equipment. He opened the refrigerator door to look inside. Nothing much there except coffee and a bottle of wine. Stale now, one must presume.

'She didn't live here in any real sense,' explained Darcy, who plainly felt the conducted tour was his responsibility as guide. 'Lived with Marlowe in his place.'

'Let's hope Marlowe has calmed down.'

Darcy shrugged. 'I think his sister has a calming influence. May have fed him a sedative of some sort, wouldn't be surprised.'

'Any indication either of them were on drugs?'

Darcy shook his head. 'None, and you can bet we looked.' He opened the door to the bathroom. 'Not even an aspirin.'

The bathroom had a shower as well as a bath and showed

the only sign of feminine habitation, with scented soap, bath oil and toilet water all in a matching perfume.

The bedroom led off the bathroom; it was small with a low bed. The bed, however, was large and luxurious. Coffin turned to Darcy with enquiry.

'Yes. Her sister said she had a succession of lovers. It was the way she lived. Easy to anger. Always a bit violent but soon got over it. She loved the girl, but was realistic about her.'

'What was the sister like?'

Darcy appraised her: 'Large, easy manners, very well dressed; I should say she had a temper too. Not totally nun-like, either.' He couldn't repress a small smile: he had liked Griselda Layard. He had an idea that she had liked him also. The home life of the Layard family must be interesting.

'There is nothing to suggest she was killed here?'

Darcy shook his head. 'No sign of a struggle. As you can see, all is in order.' He looked around the room where a faint show of white powder still remained on doors and windows. 'We checked for fingerprints. Just hers and a blur of others that we can't identify. Marlowe says he did come sometimes on her invitation but he hadn't been here for some weeks.'

'Do you believe him?'

'I can't show that he is lying.'

'He's not your favourite for the killing, is he?'

'I fancy both of them.' Darcy set his jaw like a terrier who had just got his teeth in. 'Times I think it's Jack Bradshaw. He's the only one who knew the girl, had a motive of sorts and could have used that jacket. And then I think, well, the girl more or less accused Marlowe of attacking her once, and then he was seen around here last night.' He looked at Coffin. 'Yes. I know we lost him, but one of the local mob saw a man who fits his description hanging around here last night . . . he could have been trying to break in. And if it was he, then I have the more reason to suspect him. I will be asking him, that's for sure. And checking on any alibis he might have. Trouble is, no one seems to have them in this case, all airy-fairy, and on their own or with a sister who would swear to anything.' Grudgingly, he added: 'Equal as to motive: both in love with her.'

'Is love a motive?'

'It brings motives with it, sir. Mind you, it's a mad murder.'

Coffin made a noise that might have been assent. He moved to Jaimie's desk where he sat looking around him, studying the whole area from telephone to the printer attached to the word processor. 'Have you looked at what she had on her PC?'

'I have a girl going through it all, one of our electronic miracle workers. She will let me know what there is. I don't expect miracles.'

Coffin sat looking at the telephone and the pad beside it. She had two phones, one attached to a fax machine. He absorbed the numbers automatically. Part of his years in CID, you always remembered the telephone numbers. No messages scrawled, no useful messages on the answerphone.

He stood up and drew away from the table to take a look out of the window. A busy street scene with the red London buses edging their way forward in the traffic, while taxis seemed to weave their way in and out.

'Are you all right, sir?' said Darcy, coming up behind him.

Coffin swung round. 'Yes, sure. Just thinking.'

Darcy screwed up his eyes, but said nothing. Not good thoughts, it seemed, if he could read Coffin's face. He was a funny one. Darcy had heard Archie Young say that sometimes Coffin seemed to pluck ideas out of the air and then there was a solution. Stood up in court, too, which is more than you could say for the cases put in by more conventional coppers.

Coffin walked away from the window, saying as he did so, in a conversational way: 'Martin Marlowe's outside on the pavement looking up. I've been watching him. I was looking down and he was looking up. He saw me, I think.'

Darcy went over to the window. 'Wonder what he wants?'

'Let's go down and find out.'

They met him on the staircase. 'What do you want?' asked Darcy. Coffin kept silent. Martin stared back at them with unfriendly eyes.

'Not to see you,' he said. 'I came to look . . . She died here, and I want to know why.' He staggered backwards, grabbing at the stair rail to stop himself falling.

'No reason to believe that she was killed here.' Coffin put his hand on Martin's arm. 'We don't know where she was killed, not yet, although we will find out. Come and sit in the car if you want to talk.'

'He'd better not be sick in the car,' muttered Darcy.

'He won't be.' This man is not drunk, Coffin said to himself, or not on alcohol but on raw emotion. He could see from Darcy's face that he was thinking: This bloody actor.

'Let's establish one thing: were you here last night?'

'Yes.' Martin's voice was thick. 'And the night before that and the night before that.'

'Before the performance or not?' asked Coffin.

'After, you fool.'

'Did you try to break in?'

'No . . .'

'Someone tried to.'

'Not me . . . it's her coffin, her shroud . . .'

This was not endearing him to Darcy. 'Did you ever have a key?' he demanded.

'I had one once, but Jaimie didn't like me using it. It was her private place. Jaimie did not like invaders.'

Once inside the car, Martin became quieter. 'I want to know what you are doing to find her killer. I don't think you are doing much.'

'We are working on it,' said Darcy, still irritated.

'You think it's me, don't you? Written all over your face. Or my poor sister. Killed once, easy to do it again. I'll tell you who killed her, I know. That old pervert, that Grand Old Man, and if you don't get him, I will.'

'Are you accusing Richard Lavender?'

'Yes.'

'He's very old and feeble.'

'Somehow he did it. Hired someone, he wanted Jaimie silenced. I don't know why, but he did.' He was sweating. 'Open the car window, will you?'

170

Coffin wound it down. 'Why do you call Richard Lavender a pervert?'

'There was something rotten about him, and Jaimie knew. In the past. I don't know, perhaps not even that. She didn't trust him, she said you couldn't. Wanted to maul, I expect, probably all he could manage. She wouldn't like that.' His voice was getting thicker. 'She was straight about sex, Jaimie, plenty of it, but straight.'

He started to cry. This irritated Darcy even more. 'I am not satisfied with all you are saying. I am going to take you down to the station for questioning.'

Surprisingly, this steadied Martin. 'All right, but let me tell my sister first.' He looked at Coffin for support.

'Are you staying with her?'

'No. She has a hospital flat, I can't live with her there, not allowed. So she is with me.'

'Will she be there now?'

'Yes, she's waiting for me.'

Good sister, Coffin thought. He gave Darcy the look that meant: when we get there, you stay in the car and I will go in with him.

Dr Clara Henley opened the door herself. Coffin thought she had missed the stigmata which many long-term prisoners acquire: she was neither wary nor aggressive, she was neither anxious to please, nor dismissive; she looked lively and cheerful, but she looked older than her years, which he could understand. She was indeed older than her brother. His dependence on her showed at once, he rushed towards her and hugged her.

'Are you all right, Clara?'

'Of course I am all right. It's you that seems not to be.' She looked over his shoulder; she was cool, and it seemed she could talk. 'Good morning, Chief Commander, or is it afternoon?'

Coffin stood in the doorway, through which he could see the kitchen and the living room, both of which were, he guessed, tidier than at any time in the tenancy of Jaimie and Martin. They had lived here together and quarrelled; Martin

171

had loved her, but he was probably right in thinking that the girl was only after his 'story'.

Looking into Clara's cold eyes, he wondered if she would have been capable of killing Jaimie to stop her doing just that. It was judged that Jaimie had died in the late afternoon or early evening, hard to be precise. She had been operating, of course. Presumably that had been checked. He wondered how easy it might be to walk out of an operating theatre, commit a murder and then come back. Didn't some operations go on all day?

'I've got to go in to be questioned again,' Martin was saying.

'I think we had better get you a lawyer.'

'It would be a good idea,' agreed Coffin.

Clara patted her brother's shoulder. 'You get off, I will find you a lawyer. There's a woman I knew from college.' She looked sardonically at Coffin. 'A real college, where I started my medical training, not a cover name for prison.'

Martin drew away from his sister. 'I will go then. Thanks, Clara.' He had taken strength from her, he sounded calmer.

'I had come to that conclusion myself.' Coffin motioned to Martin to get into the car where Darcy sat, scowling. 'Doctor, what did your brother pass to you when he was hugging you?'

She kept silent.

'I saw, you know. In fact, I was looking out for something of that sort. I expected it.' He stood in front of her, his face stern. 'Come on, hand it over. I could take you down to be searched.'

'Give it to him,' said Martin from the car. 'Sorry, Clara.'

Silently, she drew a short, stubby but sharp knife from her pocket.

'What was that for? Or were you going to use it to break into the flat?'

'I wanted it for self-protection, I have been carrying it for days,' was all Martin said.

*   *   *

At the end of that day, Coffin went into the theatre to find Stella. 'I want to take you out to dinner. Let's drive, get out of the Second City.'

Stella was sitting behind her desk once again, studying the theatre accounts which always made her nervous.

'You have taken away my new young juvenile,' she complained. 'It is very awkward for us here. I only heard just before the curtain went up.'

'Is he in this production?'

'No,' Stella admitted. 'But he might have been, you lot ought to remember that theatre is not like a factory or an office: we have a duty towards the audience.'

'You do put on a marvellous act,' Coffin said with admiring affection. 'I shouldn't worry, he's probably safer where he is now, than elsewhere.'

'What does that mean?'

'I'm not quite sure,' said Coffin soberly and with conviction.

'Is he in danger?'

'He might be . . . anyway, his sister is getting him a solicitor, so I expect he will be out on police bail, after a while.'

'You think he is the killer?'

Coffin did not answer.

'But if he is, then he himself cannot be in any danger.'

'Grow up, Stella. If you kill someone who is loved, then you are in danger of revenge.'

Stella thought about it. Who was a candidate for a revenge killing? 'Jack Bradshaw?'

'Silence on that one.'

'So they are both under suspicion . . . Silence on that one too, I suppose. I am glad I don't have to write the dialogue for any play you might perform in.'

'Unluckily it is not a play,' said Coffin, turning away.

Stella walked round to face him. 'Let me look at you . . . you are worried, aren't you? Anxious. Or is it guilty?'

'All of that.'

'What do you think is going to happen?'

Slowly, he said: 'I think it is already happening. And yes, it is my doing.'

Into the silence, Stella said: 'If we are dining out, I ought to go and change.' She looked down at her jeans and silk shirt.

'Don't change, you look lovely as you are. I have booked a table at that restaurant in Basil Street. I think it's a night for being very extravagant and detached.'

Stella looked at him, and was frightened.

For him, not of him.

'If this was a play,' she said, 'you would put your arms round me and say: "Don't shiver, just think of it as a play," and the audience would nod as the curtain came down and wait for the next act. But this isn't a play and you aren't that sort of person.'

'No, my darling,' he said sadly.

The restaurant was not in Basil Street itself but in a little cul-de-sac just off it called The Pens, the origin of this name was not clear, but perhaps, a hundred and so years ago when all this was fields, sheep had been penned there.

They had a table in the window overlooking the back garden, which was tiny, paved but full of greenery which seemed to be surviving the winter weather. It was gently floodlit.

Stella settled herself at their table, and adjusted her scarf before looking around the room. She knew that her jeans, silk shirt and cashmere jacket matched the rest of the diners, who were dressed with expensive casualness.

She turned to her husband, who was thinking about the wine; not a natural wine buff – having been brought up in a world that took a pint of beer – he wanted to be intelligent about it and not just go by price.

'So why did you bring me here?'

'I thought you liked it?'

'I do. But usually I am taken here by those who want me to put on a play for them or, if I am lucky, to offer me a part in a film. TV people take you somewhere less expensive.'

'What a cynic you are.'

'Just full of experience. So why are we here?'

Coffin looked thoughtful. 'My idea was that you deserved

to get out of the Second City for a while and to have some food and drink in a pleasant ambience ... Also, I wanted to show you off a bit. You are quite a person, you know.'

Stella accepted the compliment, looked round the room again, saw that there was no one there she knew except a woman she had worked with years ago and whom she hardly recognized. Satisfying to see someone age so thoroughly. 'That's Aileen Alleen over there,' she said happily to Coffin. 'I only just recognized her. Wouldn't know her, would you? Marrying that millionaire just did for her.'

'Has she still got the millionaire?' Coffin was looking at the very young but exceedingly good-to-look-at young man who was dining with Aileen.

'I don't know if she's still got him, but I understand she has quite a few of his millions.'

'Envy her?'

'No, I would rather have my policeman, my theatre and my figure.'

They drank some wine and ate the smoked salmon. Stella thought about some of the meals they had had together, from fish and chips in Greenwich to chicken Marengo in Max's restaurant. Not to mention some of the food they cooked together in their own kitchen; in many ways, because neither could cook, the most memorable.

'Where's Augustus?' she asked suddenly. 'Did we bring him or leave him at home?'

'In the car.'

'He'll hate that.'

'Passionately.'

Stella leaned forward. 'We are talking about nothing, aren't we? What are you hiding?'

Coffin sighed. 'Well, I wasn't going to mention this tonight, but I think you might be losing an actor.'

Stella leaned back in her chair. 'Martin? You are arresting Martin for the murder of Jaimie.'

'I'm not arresting anyone ... and no, not Jaimie. Your new actor just recruited ... the police in the city he came from want him back ... He has a taste for little boys. Not recommended.'

175

Stella took a draught of wine and prepared to be philosophical. 'Worse things have happened. Now I know why he didn't bargain but took what I offered.'

'I expect he knew things were getting hot, yes.'

Stella began to eat, relaxed, she felt she knew the worst now and could enjoy her evening. It was a pity about her latest recruit but there you were, these things happened. She doubted if he restricted himself to little boys; her impression was that, sexually, he was omnivorous.

She smiled at her husband, and he smiled back.

He saw no need to tell her that he had thought it best to get them both out of Spinnergate that evening.

I think I have alerted the killer. I have turned on the tap marked violence, he said to himself. And I don't know when it will start to pour out or who will get splashed.

They ate their meal, talking quietly now, Stella enjoying the wine, Coffin drinking very little because he would be driving home.

Just as they were leaving, Coffin's telephone rang.

'Oh dear,' said Stella.

Coffin took the telephone from his overcoat pocket. He listened to Darcy explaining that both Marlowe and Bradshaw had been released.

'Not much else you could do,' agreed Coffin.

'No forensic evidence as yet to tie in to either of them. And smooth talkers both of them. Bradshaw is a clever man and Marlowe had his solicitor on hand. Fat Louie Armstrong,' obliged Darcy, who had clashed with the lady before. 'And she's clever enough for both of them.' Heavily and sadly, Darcy said: 'I will see you tomorrow evening then, sir, at the E and B?'

'I will be there,' agreed Coffin. It was one of the functions he had to attend.

Coffin drove them home to the Second City, advising Stella to lock the car door on her side and when she protested, advised her just to do it.

He was tetchy, and tense.

13

It was a cold bleak night. Richard Lavender was being prepared for bed. Like a package, was how he put it when in a bad mood.

In the evening, Janet Neptune was free, or regarded herself as so, although her great-uncle (if that was what he was) still called upon her for a hot drink, or a new book to read if he felt like it. But Janet Neptune's place was taken by a nurse who came in every evening to get the GOM (the nurse called him that: Come on, Grand Old Man, the bath is ready, and this infuriated him) bathed and put to bed.

Nurse Flint was a large, plump, pretty woman whose appearance belied her name, but was supported by the great firmness of her nature.

'Come on, dear, bathy time.'

Dick Lavender showed his teeth. 'Fussy bitch, you wouldn't have spoken to me like that when I was PM.'

Flint helped him towards bed, her hands gentle, he knew and appreciated her touch. 'No, certainly I would not. But I wasn't born then.'

The bath water was softened with soothing oils, and afterwards Nurse Flint would rub unguents into those joints where the skin was thin and likely to crack into sore spots. She was delicate about this, even as her tongue was sharp.

'You ought not to sit around on your bottom so much.'

'Where else can I sit?'

'I mean you should move around more. You can, you know, but you don't like to admit it. You could run if you had to.'

'Rubbish.'

'I bet you would if there was a fire.' She rubbed some cream into his thin flanks. 'You don't deceive me, I know you can nip around if you want to . . . I can feel the muscles.' She gave a snort. 'You pinched me.'

'I thought you might enjoy feeling my muscles. And your bottom asks for it.'

She rolled him over, but taking care not to be rough. 'You're an old devil, I wouldn't like to be shut up in a dark room with you.' She gave a low rumble of a laugh. 'Now you ought to get out more, that's my advice. Get Janet to drive you about a bit or ask that nice Dr Bradshaw.'

'Oh yes, everyone likes Jack Bradshaw,' Dick Lavender growled. He could growl. It was a low rumbling in the back of his throat like an aged lion.

'Jealous, are you now? At your age. Say to yourself it's an addiction, like smoking.' She sprayed him with a sweet-smelling talcum. She liked her patients to smell sweet, more for her own sake than theirs. 'Give it up. Cure yourself.' She added half humorously, half sardonically: 'Grow up.'

'Old age doesn't cure everything.'

'Don't I know it.' She patted him with a tissue. 'Never did anything for me.' How old was he? Ninety? Ninety-six more like it.

Soon she had him in his dressing gown, leaning against a pile of pillows.

'Tea or coffee, or I could make you some cocoa?'

'Whisky, please.'

'Right you are. And I'll join you.'

'Did I ask you?'

'No, but I have to have some reward for looking after you.'

The theory was that this sparring between them was enjoyed by both parties, but the truth was that Dick Lavender had tired of it. He no longer wanted to be jokey or the butt of jokes. The well of humour had long been dried up inside him, and he felt himself full of bitter memories which seemed to have an odour. A rank smell filled his nostrils in the day, and at night he smelt bodies, always bodies, sour and sweaty. Probably it was his own body, full of the odours of old age, but that did not make him love it more.

They drank the whisky neat and with quiet pleasure.

'Leave me the bottle.'

'I ought not. What will Janet say?'

'I will deal with Janet.' The growl came out again. Janet might have feared to hear it, but she was not one who understood all the sounds she heard.

Miss Flint obliged, leaving the bottle enough out of his reach so that he would have to get out of bed to get it, which might deter him or might not. He could move when he wanted to.

'Look,' she said at the door. 'I know you are still a lion but don't take risks. Don't roar too often.'

'God shield us,' he quoted to himself. 'A lion among the ladies is a most dreadful thing.' He felt the growl beginning and the rank smell rose inside him. 'Shakespeare is my god, you know, he educated me: Macbeth, King Lear, and of them all, Bottom, the great bottom with the donkey's head.'

'As you like,' said Miss Flint, buttoning her coat. 'You do go on about bottoms.'

He watched her go. It was going to be a bad night.

Miss Flint stood in the hall listening: she hated that sound he made, rasping and low, call it a growl if you must. She considered going back in, but no. She had done all that could be required of her.

She sped to her car, it was raining and cold. It was going to be a bad night.

Dick Lavender read for a while – Lady Thatcher's memoirs. She had it easy, he thought, should have been PM when I was, I had more vultures around. Outlived them all, though.

He dozed, and then woke up. He could hear noises as of bones cracking and a woman screaming. A little muted scream, suppressed.

He tried to get up but he could hardly move his legs. He did stagger to the door, which would not open, and then found he was floating, flying, sinking, swimming. When he got back to bed his hands felt sticky.

No more noises. Was he awake or still asleep? Were the noises outside him or inside?

Was he a performer or part of the audience?

When he woke up there was blood, dried blood, on his hands.

It had been a bad night. A very bad night.

14

There was a faxed message waiting for Coffin when he got back to his tower home in St Luke's. A tiny office had been created for Coffin on the ground floor and in this little room the fax machine and a secret, dedicated telephone lived. Stella picked it up and handed it over, there was a fax for him coming through at that very minute. See you at the E and B, Phoebe said.

'What is this E and B she's talking about?' Stella asked, having caught sight of the phrase. 'Some sort of secret society?' She was only half joking because heaven knows, she knew how many secret societies there were, some having hundreds of members and some only one or two. Sometimes you found yourself a member without knowing you had joined. Men usually had more secret societies than women but women had some very, very secret ones, hardly guessed at by the masculine world.

Coffin picked up the fax from Phoebe and shook his head. 'No, just a supper . . . Egg and Bacon supper.'

Stella raised an eyebrow in enquiry. 'Do you eat egg and bacon at it?'

'I suppose we might do,' said Coffin vaguely, his eyes on the long fax from Phoebe. 'Everyone comes.'

'Everyone?' Stella, used to the casual world of the theatre, remembered how surprised she had been at the rigid class structure in the police service, one in which different ranks ate in different rooms and did not meet socially. You had to remember that the police service was a Victorian invention and one on which the army had laid a strong hand. Officer class and other ranks was the pattern deeply imbedded in it.

She knew that her husband was trying to break this up, that he had instituted a table in the main canteen for the higher ranks at which he ate himself on occasion. But the higher ranks still had their private room in which she herself had once been entertained. Only once, women, especially actresses, need not be encouraged.

'I suppose there will be a bar,' she said, naming the one institution that no club can be without. She was leading the way up the narrow winding stairway which was one of the hazards of living in a tower. But it keeps you thin, Stella used to say to herself, as she ran upwards; she usually ran, somehow it seemed easier as your own momentum carried you forward.

'Of course.' He was still studying the fax from Phoebe, as he followed her up the stairs. 'You could come yourself one time if you liked, as a distinguished visitor . . . I have bolted and locked up, by the way, so I hope the dog won't want to go out again.' The sound of the big old locks and the heavy chains had been very audible. They were only decoration, though, a legacy from the past. Their real security was electronic.

Stella was carrying Augustus, who sometimes made heavy weather of the staircase. 'No, he attended to everything while you were putting the car away.' There was a small patch of grass and bushes this side of the road and facing the old churchyard which Augustus was licensed to use. She had noticed that there was still a barrier up over the road and one lone uniformed man still on guard. It had not been so long after all since the skeletons had been found.

She guessed that the fax from Phoebe Astley concerned the case of the bodies in the old churchyard. She had trained herself not to ask questions, but she knew a little of what lay behind the digging. Stella did not like Phoebe overmuch, but she had trained herself not to be jealous of a woman who worked so closely with her husband and whose brains and professional skills could not be in doubt. Stella never thought of herself as clever but she had understandings and intuitions that worked as well. Her mind was moving now.

Almost at the top of the stairs, she paused for breath; she

deposited Augustus by the kitchen door where he made his way promptly to his water bowl and began to lap noisily, casting reproachful glances at his owners for having eaten and drunk while forgetting their dog.

'Has it struck you,' said Stella to her husband as he joined her in the kitchen, 'that old Lavender made up this story about his father to take your mind off other things?'

'It has indeed.' Coffin threw the fax on the table. 'I have thought about it constantly.' He stood for a moment in silence. 'But what was found across the road does support his story so far.' He frowned. 'It's not straightforward though, by any means. You could say that we found more than we expected.'

The skeletal remains of a woman with the fragments of an unborn child; and close by the skeleton of a man. These were part of his puzzle. Dick Lavender had not been questioned yet about the finds, but that must come.

'I will just read through what Phoebe has got to say. You go on up, Stella.'

Stella took the dog and went up to her bedroom, where she found the cat already installed on the bed. Dog and cat eyed each other, assessed the best sleeping territory, but decided it was too late at night to fight over it.

I won't be jealous of that woman, Stella told herself as she creamed her face. 'She is a good professional, John needs the work she does, probably no one but Phoebe could do it. I admire her.'

Stella studied her face in the looking glass, focusing the light on her dressing table directly on it. A few lines here and there, not really important, the general effect was still good. Phoebe was younger than she was, many years younger, not pretty but attractive.

'He needs her in his work, I suppose. She supports him, plays the good sister. I can't do that, I back him up, but not on the work front. Very often we are at odds there.'

As now. He suspected Martin of murdering Jaimie, he probably believed that the sister Clara had helped.

Some cleaner got into her eye to make it sting. 'Damn.'

There was Jack Bradshaw lined up as a suspect; Stella

decided that he would not do, he had loved the girl, and Stella herself had seen the shock on his face when Jaimie was discovered in that terrible disguise. He could not have done that to Jaimie.

To herself, she would admit that Martin, the actor, could have done so. It would have been a performance to him.

Downstairs, Coffin sat reading Phoebe's fax. 'I have been working on the newspaper records, all of which are on micro-film, so easy to read. There are gaps, due, I suppose, to accidents of life and war. The Spinnergate paper, which was daily until the 1920s, and the East Hythe weekly paper have been the most useful. Both papers still exist but both now are weekly papers, run for the advertising revenues and not for the news.'

This Coffin knew, a copy of his local newspaper, full of advertisements for the sale of houses and offices, was on the kitchen table in front of him. The cat had shot in, leaving his bed, and was drinking from a saucer of milk placed on the table. As far as he could see she was spilling milk on a tactful and oblique but obliging advertisement from the local madam advertising her girls. As the cat slopped another drop of milk, Coffin registered that action might have to be taken on Madame Biddy LeSalle.

He turned back to what Phoebe had to say.

'I followed up all items about the names of the murdered women, Mildred Bailey, Mary Jane Armour, and Eliza Jones, shop girl. The bodies of the first three women were found over a period of some months. Going on the newspaper reports, each of the first three victims died in similar circum-stances: each woman was raped and strangled. In each case, a piece of underclothing was removed.'

Phoebe added: 'Newspapers in those days were too decor-ous to name the piece of underwear, so I think we must conclude that the killer whipped off his victims' knickers. None was found with the victim so he must have taken them with him.'

Coffin stopped reading for a moment to stop the cat walk-ing all over the fax as it spread across the table.

'The newspapers were similarly discreet over the lifestyles

of Bailey and Armour, they are called married women, but Bailey was said not to be living with her husband, and Armour said to be living in a lodging house. I think you draw your own conclusions from that.

'There was a suggestion in the Spinnergate paper for September 23, 1913, that a fourth woman, Isobel Haved, might have been murdered by the serial killer, but although I am going through the papers carefully once again, I can find no other mention of this woman. No date, no name and no place.

'How many women did Richard Lavender say his father had killed?'

Coffin scrawled a note on the fax to this effect.

Phoebe's fax went on: 'The odd woman out is Haved; she is named as a likely victim because she is missing from where she lived, a house down by the old Flemish Docks. There is an interview with a neighbour, a woman who worked in a fish shop, who says how worried she is but there is no further mention of her.'

Coffin wrote in the margin: *Is she perhaps the woman that Lavender claims he and his mother buried? And if so, can she somehow be linked with the skeleton already found?*

'There are certain facts that make me wonder how true the story that old Lavender told us could be. I mean, it's so odd that his mother should recruit her son for the job when all she wanted to do was to keep secret her husband's crime. Could she trust the boy not to talk?

'And then, how was it SHE HAD THE BODY? If I write this large it is because for me it is a large question.

'In a smaller kind of way is the worry how they got through the streets and did the burial.

'And where was Dad?'

Coffin wrote another note: *I think he said that his father had run away.*

Phoebe went on: 'I can't think why Lavender should lie, it's all so far away and long ago. Also, he got us into it – I wouldn't have been digging in the old churchyard but for his tale . . . All the same, it doesn't quite fit . . . Perhaps it is

185

because it was so long ago, and he is old. Memory, you know, plays tricks.'

Coffin wrote: *I think both of us should question Richard Lavender once more.*

Phoebe continued: 'I don't pretend to understand his mind or what lies behind the story, but whatever it is this is important to him.'

Phoebe added: 'I have kept a more complete run of events in a work diary, as usual.'

Somehow, Coffin thought, he got his need across because I listened and you are working on it, Phoebe. He sat thinking, putting out a hand to stroke the cat who had appeared again, and finally walked over to the telephone.

It was late but he did not mind disturbing Phoebe's sleep if she was there; he had done it in the past but better not to dwell on the past.

Phoebe was not there, so he left a message on her answering machine, telling her to get a copy of her diary on to his desk early tomorrow. And yes, they would meet at the Egg and Bacon supper where they would be able to talk about Richard Lavender. More and more the strangeness of the whole business was unfolding before him. He had been hypnotized by the old man. No wonder he had become a Prime Minister, he was a spellbinder.

He sat thinking about Richard Lavender while continuing to stroke the cat. 'There's death, there, cat,' he said, looking into the bright-green eyes. 'I can smell it.' He had learnt in his years dealing with murder to recognize it: you didn't get it in your nose like ordinary smells but down your throat and on your chest, miasma ascending to your brain.

You could call it conviction, if you liked, but to him it had always been a stink.

The cat sped down from the table and disappeared. Then Coffin went to bed. As he cleaned his teeth, which always seemed a vital preparation either for sleep or insomnia, and he was practised in both, he allowed himself to wonder where Phoebe was spending the night.

Stella was asleep with her arms tucked neatly around her. Even in sleep she was neat and graceful. She had left a bedside lamp on so she wore a black silk mask to shield her from the light. This gave her an air of mystery.

She dispelled this instantly by remarking: 'I'm not asleep.' She did not remove the mask. 'Phoebe all right?'

'I reckon she is.'

Stella laughed. 'I reckon she always is. But tell me, I must ask again or I won't sleep, are you planning to arrest Martin?'

'God knows.'

'God may,' said Stella, 'but that won't help me with my new production, will it?' She rolled over on her side and composed herself for sleep. 'Oh well, if you won't help me I shall have to have a word with God. Please send me a handsome young actor, English-speaking, please. Oh yes, and thin, as the costumes are already made.'

Coffin touched her on the shoulder. 'Take that mask off and look at me. You don't believe Martin is guilty, do you? Or you wouldn't be joking about it.'

'I don't know if I was joking, my productions are a serious matter to me, but no, I don't think he is guilty, nor his sister. Not that it would stop your lot arresting him.'

'I can't just act on your faith,' said Coffin gently. 'I wish I could. But I will remember it, I call you a good judge of character.'

Stella allowed herself a laugh. 'I don't know about that, but I am a jolly good judge of a character actor.'

'Do you mean Martin is acting?'

'No, I don't. As a person he is what he seems to be. I mean Phoebe Astley: I judge she is acting a part all the time when she is with you and you ought to think about that.'

They lay in bed side by side, coldly separated by Phoebe Astley.

In the morning it was better. Over the coffee and hot toast which Coffin had learnt to produce, they talked. Not mentioning the murder of Jaimie or whether Richard Lavender's story about his father had somehow provoked this death, but tacitly admitting that both of them were disturbed and anxious.

'You've kept your nerve better than I have,' admitted Coffin.

'Did you have a nightmare?' asked Stella with sympathy. 'You were muttering in your sleep.'

'I don't need nightmares, I have them during the day.'

'I have to go to a meeting in London this morning,' said Stella. 'My agent, you know how it is. And then I will get my hair done. It needs it badly.' She reached out to put her hand on his. 'You know who Jaimie's killer is, don't you?'

'Think so. No proof, though.'

'But you will get it,' she said, studying his face.

'I think I let the killer guess . . . and that could be dangerous. You can never predict what an unstable person will do.'

'This killer is unstable?'

'My guess is yes.'

'How do you know?'

'By direct observation, but there is a powerful emotion at work.'

Stella looked at him. 'You couldn't name it?'

'Self-hate, I think,' said Coffin.

Stella drove away for her appointment, thinking that sometimes her husband frightened her. Not for herself, exactly, but for the human race in general: he was so alarmingly clear-eyed.

She parked her car near the Spinnergate underground station where her old friend Mimsie Marker was, fur-hatted for the winter, but ears alert for the gossip she collected and passed on. Invented it sometimes, perhaps.

Mimsie handed over *The Times* and a copy of *Vogue*, the American edition, Stella's chosen, and smiled at her.

'Lovely morning, dear, isn't it? Cold but bright.'

Stella nodded.

Mimsie was pleased with life. 'Off to town? Lovely, give Piccadilly Circus my love.' Mimsie acted as if she was stuck in Spinnergate but she was believed to be rich. 'What a blessing your husband has been since he came here.'

'Oh good.'

'Some smashing murders we've had since he came. Very good for trade. Selling papers like hot cakes.' Mimsie looked down at the racks, which were already nearly emptied, early as it still was. 'Dead Dolly Murder,' she read from one newspaper.

'But that's revolting,' said Stella.

''Course it is, people like being revolted.' Mimsie was forthright. 'At second hand, mind you, not face to face, but something to think about on the train, that's it.'

Dead Dolly, Stella thought, a circulation raiser.

Phoebe's diary itself was on Coffin's desk when he got there that morning. He was familiar with the physical appearance of the book, smallish, dark blue, heavy, because all his officers kept one.

'Couldn't manage a photocopy in the time. Have the original.'

He picked it up, it smelt faintly of Phoebe's scent. Also of cigarettes – so she was smoking again. After a cancer scare she had given up the weed but her nerve must be back again, or she had given up worrying.

He turned the pages, searching for the entries he wanted because Phoebe had been engaged in other enquiries at the same time as the skeleton in the old churchyard.

He observed gratefully that the arson and fraud case, for it was both, on which she had been occupied was on the point of going to the office of the Public Prosecutor and thus, he hoped, to the courts. He had taken a dislike to the mean-hearted entrepreneur who had embarked on the fraud. She had also, and here his feelings were mixed, got quite a way into the investigation into the possible corruption of a colleague of them both. Hell, he thought, it's coming positive.

One of life's nastier boils was about to be lanced, painfully too. He had never perhaps totally trusted the man but he had liked him.

No wonder Phoebe had looked so peaky sometimes, she too had liked the man. Still, dirt has to be washed away, and they were both of them ruthless when required.

One of the things he loved about Stella, possibly that which made her so valuable to him, was that she was not ruthless but had a kind of silent skill that made ruth unnecessary to her. She walked round dirt, it did not come near her; she saw it from afar and kept her distance. Not many people have that skill. He rather thought the quality was called integrity and if some of it rubbed off on him he would be the better for it.

All the while these thoughts were rumbling through his mind, he was reading what Phoebe had recorded about the murdered women of so long ago.

The strange thing was that it did not read like an historical novel.

The characters, the bodies of Mildred Bailey, Mary Jane Armour and Eliza Jones were alive and moving. They were not ghosts, although dead so long ago.

Mildred Bailey had been a seamstress to a London Court dressmaker, she was good with her needle but the wages were so poor and, when the Season was over, workers like Mildred were often laid off. It was a tough world, so that she had to make money how she could. She was twenty-six when she died.

She lived, Phoebe did not write of her in the past tense, with a widowed mother and an invalid sister, they too sewed for dear life. The house was in a Dike alley which no longer existed, having been knocked down for a new road through Spinnergate in 1922.

Mildred's body had been found just around the corner from where she lived. It was not investigated until the next morning. She had been seen but passers-by (and there was always someone around in those poor streets) had thought she was drunk.

This first death had not initially got the publicity that came to it when Mary Jane Armour's body was found; she too was strangled and left about like a bit of litter. In her case she was deposited between a horse trough and a drain.

Mary Jane was only seventeen, a poor little drab who had worked as a cleaner in a local hospital, long since gone, swallowed up by two wars and the National Health Service but good in its time and dedicated to sick seamen. She too earned extra money to pay for her lodgings in the only way open to her.

When her body was found, and that of Eliza Jones, the idea of a multiple killer, a new Ripper, sprang forth.

Perhaps Edgar Wallace played his part there; it was the sort of story he delighted in.

Isobel Haved was different from the other girls. She was older, thirty-two that summer, and she was an elementary schoolteacher for the London County Council.

Her body was never found but she was believed to be the fourth victim of the killer; she was very regular in her habits and her landlady could think of no other reason for her lodger's disappearance. 'She was a pearl of a girl,' Mrs O'Hanaran had said to the reporter. 'I am afraid he got her.'

One curious thing: the landlady left it three days before she reported her lodger missing. In fact, it is not clear if she ever did so, it being the teacher's headmistress who went to the police. She was anxious and afraid.

I am afraid he got her, to quote the landlady. Who was He? Phoebe's study of the newspapers revealed that several men came under suspicion.

Charles Heddon, ship's carpenter but unemployed at the time of the murders, came under suspicion first because he had been drinking in the public house, the Anchor, near to which the first body was found. He was known to be a violent man whose wife had left him; he had been seen talking to Mildred Bailey on the night of her death.

But he was able to prove he had spent the night in his sister's house. Nothing was found to indicate he was the killer.

Ralph Dream, a seaman without a ship, was another suspect, he had known both Mildred and Mary Jane, and so sharp was the public feeling by then that he was mobbed and had to be rescued by the police.

Nothing could be proved against him.

Phoebe went on: 'Various other names came up.' She gave a list.

Peter Picker – may have been Picquet, he was half French, a street musician.

Jerry Browning, butcher, he was employed by a local shop and went regularly to Smithfield.

Frederick Tramer – unemployed dock worker.

All these men were taken in for questioning and were let go. No proof. Phoebe's comment: poor police work?

It was at this point that Phoebe began to express her doubts about Richard Lavender's story.

'There is no mention of the Lavender name. All right, he never came under suspicion, but a mention would have been satisfying.

'Also, all of the victims lived well away from where the Lavenders lived.

'Well, OK, if you are a killer then it is wise to operate away from your own territory. I see that, but I wonder . . . ?'

Phoebe Astley had attached a note:

'I know we have the remains of a woman where Richard Lavender claims he and his mother buried her.

'There is also another body there. The forensic evidence is not very helpful, but the man may have been a soldier.

'All in all, I find Richard Lavender's story flawed.'

Coffin sat at his desk, considering what Phoebe had got; she was still digging away. To her note, he added his own:

You are right, it is interesting about the landlady. Go on searching to see what you can find.

Then he put the diary in a sealed envelope (Phoebe had sent it *en clair*, she was often casual about security) and had the diary sent back to her; they would meet that evening at the Egg and Bacon supper.

While Coffin was reading the diary and considering what Phoebe had turned up, Richard Lavender was lying in bed. He was half awake and half asleep. It was dark as yet on this cold November morning and since Janet had not come in with his morning tea he decided that it must still be early and went back to sleep again.

In the night he had stirred, thinking he heard movements in the flat as if someone was walking around. He had called to Janet, hadn't he?

Or he had tried to. It was probably all a dream, he dreamt

192

a lot one way and another. He had had a restless, wretched night, full of bad visions. His hands felt sticky and his body ached this morning as if it had had no rest. Old age, he decided, half joking, as he tried to relax, was hard work.

Better to ignore the nightmares, they soon faded with the morning and he forgot them until night came. He had had them all his life, even before that drama of which you did not speak, although no one knew of them except his mother. Well, she gave them to him, didn't she? He regarded them as her gift. He had never let his wife know, yet she might have guessed but been too tactful to mention it. She liked being the wife of a famous man and would not have wanted to spoil it in any way. A pity she had died young, he missed her now when it was too late. His second wife had been rich, of course, and bought the Rolls Royce which he still had but rarely used.

The dreams were always about death, natural enough, considering his family history, and he did not think the less of himself for having them, but he kept quiet about them. A political leader must be a strong man, even ruthless, and he had push enough for two, leading his party forward into reforms, some of which they had not been prepared for or welcomed. He had fought his way to the top from nothing, beginning as a kind of errand boy to a local MP, and was entitled, he always felt, to both his dreams and his nightmares. He had been PM for only one Parliament, but a great one, that all agreed. The next election had seen his party out, and the opposition in with a huge majority which was probably always the fate of a great Prime Minister, whereupon he had retired. Glad to, he had got where he wanted, leave at the top was a good idea, he was no longer young, he had a pension and his wife was rich. There were no children, a son had died as a baby. No close relations, either. He had been an only child as had his wife; Janet was the granddaughter of his mother's brother. Janet had come to them as a girl to help his wife as her secretary, and stayed – she was useful, if a bit of a bully.

He lay back on his pillows, tired after what had been a restless night. There had been those noises. Had it been he himself walking about? He had been known to sleepwalk, which was another thing he kept quiet about. Sometimes in his sleep he had the sensation as if his hands were pressing hard on warm flesh, and with those dreams there was blood as well. He knew he had these dreams, the thirteen-year-old Dick Lavender inside knew whence they came.

Before he died himself he wanted to get one secret out of the past and into the light. When it was there, in hard fact, then anyone who wished could write about it. This was what lay behind his request to John Coffin, the Chief Commander of the Second City Police, a man whom he had known at once he could trust in one way and not in another.

John Coffin would do what seemed right to him, he was not to be controlled by an old man, even if he had once held the keys of power. An old man who still had inside him that boy, Dick Lavender, aged thirteen, who had seen and done things that no one should do. That boy would not die but must come out into the light.

Dick Lavender tossed and turned in his bed. 'I would have brought it all out anyway, but once that girl came prowling around, I knew it was time.' A politician knew the value of timing.

She had been known to him as Marjorie Wardy but it seemed her real name was Jessamond Layard, a much prettier name and pretty young woman. He had wondered how she had got on to what had been so carefully hidden?

A mystery in itself now she was dead.

He opened his eyes to the dark November day again. He turned on the light and reached out for the silver vacuum flask of iced water. As he did so, he saw that there was blood on his hands. Blood on the sheet in front of him, too.

'Janet,' he called out. 'Damn it, Janet, where are you? I am bleeding.'

Perhaps this was death coming, God knows he felt bad enough.

Janet did not answer so he got up and put on his thick winter dressing gown and stumbled out round the flat, calling for her.

'Janet, Janet.'

She did not answer.

The place was cold and dark, with no sign of Janet anywhere. Her bedroom light was on, with clothes tossed to the floor as if she had got up in a hurry.

It was at this point he realized that he was not bleeding and never had been bleeding – the blood belonged to someone else.

Slowly and with difficulty, with shaking hands, he got himself dressed, putting on a thick tweed suit and shoes and socks. He forgot the shirt and had to go back and insert himself into that, he ignored a tie. He had forgotten underpants and vest too but he decided not to bother.

Then he crept out of the door and down the stairs. No one was around, it must be later in the morning than he realized. Or perhaps it was earlier, time had vanished for him.

He was not even sure why he was walking down the stairs or what he hoped to find. At the bottom, he sat to think about it.

He was looking for Janet. That was what he was doing.

He crawled out into the street where a soft dark rain was falling. Still there was no one to be seen. No one walking along the pavement, no cars passing. It was always a quiet corner but today it seemed dead.

There were several cars parked in the forecourt, including Janet's little white van. Bemused as he was, he thought that must mean she was here.

The van door was partly opened so he took a look, but there was nothing there. Except he saw a smear of blood. The garage where she put the van at night was close by. He pushed at the door which gave easily before him. The light was on.

Inside was Janet, she was lying on her side with blood on her.

The old man knelt beside her, wondering what to do. He crouched there, he did not know for how long. Time seemed to have stretched itself out into something long and thin.

He sat there until a young constable pushed his way into the garage.

'Now, now, Grandpa,' he said. 'What have you done now?'

15

The Egg and Bacon supper took place in the evening in the
senior officers' dining room. This room was long and narrow,
a bit like a short tunnel; in fact, its habitués called it the tube.
'Going down the tube,' they said. 'Or 'Up the tube'. It was
painted pale yellow with a serviceable dun-brown carpet.
One wall bore several pictures of the Second City painted by
a local artist in bright colours. No one ever looked at them.
By the door and with the light from the window full on it
there was a photograph of a man in spectacles and with a
big moustache. He was called Jack the Ripper by the senior
officers but he was, in fact, an early Chief Constable of the
Force before the formation of the Second City, and his portrait was there because it had survived the Blitz and was one
of the few portraits they had. Coffin always hoped that *his*
portrait would not figure there one day.

He came late to the supper, he had learnt from experience,
not to mention his own memories of such functions in his
junior days, that it was more tactful to let his men get a few
drinks inside them before he appeared. Then he knew to
leave early. He could smell that there was egg and bacon to
eat, but he knew from past suppers that there would be cold
beef and pork pies and apple tart with ice-cream. Hot mince
pies too, probably, as Christmas was approaching.

Looking round he could see George Darcy and Archie
Young. No sign of Phoebe, it was to be hoped she would
turn up, they were short of women in the senior ranks. He
saw that one Federation representative was there, talking to
a woman from the uniformed branch who had been given
an award for bravery; she had rescued a child and a dog from

a blazing car, the child had bitten her. That was police life, she had said, you always got bitten by the one you didn't expect.

Coffin was glad that the Fed rep was talking to her and that the pair seemed happy, but this occasion was really meant to be one when the senior officers mixed in a friendly, relaxed fashion with the other ranks. It was also an occasion for entertaining important visitors like the attaché from the German Embassy who was in charge of his country's secret service in the UK, and the writer who was working on police history, and a superintendent from the Danish police seconded to the Second City. Coffin let his gaze run over the guests, knowing he must do his duty and talk to each.

Stella had telephoned him just before he came to the party. 'Just back.' She sounded cheerful.

'Saw your agent?'

'Mmm.'

'Anything interesting coming up?' He knew her casual voice. It meant there was something good in the offing.

'I have been offered a series.'

'But that's good.'

'They want to see me. I don't audition,' she said loftily.

'Of course not.' He knew she wanted him to ask. 'What's the part?'

In a neutral voice, she said: 'Woman detective. As before. I'm a success in the part, it seems.'

'A private eye?'

'No, nothing like that . . . with a force in southern England. Downsville or some such. Very similar to my earlier part, but this time I am the most important character.'

'Almost a character part,' said Coffin.

'Don't laugh; I am thinking about it. See what the money offer is. But you know the risk with these things, if it's a success then you get labelled, and if it's a failure then that's a downer too . . . Of course, having my theatre, I can fight off being typecast . . . I can play Hedda Gabler or Medea next time round.'

'Of course you can.' He could tell she wanted to take the part, had probably already agreed to do so which meant she had an idea that the money was good. 'Who is writing it? Pinter, Plater?'

'No, no, of course not. No, it's a woman – Geraldine Diss. A new girl but good.'

'You do it then,' he advised, looking at his watch. He ought to be off to the E and B supper. His answerphone was flashing on the other line, and a page was coming through the fax, but he decided to ignore them both. There had to be an end sometime.

'Martin came to work today. I gather he did a good performance, he's a real professional.'

So he might well be, thought Coffin, at more than one craft.

'His sister was in too. I like her very much. I find it hard to believe she killed her father.'

'It happened.'

'They were so young. You know she told me that Martin really can't remember anything much about it. She has told him, of course, and so did a lot of other people. The psychologist man said he mustn't be allowed to repress it. Bad thing, distort his adult vision of life, give him nightmares. Probably break up his sex life.'

'Something did,' observed Coffin, thinking that his own life had probably been distorted early, and was he better or worse for it? 'He and Jaimie quarrelled violently and she is dead.' Better perhaps if they hadn't met.

'Clara thinks that Jaimie made a play for Martin so that she could get material for a book on him and Clara and the death of their father. It was going to be a kind of double book. Martin and Clara on one side and Richard Lavender and his mother on the other. She hated the idea, she had a great struggle to get into medical school, special dispensation really, she didn't want anything brought out again and I don't blame her.'

'How did Jaimie know about Dick Lavender? Supposed to be a deep secret.'

'We know she did find out ... it was why you were brought in.'

Coffin was thinking. 'We know she was working on this

book, but the typescript pages found in her office were sparse and not very revealing.'

'She probably had it on a tape . . . and that might be why there was this quarrel,' said Stella carefully. 'I mean, he might have taken it.'

'You mean you know he did?'

Stella kept her voice smooth. 'Just guessing.'

'And did he destroy it?'

'That I couldn't say, but I shouldn't think so, would you?'

Coffin was silent for a second. 'Thank you, Stella.' He paused. 'And if you should see Dr Clara you might suggest that she hand over the tape . . . Just guessing, of course.'

She was asking to be murdered, that girl Jaimie, he thought as he put the telephone down. Might be worth looking into her background. She came from a large, comfortably off family but abuse and misery could happen even in such a family.

George Darcy was looking at him from across the room; Coffin nodded at him. 'Come over.'

Coffin was used to standing alone at these functions, drinking the strong brew that was the favoured tipple, and waiting for someone to talk to him. Men drew back, no one wanted to seem to be currying favour, subservience was not the name of the game. Presently, if he waited, one of the more senior uniformed officers would take up his duties and walk over to talk. The CID men being by nature more free-ranging souls would probably ignore him altogether.

You didn't make friends by clawing your way up the promotion tree. He totted them up: Archie Young, he was a friend, George Darcy could become one. And Phoebe, goodness knows what she counted as, but she wasn't here yet, anyway.

She was arriving though. Even as George Darcy came towards him, Phoebe pushed through the door. She was laughing and talking to the woman who came with her, no one Coffin knew. She raised her hand to Coffin but turned aside to get a drink for herself and the visitor.

Darcy saw Phoebe too. 'Got a message for Astley; she sent

a piece of fabric to the Department of Fashion at the university to see what they could add to what forensics had to say, and when I went along to see what the verdict was on that jacket, the research assistant, Dr Mary Farr, passed the word along on that too. It's an interesting place down there; have you been, sir?'

'I went once when it was opened.'

'Had an open day, didn't they? Took my daughter, she fancied the course, but she chose dentistry in the end, don't ask me why.' Thoughtfully, he said: 'Of course, she was going out with a dentist student then, that may have been the reason.'

'Did she marry him?' This was a party, you couldn't just talk work. Some gesture to social behaviour had to be made.

'No, hasn't married anyone. We're old-fashioned now, sir, you don't marry.'

The courtesies having been observed, they got down to the business in hand.

'What did you get from Dr Farr?'

'On style, cut and technique she dated in the first two decades of the century . . . we had already been told that, but Dr Farr has been working on a group of journeymen tailors who lived in Spinnergate in that period – Edwardian and just later. They were Jewish workers, immigrants very often; she believes this is one of their jackets. It seems that they often put their names inside, and she has found, in the seam of the right sleeve, just by the cuff, a tape on which can be read the name J. Silver. He had a room in Spinnergate High Street, and he appears on local records until 1922. He died or moved away.'

'Confirms what we thought. The jacket is genuine and the name of the owner is genuine.'

'We shall have to talk to Richard Lavender, sir, and his housekeeper. One or other of them must know more than they are saying. Coincidences do happen, but . . .' And he shrugged. 'Not acceptable, sir.'

'Lavender is very old and frail,' said Coffin slowly, burdened as he was by the knowledge of Lavender's past history and all of Phoebe's present doubts on the old man.

'He's got some explaining to do. And he could be more mobile than he looks.'

'He had reason not to like the girl,' Coffin admitted. 'Did you find anything she had written on him in her office?'

'Not a lot, a few notes. I don't think she had got very far.'

'She might have had a lot on tape.'

'We ran through what there was,' said Darcy. He was not slow to pick up what the Chief Commander meant. 'You think there is another tape that we haven't got?'

'I think there is another tape which contains material on Martin Marlowe and his sister and also on Richard Lavender.'

'Two for the price of one,' said Darcy cheerfully.

Coffin, who yet liked Darcy, thought he was the sort of man who would have gone to a public hanging with good cheer.

'Where is this tape, sir?'

'I am hopeful,' began the Chief Commander when he saw Phoebe Astley with her companion was bearing down upon them.

'Sir, hi; George.' Phoebe was wearing a smart tweed suit of black-and-white check and was in a vibrant mood. She turned to her companion, a sturdy middle-aged lady in work-manlike slacks and a thick sweater. 'This is my friend, Rosemary Earlie, she is an expert on local history, and she has been helping me with my searches of the local newspaper.' Phoebe said: 'I believe I am getting some positive ideas, but they may not be ones we expected. I have a bit more work to do and then I will come to you with it. If I am right, it deepens the puzzle of old Lavender.'

'Deep enough already,' muttered Darcy into his beer. 'Can I get you drinks, you two.'

Phoebe gave Darcy a sharp look, but she said thank you, yes, beer for us both. Then she turned to Coffin.

'But Rosemary has been a real help.'

'Oh, thank you, Miss Earlie.'

'She is an archaeologist working with the Spinnergate Preservation Society.'

Coffin held out his hand which Miss Earlie took in a strong grip. 'Not much left to preserve, is there?'

'More than you might think.' Miss Earlie had a deep, firm voice.

'Roman and so on?' Coffin was wondering why Rosemary Earlie had been produced. He looked at Phoebe with enquiry.

'Roman, certainly, but I am more interested myself in later periods.'

Phoebe broke in: 'I'll tell him, Rosie, he's quite an intelligent chap really. John, a row of houses just around the corner from where Richard Lavender lived as a child were hit by a bomb from a zeppelin raid in that war . . . the ground was more or less cleared and a small warehouse was run up over the top. It has now been knocked down in its turn . . .'

'More or less cleared?' asked Coffin.

'He's quick, isn't he, Rosie? Yes, some interesting remains were left . . . there is what remains of the basement kitchen of one of those houses.'

'Seems very well preserved,' said the archaeologist. 'Just covered in and left to the dust. A bit like Pompeii in a way.'

'The family that lived there probably knew the Lavenders.'

Where does that get us? thought Coffin. I am not looking for historical artefacts.

Across the room, he could see George Darcy edging his way through the crowd of his colleagues, he was frowning and abstracted, ignoring any greeting thrown at him as he passed.

He came up to Coffin, and muttered in his ear. 'Can I have a word, sir? Outside, I think.'

Phoebe stepped back. 'Come and get a drink, Rosie.' But her face was watchful. She wanted to know what was going on and meant that she should, too.

'What is it?' asked Rosemary Earlie, who found police ways and manners of interest. She was observant of how people lived, whether alive or dead.

'Death and destruction,' said Phoebe lightly. 'Have to be, I should think.' But she meant it. 'George Darcy does tend to take things heavily.'

Outside the door, George Darcy got it out quickly: 'Just got a message: it looks like another murder.'

*　　　*　　　*

In a few short sentences, Darcy explained: Old Lavender, Janet Neptune ... found in a garage. At present in Spinnergate Hospital.

Yes, the Chief Commander ought to have been told before. Sooner, soonest.

'It's a bit of a cock-up, sir. You ought to have been told sooner ... but it seems the old man sat there by the body, not doing anything. And then the first thing to do was to get him to hospital. Her, too.'

'All that side is under control?' Coffin enquired. 'Who has talked to Lavender?' The two men were on their way to Lavender's apartment.

'Sergeant Bishop from Spinnergate West, he has the CID desk there at the moment, he comes under my control ... but there wasn't much point, the old man being virtually speechless – he was in shock. He will come round, they think.'

Coffin was silent. Then he said: 'I blame myself.'

Darcy found no comment to make on this since he did not understand it. 'There was blood on the old man,' he said.

'How much?'

'Not a lot, but enough. Not his blood, there is no wound on him.'

'And of course, he can't say where it came from.'

'Not at the moment, sir, no. He will be able to talk later, but whether he will make sense ...' Darcy shrugged.

'He's not senile.' Coffin was sharp. 'Or he wasn't a few days ago.'

'I think he's not clear what he's been doing. He has muttered a bit, apparently.'

'Saying what?' asked Coffin, still sharp, as the lift bore them up to the top floor where Lavender lived. A WPC let them in. She knew both of them by sight.

'Seemed to blame himself ... thinks he did it.'

'You seem to have heard quite a lot in your telephone call.' Coffin was still sharp, sharper, indeed.

'Bishop thought it was important for me ... and you, sir, to know as soon as possible.'

Coffin acknowledged this with a quick nod, and a request to see Lavender's bedroom. Still in a mood, Darcy accepted, and tried to be calming back.

'This way, sir.'

'SOCO's been in,' said the WPC, aware she was stepping in troubled waters and anxious to get a foot on solid ground.

Coffin accepted this without a word. 'Photographs?'

'Yes, sir. And the garage downstairs.'

Coffin parted the yellow tape that had been placed across the bedroom door. He could see the bed, with the blankets thrown back, the top sheet had fallen across them, displaying the blood.

A long streak of it.

'Not a lot of blood.'

Darcy nodded. 'So I was told. Some on his pyjama jacket and more on his hands, apparently. All dried.'

'And he has no wound?' Coffin was talking aloud, needing no answer. 'Get the bloodstained sheets down to forensics as soon as possible. And his pyjamas.'

He stood there looking at the room, then he turned on his heel to take a tour of the flat.

There was a certain amount of disorder everywhere, as the old man had blundered around in it in the dark. Or in his sleep. But the worst mess was in Janet Neptune's room where the blankets and sheet were twisted together in a heap on the floor. The looking glass on the dressing table was cracked, and a bowl of flowers overturned.

'She got out of bed, or was dragged out, and then there was a struggle,' said Darcy.

'Could be.' His tone was neutral, detached. Coffin was walking round the room, trying to assess it all. A muddle, but what sort of muddle?

'Looks that way to me.'

'Been photographed?' the Chief Commander asked the WPC.

'Yes, sir. There's a lot more to do, they are coming back to do an in-depth survey.'

She had the jargon, Coffin thought. 'What's your name?'

'Bailey, Avril Bailey, sir.'

Coffin smiled at her. 'Been here all the time? I thought so. Hang on a bit longer, I'll see you get relieved.'

'I don't mind, sir.' She was cheered, the water had been stormy but she had walked on the water, she had done the right thing. People said the Chief Commander was a nice man, and in spite of that first grim look, they were right: he was a nice man. 'I'm all right.'

Coffin turned to Darcy: 'The hospital now, George.'

Darcy too was relieved, he too had put his feet on the right spots, so it seemed. He was George now, first-name terms. But he would still watch his step.

'Seen all you want to, sir?'

'I've seen what I want, yes.' He was already running down the stairs. 'Have the stairs been looked over?'

Darcy had to admit he did not know, nor if the lift had been examined.

'Should have been.'

The sharp mood was back, and Darcy wisely kept silent; he had the uneasy feeling that he was not seeing what John Coffin had seen.

'Think there was a real struggle in that place?' the Chief Commander asked as he got into the car.

'You don't?' Darcy said.

'No, and no and no.' Coffin was silent and then said: 'When Dick Lavender was found beside Janet Neptune, he thought she was dead. He has since muttered about murder. That's right, isn't it?'

'It's what I was told.'

'But she isn't dead, is she? Wounded but not dead.' Coffin spoke to the driver. 'We can get on now. To the University Hospital.' This was the preferred name of the old hospital, now part of the new university.

'I suppose he thought he had killed her.'

'I'm sure he did. I'm sure he did think so.' Coffin waited for the car to start moving before getting hold of the car phone. 'Give me a minute, George . . . Stella?' Stella, for once where he wanted her to be, at home, answered his call. 'Stella, can you tell me where Martin Marlowe was last night?'

'He did his performance, you know that, I've told you.'

'And after that?'

'I don't keep an eye on my actors,' said Stella tartly. 'But as it happens I do know that he was at a birthday party with one of the cast which seemed to go on all night, judging by the hungover way most of them were behaving today. But Martin has since done a matinee and a full evening show.'

'Thank you, Stella. Keep an eye on him for me.'

Darcy let a moment elapse before he said: 'What's on your mind, sir?'

'Just clearing the ground.'

Clearing your ground and muddying mine, Darcy thought. I don't know what to make of it now. Nor of you, sir. This must be what chaps mean when they say you can see through a wall, but you build the wall yourself first.

The University Hospital was an old hospital with a new name; it had once been a poor-law hospital, taking in the indigent and sick, but various social reforms had put a new hat on it, provided more funds, a few new buildings, including an operating theatre and a paediatric department. It also had a flourishing clinic to deal with sexually transmitted diseases. 'Very much an expansion area,' the cynical, worldly pathologist Dennis Garden had said. As part of the new university with a medical school, the hospital had gone up in the world. It had status and a much enlarged staff. It had been much loved always in the neighbourhood where it was deemed almost a bit of luck to die in the old Pickle Road Hospital, as it once was, and it was a piece of luck that came the way of many in the old days. Rates of survival had definitely gone up.

Richard Lavender and Janet Neptune were both in private rooms on the same floor, the fourth, the top floor.

'The old man first,' said Coffin. The door was guarded by a uniformed constable sitting on a hard chair; he was talking to a nurse. He looked up, and recognized both men, standing up and saluting. Always be polite to top brass was written on his heart, his father having been a successful soldier.

'Nurse here says that Mr Lavender has woken up. I was

to tell Sergeant Bishop as soon as that happened, he needs to talk to him.'

The nurse protected her patient. 'I am not sure if he is up to much questioning at the moment. You will have to clear it with the doctor.'

'Wouldn't dream of doing anything else,' said Coffin, opening the door to Richard Lavender's room. At once, a voice, surprisingly stronger than might have been expected, called him to come in.

'How are you feeling?'

'Better. But I am glad to see you. Thank you for coming, I knew I could trust you. You know what has happened?'

'I know there has been an accident.'

'Kind of you to call it that, but I hope I am able to face facts.' There was desolate sadness in Dick Lavender's voice. 'I killed her. There was blood on me. I dragged her from her bed and killed her.'

'Supposing I told you Janet was not dead.'

'I would thank God that I did not kill her.'

The nurse was fussing at the door. 'Doctor is on his way,' she called.

Dick Lavender went on talking, almost to himself but his eyes on John Coffin. 'I heard noises in the night, banging, shouts . . . I thought it was a nightmare. Then when I woke and saw the blood on me, I knew it was real. But it was not my blood. I had got up, attacked Janet.' He paused, as if puzzled. 'She wasn't in the flat, though . . .' He passed his hand over his face. 'I couldn't find her.'

'You did find her, though.'

'She was bloody, the blood was hers. Her wound, her blood on me. I had no wound, I did not bleed.'

'You are bleeding now,' said Coffin. 'Bleeding inside you.' He came close to the bed, and put his hand on Dick Lavender's thin cold fingers, which moved to grip his tightly.

'You tell me I did not kill her?'

'You did not kill her,' said Coffin. He took his hand away and moved from the bed as a severe young doctor appeared at the door.

On the corridor outside, Darcy said: 'I noticed that you said he did not kill her, not that he did not try.'

In a sober voice, Coffin said: 'For what happened to her, I blame myself. Stupid, stupid girl.' He marched off down the corridor, leaving a perturbed George Darcy to follow him.

I think I could write a book about this man, George Darcy said to himself, as he followed. What should I put in it: sharp mind, pleasant manners except when crossed, can control himself but doesn't always. Oblique way of talking, asks questions but probably knows the answers himself before you do. Sees further into the mist than you but sometimes leaves you staring into it without help.

As now, he added, as he marched after Coffin's retreating figure – he seemed to know where he was going.

Do I like him? Yes, I do.

Along the corridor, Janet Neptune's door was marked by a WPC who was sitting with her legs stretched out in front of her and looking bored. She yawned, and then yawned again. There was an empty cup and saucer on a tray on the floor. As soon as she recognized the two men she leapt to her feet, giving the tray a kick so that it went noisily rattling down the corridor.

The door of Janet's room opened at once, an angry face with a shock of red hair with a white cap on it demanded silence.

Coffin braved the storm. He identified himself and asked to see Miss Neptune.

'I know who you are,' said the red-headed nurse irritably. 'You gave me a medal about two years ago when you handed out awards at the Nursing College. Sister Bardy, not that you'd remember that.'

'Yes, I do.' Coffin had been studying her face. 'You got the medal because you went into a collapsing house, an airplane had landed near it, and you went in to give painkilling injections to a boy of ten while he waited to be cut free. You deserved that medal and more.'

'You've silenced me,' said Sister Bardy, showing no signs

of actually being mute. 'Smooth talk, smooth talk, I noticed it then.'

'Thank you.'

'No thanks needed. A mere courtesy.' Both parties were enjoying the sparring. 'I suppose you have come to see my patient. I'm not sure if I ought to let you in.' She managed to notice George Darcy, to whom she gave a wide smile which he returned sheepishly.

'But you will?'

'I will have to ring through to the doctor.'

'How is she?'

'Not too bad, not bad at all. The blow to the head was nothing, probably did it herself falling against the wall, but the body wound although not deep made her lose blood . . . If she had been discovered earlier it would have been nothing much.'

'I think she was meant to be found earlier,' said Coffin.

'Oh well, if you think so, you'd know.'

'Is she conscious?'

'Oh my, yes. Talking and complaining.'

While she was talking, Sister Bardy had quietly opened the door behind her. 'Five minutes and no more.'

Janet Neptune was propped on several pillows, a stretch of plaster ran across her left temple, her hair was cut back at that point, the left eye was bruised, and the cheek below it. She was wearing a white hospital shift with the hint of bandages around her waist.

She stared at the two men with no friendly expression. 'Now you see what has been done to me. I was attacked.'

She looked at John Coffin and he answered her: 'Can you remember what happened?'

'I have already told what I could to that sergeant.'

'I am afraid you may have to go through it all several times. Can you remember?'

'More or less.' She put her hand to her head. 'You don't remember all the details when you've been hit on the head . . .' She frowned with the effort of remembering. 'It started when I heard noises . . . like someone banging around the flat . . . I went out into the hall, it was all dark, and there was a sound like an animal growling.'

She stopped.

'Don't go on if it hurts you.'

'I think I ran to the door to get out because I was frightened; I didn't want to be inside with whatever there was. Then something hit me on the head . . . I don't remember much else, except a sharp pain just below my ribs . . . that was when the knife went in. I must have become unconscious soon after.'

'You were found in the garage.'

'I must have got down the stairs, I suppose . . . or perhaps I was dragged. I may have fallen. I don't know about the garage, I must have been dragged or carried in.'

'The state of your clothes will give us some help,' said Coffin.

She looked around vaguely. 'I don't know where they are. I don't remember what I had on.'

'We will find out,' said Coffin soothingly.

'I might have told them to throw them away.'

'I don't think they will have done; they know the rules in cases of violent attack.'

'I ought to have been found sooner, I was there for hours,' said Janet angrily. 'I almost died. I was meant to die. He did it, you know, the old man. He's mad.'

Coffin was silent. Then: 'I did warn you.'

Janet did not answer; instead she closed her eyes.

Sister Bardy put her head round the door. 'Five minutes are up and the doctor is coming here fast.'

From under closed lids, Janet said: 'Take your running mate with you.'

Coffin took the silent Darcy by the arm. 'We'll go.' At the door, he paused, and turned back. 'Janet, what became of the pink chiffon?'

Still with eyes shut, she said: 'I am going to have it dyed black.'

As they walked to the car, Darcy asked what was it about the pink chiffon.

'I just wanted to put the question,' said Coffin. 'See what she said.'

In the car, George Darcy said: 'Was it attempted murder?'

'In a way, yes, I think so, don't you?'

'I don't know what to think.'

'I think the forensics on the clothes and blood will be helpful.'

'Yes, sure. And was her attacker also the killer of Jaimie Layard?'

'Oh yes,' said Coffin. 'Can't you see that?'

No. I can't, you enigmatic bastard, thought Darcy. It seemed a long time since that Egg and Bacon supper at which, now he came to think about it, he had had nothing to eat and very little to drink.

16

Once they were in the car, Coffin fell silent, but the chief inspector meant to have it out.

'I don't know if I have got this right or not,' said George Darcy, now filled with an irrational anger, and feeling there were secrets here that he was not being told. 'But Janet Neptune is accusing the old man of attacking her with a view to killing her.'

Coffin nodded. 'That's right, she was certainly doing that.' Among other things.

'And Richard Lavender, OM, former Prime Minister, is accusing himself.'

'He is indeed.'

'What a bloody mess. I suppose' – he couldn't stop his fury showing in his voice – 'I suppose it has some connection with the business that is keeping Phoebe Astley so busy?'

'It is connected, but not as directly as all that, Darcy.'

'I knew the woman Jaimie was working on the background of Richard Lavender's life, I knew that Phoebe was digging up something to do with his past. We do communicate. Word gets around and Phoebe isn't the closest with the latest.'

'No.'

'But the dead woman was also investigating the story of Martin Marlowe's murder of his father. It seemed to me, and I thought you took the same view, sir, that she had got to know him because of this, he had found out, they had quarrelled, he had beaten her up and later killed her. That story fitted the facts until that jacket on the dead girl, part of her transvestite I-am-a-guy get-up was discovered to have belonged to Richard Lavender's father.'

Coffin said apologetically that he had operated on a need-to-know basis with old Lavender; the old man was a former Prime Minister after all, he still had heavy guns behind if he chose to use them, and he had requested silence. 'Silence, of course, was never going to last. I suspect he knew it.'

'The tom-toms do work, sir.' They were nearing the Central Police Station, the night air was heavy with rain with the hint of mist as well. The Egg and Bacon supper must be long over. What Darcy wanted now was to get home to his wife, and have a meal and a drink, but first he might shoot the Chief Commander dead in the head.

Verbally, of course.

'We knew a lot, sir. Word passed round the canteens and the senior officers' room, but there was a hole in the middle: what we didn't know. That old Lavender might by now be a dangerous senile murderer. I suspect you did know, sir.'

There, he'd had a shot at the Chief Commander's head, and lived to tell the tale.

'Not as straightforward as that, George, but yes, I do wonder about Lavender's state of mind. He is guilty, he wants to show his guilt, and I think that is why I was called in.'

Darcy ground his teeth. Still talking in riddles, he thought.

The car was drawing into the front of the main block where Coffin had his office. It was late enough for the building to have quietened down.

'Come into my office, everyone will have gone, and have a drink and I will talk.'

Paul Masters was leaving as they walked in. He raised an eyebrow at the Chief Commander. 'I am just off, sir.'

'Right. The Egg and Bacon go well?'

'Chaps seemed to enjoy it, sir. You missed the main celebrity, Lennie Chickenfeed.' Lennie was a comedian who lived locally and did a lot for charity.

'Sorry about that, but I was called away.'

'He understood. I think you may find yourself figuring in his next joke, though, sir. I could see him working on it.'

'It's what I have to suffer,' said Coffin with good humour.

Paul Masters greeted the chief inspector and said goodbye in the same sentence before collecting his briefcase and going out of the door.

'Good man,' said Coffin absently. 'He's clever without being too clever, he'll go right to the top.' Whatever would count as the top then. 'Whisky?' He was already pouring out two good doses.

'Thank you.' Darcy was uneasily aware that his stomach needed a lining of food before it got whisky poured on it.

'I was recruited,' began Coffin, 'yes, I use that word. I was recruited by the old man who has lost none of his wiles, a politician through and through, and I did not know what I was really being recruited for. I am beginning to realize now.'

Darcy could feel the heat of the whisky hitting his brain. Certainly he felt more cheerful.

'Old Lavender sent Jack Bradshaw, who was writing his official life, round to see me. He had a secret to tell me: his father had been a serial killer of women in the years before the Great War.'

Darcy nodded. 'A word of that has been going the rounds. Seems fantastic.'

'He said that he, then a young boy, and his mother buried the last victim. They buried her in the nearest they could get to holy ground: the rough land at the edge of the old churchyard of St Luke's. In other words, opposite where I live. I suppose that may be why I got the job. He wanted me to find her body, and, I suppose, see she got a proper burial. I don't know if he thought I could pop out to do it myself, perhaps he did.'

'You gave the job to Phoebe Astley.'

'I did, because there was more to it than just finding a body. He had his burden of guilt to clear, he wanted to find out who his father had killed. He wanted it brought out, Bradshaw could write about it under his control, but he did not want it to be written up by the young journalist who called herself Marjorie Wardy, who had been interviewing him. She seemed to have learnt about this deadly saga.'

'How did she do that?'

'I can guess who told her, and that knowledge was the

death of her . . .' Coffin drank some whisky and poured some more. 'Stella doesn't like me to drink this stuff . . . so I don't, much, but I keep a bottle because there are times when it is the only drink –' He stopped saying: the only way out.

'There was, as they say, a subtext. Lavender did not tell me that he had this nightmare that he could be a killer.'

'You can't inherit murder,' said Darcy, on whom the whisky was working.

'I suppose you can inherit the genes, the character. He was a ruthless politician, so they say, but I never heard that he killed anyone. So we come to today: when Janet Neptune accuses him of the attack on her, and the murder of Jaimie Layard, and when he accuses himself of attacking Janet Neptune.'

Coffin drained his glass, recognizing as he did so that it was probably time to get home to Stella.

Darcy frowned and put his glass down. 'She thinks she was attacked by the murderer of Layard.'

'I think she was,' said Coffin.

'And she accused old Lavender.'

'She did.'

'So what is your advice, sir,' asked Darcy, aware that he was in charge of the investigation into Jaimie's death. 'Does that mean Bradshaw and Marlowe are out of it? It seems to me there is still reason to suspect both of them and that this episode doesn't change that.'

Coffin stood up. 'My advice is to keep a watch on both Richard Lavender and Janet Neptune, even in hospital. And trust that a thorough forensic survey will give you some help.' He tidied away the whisky bottle and put the glasses on the table by the door. 'You can keep an eye on Bradshaw and Marlowe as well, if you like. Let's get off home, both of us.'

Darcy followed Coffin out of the building, noticing that the Chief Commander turned off the lights in his office as he left and locked all the doors.

'You know who the murderer of Layard and the Neptune woman's attacker is, don't you, sir?'

Coffin said nothing until he had reached his car. 'Want a lift home?'

'No, thank you, sir, got my own car here.' Thank goodness he had not drunk any more whisky.

'And the answer to your question is, Yes, I do think I know, and I believe you do by now. It's your case, your team that will have to do the dog work to prove the killer guilty. It may be one of those cases where guilt can never be proved, but my advice is to remember the old nursery advice from mother: to trust the doctor.'

Darcy gave him a long hard look. 'I see what you mean.'

'I thought you would. Push them, and let me know what you get. Meanwhile, I have a feeling that Phoebe Astley is about to go in for surgery on her own account.'

When he got home, Stella was awake, in the kitchen drinking tea in company with the cat and dog, both occupied with their own food bowls.

Stella poured herself some more tea. 'You look the tiniest bit drunk,' she said to her husband.

'Only with worry and misery,' he answered.

'You can take Augustus out for his late-night walk, that should settle you.'

'Can I have some tea first?'

Stella poured him a cup of the good rich Indian brew they both preferred. 'The worry I allow you, but what's the misery about?'

'I think I may have to let a killer walk free.'

Stella stood up. 'I will make you a sandwich, I reckon you are hungry as well as miserable. Have you eaten?'

'Come to think of it, no.'

'A sandwich and a cup of tea and a walk with Augustus will sober you down; you have a small dose of the whisky blues.'

The sandwich arrived on a plate with a blue napkin; he realized he was hungry. 'What's in this?' he asked with bite two.

'Smoked salmon and cream cheese.'

He ate it quickly, drank two cups of tea, then looked at

Augustus. 'I suppose he does want to go out? It's a dirty night.'

For answer, Stella attached the lead to the dog's collar. 'Drag him.'

Coffin walked round the tower in which he lived, leaving behind him the three theatres: the Stella Pinero and the much smaller Experimental Theatre, opposite to the Theatre Workshop. He had to hand it to Stella, who had put every inch of the old St Luke's Church to use and to profit.

The rain had stopped, the mist was clearing, not such a bad night after all. Augustus plunged forward eagerly, night smells were rich and good.

They walked the narrow stretch which bordered the pavement; across the road was the old churchyard. No one was on duty protecting it, but the site where the skeleton had been found had been wired off.

He could see that someone else was there, moving among the trees of the old churchyard. 'Come on, Augustus, let's take a look.'

A tall, dark raincoated figure swung round as he came up. Augustus leapt forward with a fusillade of cheerful barks.

'Phoebe, what are you doing here?'

'Mooching round, thinking.' He could see her troubled face in the light from a streetlamp. 'I didn't stay long at the E and B supper after you left . . . I know why, the word got around, and of course I was interested. Not my case, but it touches what I am doing, what I have done. So I went back to work. I told you I had got on to something . . . one of the local newspapers of December 1914, spoke of a man being arrested for the murders. I wanted to see if I could find anything more.'

Coffin let Augustus off his lead. 'Yes?'

Phoebe took a deep breath. 'In December 1914, a man called Henry Phillips was arrested for three murders: those of Armour, Bailey and Jones. He denied knowing anything about Haved but confessed to the others. He was brought before the magistrates and committed for trial at the Old Bailey. They were quick about things then – he was tried and found guilty soon afterwards, and hanged. He was not Richard Lavender's father.'

She looked at Coffin, her face full of fury. 'Where does that leave us? Did he believe it ever? Was he lying all the time? What is he?' Her voice was full of feeling. 'I liked what I was doing. I believed in it . . . but now . . . What is he, some kind of monster?'

'I think he may be,' said Coffin sadly.

Chief Inspector Darcy was on the telephone early next day. 'Medical report,' he said briskly. 'Dick Lavender is coming round nicely. The doctors say he has good muscle tone . . . that means he can get around and do pretty well what he likes, not frail at all for his age. He probably had a sedative dose on the night of the attack, made him dopey.'

'You had better find out where that came from.'

'We will,' said Darcy with conviction. 'He had some painkiller for arthritis in his knee . . . could have been that. Janet Neptune is recovering well, the blood loss well made up. The wound itself not dangerous, she was unlucky in not being found earlier . . . Should have been, we had police check up on the area as you know, but there was a fight in the High Street . . . delayed the constable. Shouldn't have.' Darcy added tersely: 'I've dealt with that.'

'Right,' said Coffin thoughtfully. 'Not quite enough evidence for you to move.'

'No, I am waiting for the forensics. Told them to get a move on.'

'See the two are kept apart.'

'They have both had a visit from Dr Bradshaw . . . that is, he tried but he was told no visitors. He says he will come back.' Before he could say anything else, there was an interruption, and he came back to Coffin: 'Sorry about that, a message on the other phone: it's too late, they've already met. They met in the corridor, the old man was in a wheelchair, he was going to have a bath . . . he leapt out and attacked her. I'm going to the hospital.'

'See you there,' said Coffin.

As he drove himself to the hospital, he thought: How

power corrupts . . . even after all these years, the old man still feels it.

George Darcy met him. 'Strong as a horse,' he said gloomily. 'They say he could have killed her if they hadn't stopped him.' He shook his head. 'Don't know why he didn't.'

'I know why,' said Coffin, 'and so do you. Wasn't what he was after.'

'The doctor said he might have a heart attack or a stroke . . . they've put him out, given him something. We can't talk to him.'

'And Janet?' Coffin was marching down the corridor towards the lift.

'Oh, we can see her.'

Janet Neptune was sitting in an armchair by the window. Her face was still swollen, but her eyes were bright and fierce. 'Well, well, now are you going to arrest him . . . ? You know who the murderer is.' She was looking at Coffin.

'Yes, I know who the murderer is.'

'I should think you do. Well, are you going to arrest him?'

Coffin drew up a chair to face her. Darcy stood by the door. 'No, I am not going to arrest him. And you know why.'

Janet moved her head to stare at Darcy. 'What's he doing here?'

'It is Chief Inspector Darcy's investigation, he is in charge, he has some important medical evidence.'

Janet snorted. 'Doctors!'

'I am not going to arrest Richard Lavender for the murder of Jessamond Layard –'

'Jaimie,' interrupted Janet. 'Don't be pompous, we called her Jaimie. Or Marjorie.'

'I am not going to arrest Richard Lavender because he did not kill her. You did.'

The colour went out of Janet's face, leaving the bruises on cheek and eye socket, livid and stark. She said nothing.

'I always suspected you . . .'

He saw her swallow.

'You were holding back, I could sense the emotion. You were the one who knew where that old jacket was and used

219

it to incriminate Lavender. You killed her and dressed her up as a guy because you hated her ... Your van is being gone over now, Janet, and I am sure we will find fragments of clothing there, scraps of this and that to prove the body travelled to the car park in that van. I think you killed her in the garage here. They are looking there this very minute.'

'I really ought to laugh,' said Janet. 'I hardly knew her.'

'You knew her; I saw Jaimie's telephone number on the wall of your bedroom. After I saw that number, I warned you to be careful, but you don't take warnings, do you? So what you did was to try and break in to Jaimie's workplace because you knew she had a disc with all the private notes on it, you knew you would figure on that. And when you couldn't get in, you fabricated an attack on yourself, incriminating the old man.'

'I was attacked.'

'No, the doctors say that your wounds could have been, and probably were, self-inflicted. You gave the old man a sleeping tablet to keep him quiet and then performed on yourself.'

'I nearly died.' She was shaking, her whole body vibrating so the table by her shook too.

'Only because the policeman who should have checked the area was late.'

George Darcy tried to interrupt. 'Enough questions, sir?'

Coffin shook his head. 'Why did you do it, Janet? I think it was jealousy ... You were in love with Jack Bradshaw. What about the pink chiffon, Janet?'

Darcy tried again. 'You are going at this very hard, sir.'

'I want it out,' said Coffin. 'Come on, Janet, that was the motive, what lay behind this brutal killing. You loved Jack Bradshaw and he dropped you for her.'

He had found the key. Janet began to cry. 'No, not him, I didn't care for him. It was Jaimie – you wouldn't understand how I felt but I loved her. Every way you can love, I loved her.'

Coffin sat back in his chair. 'Did you? Is that how she got the information about the old man's past? You were family, families always know more than they pretend. You knew the murder story.'

'Old pig, I never liked him, he treated me like his slave . . . But I was working on him, I sent him letters and horrible flowers . . . I was going to punish him.'

She's not quite sane, Coffin thought. 'Why did you kill Jaimie?'

'I thought she loved me,' said Janet in a harsh whisper. 'You might as well know now. I was planning, I won't tell you what I was planning . . . I showed her the pink chiffon . . . "For us," I said, "you'll like me in this. Or you can wear it and I will kill you in it."'

Darcy made an inarticulate noise, but Coffin was quiet.

'And then she laughed at me.' A note of vicious anger came into Janet's voice. 'She laughed at me. "Pink chiffon," she said, "do you think I am going to make love in pink chiffon?" Then she laughed, and she said to me that if I knew anything at all about making love I would know that pink chiffon just got in the way and that bare skin was what you wanted. "You old virgin," she said, "pink chiffon, bare legs in a bed is best."'

'That wasn't a nice thing to say.'

'I hated her then but I didn't show it. I waited, I waited, I gave myself one treat. I got into her work flat and broke things up, made a mess. She blamed Martin. So when I had killed her, I dropped him in a bundle of her bloodstained hair as a treat. She was pregnant, you know, I could tell it in her face. There's a look in the eyes.'

'Is that so?'

'Yes.' A nod. 'And then she needed one more bit of help; she knew about the jacket I had found in a trunk, she wanted to see it. "Come and have a look," I said. She said: "I'll see I have a quarrel with my young man and come down to you." He was just a toy, you see, it would have been a real relationship with me. It was night, a dark November night, no one saw her. "Meet me downstairs," I said, "that's where the trunk is." When she came, I was all ready, and I killed her.' The tears were flowing. 'Killing isn't easy, you know, don't think it is; I tried once before . . . came up behind her

221

when she was walking one night ... got my hands on her ... but I couldn't do it then, she didn't know it was me, blamed him. And when I did do it, kill her, I mean, well, I suffered. I walked the streets in the dark ever so often afterwards, looking at the car park ... going to where your lot were digging up other bodies ... It was all death, all around me.'

'And dressing her up?' asked Coffin. 'And the car park? Why the car park?'

'Well, it was near Guy Fawkes night, wasn't it,' said Janet simply, her tears drying. 'And I couldn't just leave her around.'

'You were hard then, sir,' said George Darcy as they left later. Janet was in her room in the charge of the medical staff with a uniformed constable inside the room and another outside.

'I felt hard. I was angry at the name handed out to the murdered woman: My dead dolly, and I suppose a little of it rubbed off on her killer.'

'Dead dolly? You heard about that?'

'Of course I did. Someone always tells me that sort of thing.'

'What about Richard Lavender, sir?'

'There is still something to come out there. He has his own explaining to do.'

Coffin knew that Stella was attending a performance in the Workshop Theatre that night, so after tidying his desk, and receiving a message from Phoebe Astley that tomorrow was 'archaeological dig day', he tucked himself in the seat beside Stella.

She looked up at him. 'Here you are,' she said with a smile.

'What's the play?'

For answer she pushed a programme at him. 'You won't know the name, or the author, but I think it is good.'

Coffin said: 'Is Martin Marlowe in it?'

'No, he's not in this. Do you want him?' She was alarmed.

'It's all right, don't worry, Martin is clear; we have a confession from the killer of Jaimie Layard ... But I have a question to ask him.'

'You can do it in the interval, he's over there.' She nodded her head. 'A row back.'

Coffin tried to watch the play, which was a translation from a Czech original, a comedy, but he found he could not laugh, his mind kept seeing Janet's face.

In the interval, he went to the bar with Stella where he got her a drink, then walked across to where Martin stood with his sister Clara. He looked alarmed when he saw the Chief Commander.

'It's all right,' said Coffin, 'I'm not coming for you; you are in the clear. We have Jaimie's killer, and a confession.'

Martin said in a nervous voice: 'Anyone I know?'

Coffin nodded.

'Jack Bradshaw? No? Then it's Janet Neptune.'

'Why do you say that?'

'I'm right? She's the only other one who had a real relationship with Jaimie ... I always knew, it was part of our quarrel.'

'I wish you had told me before,' said Coffin with feeling. 'But I have a question to put to you: do you have a disc from Jaimie's PC with her notes on it? Perhaps even a synopsis.'

Martin shook his head but he looked towards his sister.

'So Clara has it?'

'Yes, she went to collect it the night I quarrelled with Jaimie ... one of our quarrels, the big one ... Jaimie had stuff in it about me and Clara. She had a key, I think she had it cut herself . . . she got there before Jaimie could remove it.'

'But Jaimie was already dead,' said Coffin. You haven't grieved for her so very long, he thought with some sadness for the girl. But then you were only her toy. Did you know that? 'You and your sister bring the disc to me tomorrow. In my office.'

Afterwards, he said to himself: That's where I went that day in November, back into 1917. I walked into it. 1917, because that was the date the German bomb fell on the row of houses, destroying the top two floors but leaving the basement kitchen of one house untouched.

I was glad to take that walk in the past.

A dusty walk it was too. The basement had been covered over by a warehouse that was hurriedly put over the top in a shoddy, get-on-with-it-quick kind of way. Wartime conditions, it is to be supposed. The warehouse itself survived another war and more bombs before being knocked down to make a row of houses. History going in a circle.

'It often does that,' Coffin said to Phoebe as they parked his car a short distance from Flemish Dock towards Flanders Street where the warehouse was already down. 'I have noticed that myself in my lifetime . . . Sometimes you feel you are back where you started.'

'For once the past has come up with some answers for the present,' said Phoebe. 'What I have found is very, very helpful.' Then she said: 'I am glad you got a confession from Janet Neptune.'

'We need the forensic evidence from her clothes, the van and the knife . . . she used the same knife to stab herself as she attacked Jaimie Layard with, but yes, I think it will stand up in court. I don't think she will argue.'

'She nearly got old Lavender,' said Phoebe. 'What a family. Talking of history, we don't know all the history there, but we are about to learn some.'

The developers of the area whose board announced a row of executive houses with access to the docks with berths for yachts had agreed to suspend operations while the Archaeology Department from the university did a quick survey.

Rosemary Earlie was waiting for them. 'It's dusty down there,' she said apologetically. She was wearing a thick smock-like garment over jeans and a sweater with her hair covered in a scarf.

'I can bear it,' said Coffin. 'How do we get down?'

'Climb.' She indicated a ladder down a hole. An electric line ran down it with a lamp at the end. 'Phoebe has already been down.' She grinned at the Chief Inspector. 'Never thought I'd be taking a copper down here, not to mention the top brass.'

Coffin descended first, feeling his way carefully. He stood at the bottom on what had been the old kitchen floor of the house; it was paved with stone squares. The walls had once been whitewashed and were now dark brown with dirt.

'They've had rats,' he said, looking at the droppings on the floor.

'Oh yes,' said Rosemary cheerfully. 'Generations of them. Probably been here longer than anyone else. You expected it in those days near the docks . . . ships, you see. The rats came ashore with the crew.'

Phoebe stood beside Coffin. 'Look around.'

A big wooden dresser lined one wall, the doors had fallen off so that the tins and bits of china could be seen. The bomb had done some damage, but had not destroyed everything breakable. Coffin could see a large china mug with PRESENT FROM MARGATE written across it. He picked it up and as he did so, the handle fell away. Rosemary caught both bits skilfully as he dropped them. 'Artefacts,' she said. 'Got to preserve it.'

'Sorry.'

'It's all been photographed and now I am doing maps and naming and numbering everything. We would like to keep it as it is and it may be possible. We are negotiating with the developers; they have been very helpful so far.'

In one corner was a stone sink with one brass tap above. 'Probably the only water in the house,' said Rosemary.

A wooden kitchen table filled the middle of the room. It looked as if the rats had been living on it and off it since the bomb dropped.

'No windows,' said Coffin.

Rosemary shook her head. 'No, a true basement, very common it was when this house was built, in about 1820. Tapers and candles at first, oil lamps and then gas.' She nodded towards the sink. 'A fishtail gas jet.' There was even a box of British Bulldog matches on a shelf next to it.

A dusty black oven with an open fire beside it lined the third wall. A kettle still stood on the top of the oven.

'Probably going to make a cup of tea when the bomb dropped,' said Phoebe.

'Were the people of the house killed?' asked Coffin.

Rosemary shrugged. She didn't know, perhaps did not care very much. It was artefacts that she treasured. 'Leave you to it,' she said. 'Come up when you are ready.'

Coffin stood in the middle of the room and felt the past sweep over him. There had been poverty here, but also he had a sense of happiness and love. A decent working-class family house this had been and he did not want to take away from its dignity.

Phoebe pulled open a drawer in the kitchen table. Inside he could see a dusty litter of papers.

'Letters,' said Phoebe. 'This is what we came for. Postcard first.'

The card was postmarked Blackpool, June 1917. It was addressed to Mrs Pershore, 5 Flanders Street, Spinnergate.

Having a happy holiday and riding on the donkeys. That is not me on the Big Dipper. Alice.

There was a picture of the beach at Blackpool with a view of the Big Wheel in the Pleasure Gardens behind.

Coffin read it, and placed it carefully on the table.

'Alice wrote again; I guess she went on holiday with a soldier.'

She held out another card, a plain postcard, dated August 1917; it had been posted in Woolwich, S.E. London.

I need help, Edie, you know what I mean. What's the address you know for that woman? Please write.

Coffin read it and raised an eyebrow. 'Does she mean what I think she means?'

'I am sure she did.' Phoebe handed over a page of a letter, neat pencilled handwriting covered it.

You are in a pickle, Alice, fancy getting yourself in trouble with Ted in the trenches. I don't know about that address, Mrs L. hasn't been seen around lately. I don't think she liked the zeps. If I can find out where she went, then I will let you know ... but Alice, she did have accidents. I know one woman was left very poorly, and Mrs O'Hanaran said that she never saw her nice lodger again after she went to Mrs L. with her trouble. She thinks Miss H. is dead . . .

There was no more to the letter. The bomb had fallen before it could be finished and posted.

'I reckon Alice was lucky not to end up with Mrs L.,' said Phoebe, taking the page away. 'Or she might have got buried next to Miss H. in St Luke's churchyard.'

'We mustn't jump to conclusions too readily,' said Coffin.

'Oh, come on.'

Coffin picked up the letter again. 'I wish we could talk to Edie.'

'Sounds all right, doesn't she? A nice, kind woman. But she knew what she was talking about and she has told us.'

'So Mrs Lavender was an abortionist. And she had her casualties.'

'They all did then,' said Phoebe. 'Tough times. Knitting needle or wash out with Lysol. You were lucky to come through that still walking and talking. And those that did probably still had the baby as well, not all abortions worked but a lot of damaged babies popped out into the world.'

Coffin felt as if he could not breathe down here. 'Let's go up.' Once in the cold winter air, he thanked Rosemary, asked if he could have copies of the postcard and letters, then walked off to his car.

'You realize what Mrs Lavender did? She would rather let her son think his father was a multiple murderer than admit to being an abortionist herself.'

'Will you tell him?' asked Phoebe.

'Of course. He asked me to find out and between us, we have,' said Coffin grimly. 'Besides, don't forget: there was another body in that patch of ground. There was the body of a soldier.'

His last words to Phoebe were to get a short report typed and sent over to him quickly. Today.

When he got back to his office, it was to find that Paul Masters was talking to Clara Henley.

He stood up when Coffin came in. 'You know Dr Henley, of course. She says you asked her to come in.'

Coffin wrenched his mind away from the Lavenders. 'I did. Please come in.' He led the way into his own office, thinking that Paul Masters looked disappointed at losing the good-looking doctor.

Clara began hesitantly, as if speech was still a problem with strangers, but once started it began to flow.

'I brought you the disc I took from Jaimie's office. If you wonder how I got in, I had had a copy made of Martin's key while he still had it. I always intended to search her flat. I thought she was using Martin as well as encouraging him in violence ... she clawed his arm, you know, you could see the nail marks, she was like a cat. No, I like cats and I didn't like her. I thought she was seeking violence to make a good story when she wrote it up ... I took what I could. The police changed the lock later ... I did not know she was dead, of course.' Clara put the disc on the table in front of Coffin. 'I wiped out what she had on the hard disc. One thing about a scientific training is it teaches you to cover everything.'

'Thank you.' Coffin took the disc. 'But you haven't wiped this?'

Clara shook her head. 'Science again ... I couldn't quite bring myself to do it ... I ran it through. Some stuff about Richard Lavender, not a lot and bit cryptic, she was still working on it. But a lot about us, Martin and me and our mother.' She paused, then said in her soft voice: 'She had caught on to something that I thought Martin did not know, or had forgotten, because he was so young at the time. I didn't want it brought out. It was all so horrible but in the past. I wanted it buried.'

'The past won't always stay buried,' said Coffin.

'There was something else too in the tape. She noted that she was pregnant. By Martin. Or so she guessed. But that she would have an abortion. She didn't want a child at the moment and certainly not the child of a murderer. I hated her for that. Did you know about the pregnancy?'

'Oh yes, it came out at the autopsy. We kept it quiet.'

'Thank you, I haven't told Martin. I am not sure how he would take it. I admitted killing my father and I was punished

228

for it. But I didn't do it. My mother did it and I knew I could bear punishment and survive whereas she couldn't.' Clara looked up at Coffin and smiled. 'I was young, there was a lot of sympathy for me and Martin, I knew I would come through and so would he . . . Besides, we had done a terrible thing too.'

'What was it you did?' A tough lady, Coffin thought, lovely to look at, as Martin was.

Clara's voice, always soft, dropped even lower so that it was almost a whisper. 'My mother stabbed my father, she stabbed him three times, and then she made first me and then Martin pick up the knife and stick it into each wound. "Dig hard," she said. "Dig hard." I thought Martin had forgotten; he had not, or he remembered after a while. As you say: the past won't lie down.'

'It would have cleared you.'

'But at what price?' She shook her head. 'I couldn't face it. I have built a new life, and so has Martin. We know the truth and that is hard enough to bear.' She stood up. 'I would like to have the disc back.'

'I don't know about that, I'm not sure what the legal position is, you may have to talk to Jaimie's executor. If she made a will. You may be able to get a copy.'

Clara thanked him, told him how happy Martin was now he was working for Stella and left. Outside, Coffin heard Paul muttering something about a drink, or lunch.

Coffin worked on through the day. He skipped lunch, did not open the drawer with the whisky bottle in it, cleared his desk of all current letters, chaired a committee meeting on pay, and, finally, in the early evening rang up the hospital to ask if he could talk to Richard Lavender.

Consent was given. The old man was more himself, he had calmed down and was in no need of sedation. The doctor implied that a lot of the violence might have been a reaction to some of the sedatives given him previously. 'We are not quite sure what drug was given to him the night of the so-called attack on Miss Neptune . . . but it could have disturbed Mr Lavender. Age does make a difference to how you can take drugs.'

And I am about to disturb him even more, Coffin thought, as he put on his thick overcoat, and went out into the November night. It was the worst sort of November night with rain turning to sleet, backed up by a hint of fog. Thameside weather at its worst.

Richard Lavender stood up when Coffin came in; he was dressed, there was a book on his bedside table, while he had the evening newspaper in his hands. A small television set was on the table.

'Jack brought me in the TV,' he said, seeing Coffin's eyes rest on it. 'I didn't realize how much I missed it. An old man's best friend.'

Richard Lavender had rejoined the world.

'I understand that I have been behaving badly ... It's all a blur. A little whiff of madness, I suppose. I must hope it won't come back.'

'No reason it should.'

'No ... it's bad about Janet. I feel to blame.'

'You were not. She was caught up in a muddle over her own sexuality, that was the root of it.'

'I'd be glad to believe it.' He sighed. 'She has been good to me, now it is my turn to help her. I mustn't talk as if she was dead.' He straightened up. 'Well, you come with news?'

'Yes.' Coffin patted his briefcase. 'I have had a very short report made of the work Chief Inspector Astley undertook on my orders. I will leave it with you to read.'

'You are formal.' Lavender frowned.

Coffin got the report out, it was neatly bound together. 'A skeleton was found where you believed you and your mother had taken a body. There was the remains of a foetus with that skeleton. Your father did not kill any women, the so-called Spinnergate Ripper was found in 1914 and confessed. He was hung.'

'I was sick then, in hospital. I had diphtheria, and I was in the Old Brook Fever Hospital,' muttered Lavender.

'So you didn't hear, and if she knew then she did not tell you why she had lied to you. Because she did lie. Other evidence, all very slight but suggestive, leads us to believe that your mother acted as an abortionist. The woman buried, probably a woman called Isobel Haved, died as a result of an illegal operation. Probably in your house.'

Richard Lavender leaned back and closed his eyes. 'I have to believe you,' he said. 'But I must come to terms with this. It will take time.' He opened his eyes and Coffin saw pain in them.

'It's not all. There was another body nearby. The remains of a man, probably a soldier, he had a lame leg.' Coffin looked at Richard Lavender. 'Do you know anything about that body?'

Slowly, Richard Lavender heaved himself up from the chair to hobble to the window. For a moment, he stood there in silence, then he turned.

'Who sups with the devil, should take a long spoon. You are not a devil, Mr Coffin, but you have a mighty long spoon.'

Coffin did not answer, this was something the old man had to get through on his own.

'You must remember that I loved my mother and believed what she had told me. My father had left us both. In the winter of 1914 the war had only just started but the killing fields of Flanders had started to reap the dead. My father came back to Spinnergate . . . he was in uniform and limping. He was a deserter, self-injured and wanting shelter. Remember, I only knew what my mother had told me . . . he seemed abhorrent to me both as a murderer and as a deserter. My mother was not at home, so I got behind him and throttled him, I was a big strong boy and he was a littleish man. Lame and frightened.'

'And you buried him in the old churchyard?'

Lavender bowed his head. 'I put him in the pram we had used before, wrapped him up in an old jacket of his own . . . it was a dark night, and I buried him in the old churchyard . . . I buried the coat, then I remembered that it had his name in it, so I dragged it out and took it home . . . It's amazing what you can do when you have to and I have always been strong and determined . . . Later, much later, I told my mother, and she packed up the house and took us away.'

231

Coffin stood up. 'It's what I thought. If you hadn't told me, I would have told you.'

'What now?'

'I don't know, I don't believe any case could be brought against you, so I will leave it in your hands, to do what your conscience tells you.'

He walked out, leaving Richard Lavender, once a Prime Minister, staring after him.

Stella was at home wearing bright-pink silk trousers with a cream silk shirt; she was pretending to cook dinner. Which in her case, meant ordering it from Max's and putting it in the oven. Or, if it was meant to be eaten cold, in the refrigerator. Tonight, because of the raw evening, it was the oven. She had already burnt a finger and was looking thoughtful.

She was pleased to see her husband and greeted him with a kiss. 'You can open the wine.'

He returned the kiss, adding a hug of his own; he was glad to be back in the world of loving relationships. He picked up a stick of celery and began to chew it. 'I am rather off family life at the moment. It's lethal.' He swallowed the celery, which was bitter. 'What do you say about a man who kills his father, a mother who makes her children stab their father and a woman who kills another woman and sends accusing letters to an old man with cut-out letters from a newspaper, and gives a packet of bloodstained hair to a young man?'

'Is that what she did?'

'Yes, leaving fingerprints. Those prints and forensic evidence from the cloth fragments and blood on a dark cape she wore will convict her. Do you know, she said she went tramping round the old churchyard before we found the skeletons; I knew someone with big feet had walked there, I saw the tracks. She came back later too, just to stare, a real night walker. She knew so much all the time about old Lavender; there was more family talk, I guess than he ever knew. His mother may have talked to her sister and so on down the family. Janet knew what the old tweed jacket was when she found it in the trunk, that's for sure.' He took a deep breath; he was glad he had all that out to Stella, it wrapped this horrible business up and put it in the past. 'I suppose you want me to take the dog out?'

'No, Martin and Eden took him out for a lovely walk by the river before they went off to dinner.'

She kept a straight face as Coffin spun her round to take a look. 'Remember the little animal that was going to crawl out of the undergrowth to capture Martin? I think she's started to crawl.'

They both began to laugh, that was how life went on. Eden had it right after all.

Suddenly Coffin stopped laughing. 'We never found out where the empty coffin came from, and Phoebe was so sure she would ... Damn, there's always something you don't get clear. The missing bit of the jigsaw.'

A Grave Talent

Laurie R. King

Kate Martinelli, a newly promoted Homicide detective with a secret to conceal, and Alonzo Hawkin, a world-weary cop trying to make a new life in San Francisco, could not be more different, but are thrown together to solve a brutal crime – the murders of three young girls.

As Martinelli and Hawkin get nearer to a solution, they realize the crimes may not be the sexually motivated killings they had seemed, and that there is a coldly calculating and tortuous mind at work which they must outmanoeuvre if they are to prevent both further carnage and the destruction of a shining talent...

'If there is a new P.D. James...I would put my money on Laurie R. King'
Boston Globe

ISBN 0 00 649354 8

Head Count

Ingrid Noll

Nicknamed 'Elephant' by schoolmates and family, Maya is at odds with the world until she meets beautiful, sophisticated Cora. These two form an intense relationship based on a conviction that they are somehow separate from the rest of society and its petty rules. They dabble in crime and lead fantasy lives . . . then reality creeps in and explodes their illusions.

Years later, Maya is trapped in a conventional marriage, while Cora enjoys a life of luxury in Italy with a sugar daddy. But they join forces again, driven together by their refusal to conform to anything but their own desires. Inevitably, other people get in the way, and naturally the only solution is murde . . .

Beautifully written, witty and original, *Head Count* is the new bestselling novel from one of Europe's hottest crime writers.

'A first-rate example of the Eurocrime novel'   VAL McDERMID

'Ingrid Noll is often referred to as Germany's "Queen of Crime", and her *Hell Hath No Fury* shows how fully she deserves this title'   DONNA LEON, *Sunday Times*

ISBN 0 00 649767 5

Pictures of Perfection
Reginald Hill

High in the Mid-Yorkshire dales stands the pretty village of Enscombe, proud survivor of all that history has thrown at it. But now market forces mass at the gates and the old way of life seems to be changing fast. The Law can do little to stop the ever-growing crimes against tradition, but when a policeman goes missing DCI Pascoe gets worried. Andy Dalziel thinks he's overreacting until the normally phlegmatic Sergeant Wield shows signs of changing his first impressions of village life.

Over two eventful days a new pattern emerges, of lust and lying, of family feuds and ancient injuries, of frustrated desires and unbalanced minds. Finally, inevitably, everything comes to a bloody climax at the Squire's Reckoning, when the villagers gather each Lady Day to feast and pay old debts . . . and not even the presence of the Mid-Yorkshire CID trio can change the course of history . . .

'For suspense, ingenuity and sheer comic effrontery this takes the absolute, appetising biscuit'   *Sunday Times*

ISBN 0 00 649011 5